By Cook or By Crook

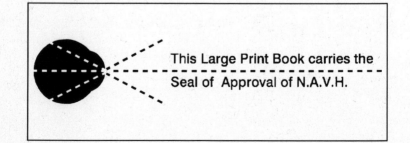

This Large Print Book carries the
Seal of Approval of N.A.V.H.

A FIVE-INGREDIENT MYSTERY

BY COOK OR BY CROOK

MAYA CORRIGAN

THORNDIKE PRESS
A part of Gale, Cengage Learning

GALE
CENGAGE Learning·

Farmington Hills, Mich • San Francisco • New York • Waterville, Maine
Meriden, Conn • Mason, Ohio • Chicago

GALE
CENGAGE Learning®

LIBRARY OF CONGRESS CATALOGING-IN-PUBLICATION DATA

Corrigan, Maya.
    By cook or by crook / Maya Corrigan.
        pages cm — (Thorndike press large print clean reads)
        ISBN 978-1-4104-7578-7 (hardcover) — ISBN 1-4104-7578-6 (hardcover)
        1. Food writers—Fiction. 2. Murder—Investigation—Fiction. 3. Large type
    books. I. Title.
    PS3603.O77322B93 2015
    813'.6—dc23   2014041264

Published in 2015 by arrangement with Kensington Books, an imprint
of Kensington Publishing Corp.

Printed in Mexico
1 2 3 4 5 6 7 19 18 17 16 15

For my parents,
Helen and Walter Roman,
who shared their enjoyment of
mystery books and good food with me

We owe much to the fruitful meditation of our sages, but a sane view of life is, after all, elaborated mainly in the kitchen.

— Joseph Conrad,
Preface to Jessie Conrad's
A Handbook of Cookery for a Small House,
1907.

CHAPTER 1

Val Deniston waved good night to her last customers, relieved that they'd ignored the elephant in the Cool Down Café. No one had rehashed Monique's rant about her husband's affair with Nadia. Maybe they'd tired of the topic after three days or avoided it with Nadia around. Though thankful that Monique hadn't shown up tonight, Val worried that her cousin had spent the evening alone, plotting how to get back at Nadia.

Exercise music from the workout room drifted into the athletic club café and set a quick pace for Val's cleanup. She poured a pot of coffee down the drain, taking a last whiff of the aroma that masked the scent of sweat. Not many takers for coffee tonight. After two hours on the tennis courts, the crowd had thirsted for juice and smoothies, not lattes.

The music cut off, and a gruff voice came through the speakers. "The Bayport Racket and Fitness Club will close at nine-thirty. Please finish your workout promptly."

As Val wiped down the eating bar, the exercise junkies who'd stayed until closing time on a Sunday night filed past the café toward the exit. A petite woman in a white tennis dress bucked the flow and rushed back into the club. Nadia Westrin carried an athletic bag large enough for three rackets, a change of clothes, and a Thanksgiving turkey.

"Thank goodness you're still here, Val." Nadia dropped her sports bag near the eating bar. Under the hanging lights, her frosted brown hair with gray roots resembled a desert camouflage helmet. "My car won't start. Can you give me a lift home?"

Val hesitated. Since the night of her accident this past winter, she'd allowed no one to ride with her after dark. Time to get over that. The country road from the club to town posed no driving hazards. Though Val didn't want to do any favors for her cousin's enemy, refusing to give Nadia a ride smacked of schoolyard tit-for-tat. "Of course. Give me a minute to finish here."

"I'm glad you agreed to play in our mixed doubles group and open the café for us." Nadia watched Val stack biscotti studded with pistachios and currants in a glass jar. "The last café manager sold everything in cellophane like a vending machine. Your fresh food is way better."

"Thanks." Val waited for the dig that would surely follow the compliment.

"Isn't the café a comedown for you, though? After doing publicity for New York chefs?"

Val clenched her teeth. Over the last few months, she'd adjusted to living in a Chesapeake Bay town, but reminders of her shattered career still rankled. "I publicized other people's cookbooks for ten years. Now I have a job that lets me try out recipes for my own book." Recipes the average person could make in less time than it took to watch a TV cooking show.

"When the tennis teams finish the season in July, we always throw a big catered party." Nadia leaned toward Val like a conspirator. "I can talk the club manager into letting you cater. It's four weeks away, but I'll need menu options and prices pretty soon."

Val perked up as if a shot of espresso had hit her veins. One catering gig could lead to another and plump up her résumé. "I'd love to do it. When do you want to talk about it?"

"Stop by my house Tuesday morning

before you open the café. I get up early. Let's make it seven o'clock."

The day after tomorrow. Not much time to work on the menus. "Okay, and thanks for the chance to cater the party."

"We always funnel business to each other here at the club. I hope that when your grandfather's ready to sell his house, you'll reciprocate and give me the listing."

Ah. The sales commission on Granddad's huge house would dwarf whatever Val earned from catering the club party. Nadia's idea of a fair trade — her lentils for your caviar.

Fifteen minutes later, Val steered her Saturn off a narrow tree-canopied road and onto Nadia's street at the outskirts of town. "Let me know when we get to your house. I'm not sure I'll recognize it in the dark."

"I appreciate the ride. I'm glad your cousin hasn't turned you against me."

Val felt her blood pressure rise. "Don't start knocking Monique. I won't —"

A black-clad figure darted into the car's headlights.

Val swerved. She slammed on the brakes and clutched the wheel in a death grip. A memory flared of an icy highway, the car skidding and hurtling toward leafless trees.

The tires grabbed the road, and she snapped back from the past. Breath whooshed from her lungs, a mix of relief and frustration. No crash this time, no blood spattered on her. But the elusive memory of the accident last winter had vanished, leaving behind a single frame when she needed the whole reel.

Nadia smacked the dashboard. "What an idiot. Who jogs at night dressed in black? If you'd hit the guy, it wouldn't have been your fault."

No fault didn't mean no guilt. Val started the stalled car. "How far to your house?"

"Just past the bend."

Val took the curve slowly, still shaky from her near miss. Pinpoints of light came from houses set back from the road. An eerie glow flickered through the bushes. Flames? "It looks like someone built a campfire up ahead."

Nadia peered through the windshield and squawked, "That's *my* place."

Val stopped across the street from Nadia's driveway. They both dashed from the car toward the fire.

The flames came from a makeshift torch, a wad of white fabric tied to a wood shaft like a giant onion on a two-foot skewer. The odor of charcoal lighter fluid hung in the still air. Val circled the torch planted in a bed of river rock near the driveway. No trees or shrubs nearby. It would take a gale force wind off the Chesapeake to spread the fire. Tonight, though, a shroud of humid air hung over Maryland's Eastern Shore. This fire would die in place.

The light from it tinged Nadia's ashen complexion orange and emphasized the frown lines in her forehead. "Who put that here? What is that thing anyway? Why — ?" Her voice broke on a helium high note.

The outer layers of cloth disintegrated and the inner ones sprouted holes. The shape under the cloth became visible — oval and flat like the head of a tennis racket.

Val gasped. "A wood racket?" She'd occasionally seen one of those at a garage sale, but never on a tennis court or on fire.

Muffled pops came from the head of the torch, strings snapping from the heat.

The burning racket would make an awesome kickoff for a surprise party. Too bad no one was jumping out of the bushes, singing "Happy Birthday."

Nadia thrust her shoulders back, her posture ramrod. "Your cousin did this. She's harassed me for the last three days."

Val's jaw clenched. A few seconds ago, she'd felt her first ever twinges of sympathy

14

for Nadia. Not anymore. "You have no way to know if Monique —"

"She turned everyone against me. Blew off a team match. Now look what she's done."

Val waved away the torch smoke and the accusation. "Let's put the fire out. Where's your hose?"

Nadia flicked her wrist toward her white Cape Cod. "Hanging near the back porch."

Val turned on her key ring flashlight, headed toward the clapboard house, and unwound the hose.

She tugged it toward the fire. "Good thing you hitched a ride with me and not Althea." The flaming racket would remind the tennis team's only black player of Klan cross-burnings.

Nadia put her palms together. "Amen to that."

A car door slammed and someone bounded up the driveway. Luke Forsa entered the circle of light made by the fire. "Hey, Nadia, what's with the torch? You having a luau?" Her silence must have told him his joke had fallen flat. "I was driving by and saw the fire. You need any help dousing it?"

"Val's got the hose. We can handle it."

Luke sidled up to Val. "Whaddya know?

15

Meeting an old flame over a fire."

Val nearly dropped the hose, surprised that he remembered those kisses and fumbles after nearly two decades. Back then, his success at poker and hooking up had earned him the name Lucky Luke. Now the dashing rebel of her teen fantasies manned the grill at his mom's diner.

Luke's gaze lingered on Val's thighs, where her tennis shorts ended. The guy still hoped to get lucky. She looked down. Did torchlit legs, like candlelit faces, have a romantic glow? Not that she could see. Val gave one last tug to the hose, aimed the nozzle at the torch, and squeezed the handle. Luke jumped back from the water ricocheting off the rocks. So much for old flames.

She soaked the racket thoroughly and turned the flashlight on the charred frame. Bits of singed cloth clung to it.

"Racket flambé. Yum." Luke stepped toward Nadia. "You should have given your racket a decent burial instead of cremating it."

"It's not mine." Nadia glared at him. "How old do you think I am? Wood rackets were passé long before I took up tennis."

Luke pulled the charred racket out of the ground. Either it had cooled down, or he had asbestos hands. The racket's handle, bare of grip tape, was whittled to a point. "Lot of work, turning this into a stake and getting it to burn."

"Right on schedule too. I always play mixed doubles on Sunday and hang around the club until closing time." Nadia waggled her index finger at Val. "That jogger I took for a man could have been a tall woman. She wore a hoodie so I wouldn't recognize her."

The flashlight wavered in Val's hand. Monique, the tall woman Nadia meant, could have waited near Nadia's house for an approaching car, set the fire, and fled in a face-hiding hoodie. But so could anyone who'd played tennis tonight, or even one of Nadia's neighbors.

Val didn't want Luke, or anybody else, to hear wild charges against her cousin. "Would you get Nadia's sports bag from my car? It's parked across the street."

"You bet." He jogged down the driveway.

"Are you going to report this to police?" Val held her breath, waiting for Nadia's answer.

"I don't need the police to tell me who did this."

Val exhaled. Nadia could make accusations, but no one would believe them without evidence to back them up.

The bushes on the far side of Nadia's driveway rustled. A sixtyish woman in a black caftan emerged from them.

Tall and erect, she held a portable lantern in her upraised hand. "I saw a fire from our window. Is everything okay?" Nadia's neighbor, Irene Pritchard, made an imposing figure.

Nadia looked tiny next to her. "Everything's fine now. The fire's out."

Val stepped back from the lantern's beam. She felt uncomfortable around Irene, her former rival for the café manager job.

Irene lowered her lantern toward the charred racket. "What on earth? That's a nasty thing."

Luke joined them, gave Nadia her sports bag, and pointed to the racket on the ground. "You want me to junk that?"

Nadia picked it up. "I'll take care of it. Y'all keep a lid on this, okay?"

She held the racket away from her tennis whites and marched toward the house with Irene lighting the way. Dramatic exit. A crescendo from the cicadas in the trees sounded like applause.

Val aimed the blue beam of her LED flashlight at the driveway.

Luke fell into step beside her, gravel crunching under his feet. "You're still in

Bayport, huh? I heard you came here just to coax your grandpa to sell his house."

"That's what Mom wanted." But not Granddad. Easier for Val to side with him while living in his house than with her mother a thousand miles away in Florida. "The house needs work before it goes on the market. I don't have the time to spend on it, now that I'm running the café at the club."

"And competing against my diner." He nudged her with his elbow.

"No competition. You have a different clientele."

"I'll say. My customers would never burn sports equipment. What do you make of that flaming racket?"

"An ugly practical joke?" Or an act of revenge.

Val swiped at a mosquito whining near her ear as Luke aimed his remote at a black BMW. Fancy car. He must have made money before moving back home to rescue his mom's diner, a doomed business if Val ever saw one. But what small business in a small town wasn't doomed? Granddad had kissed good-bye to his fish market and his video store.

"Drop by the diner sometime with your grandpa. He used to eat with us everyday,

19

him and his buddies, sometimes all three meals."

Three meals of cholesterol, salt, and empty calories, the diner's staples. At least Val could check off one item on her mother's agenda: a healthier diet for Granddad.

Back in her car, she grabbed her cell phone, punched the first three digits of Monique's number, and stopped. What would she say if her cousin admitted burning the racket? What would she say if Nadia asked whether Monique had done it? If Val didn't know the answer, she wouldn't have to lie or betray her cousin. The best strategy for flaming rackets: don't ask so you can't tell.

She clicked the phone off and drove home — or what passed for home temporarily — a gabled and turreted Victorian that looked like an eyesore by day and a haunted house by night. Her grandfather's big Buick sat as usual on the street. He'd hit the mailbox backing out of the driveway so often that he happily ceded the driveway to Val's much-used Saturn.

She let herself into the house by the side door sandwiched between the dining room and the sitting room. She found her grandfather ensconced in a recliner by the sitting room window. A scene from Hitchcock's *Vertigo,* one of his favorites, played on the flat-screen TV near the tiled fireplace. The ear hooks of his bifocals nestled in tufts of white curls that fringed his balding head.

He pressed the pause button on his remote. "Humidity must be bad. Your hair's wilder than usual."

She ran her fingers through the unruly, cinnamon-colored locks she inherited from him. Eventually her curls would turn ivory like his. She pointed to a plate with telltale crumbs on the end table. "I see my apple crisp was a hit."

"A base hit, not a home run. Your grandmother always topped it with whipped cream."

Val glanced at the mahogany table in the dining room where Grandma had served so many family meals. Cream, butter, and red meat, Grandma's favorite foods, had nudged her toward a heart attack six years ago. Val knew enough not to say that to her grandfather. He'd reply that at least Grandma had enjoyed life, and Val couldn't argue with that.

She sank onto the oatmeal tweed sofa near his chair. Its cushions enveloped her like a hug from a long-lost and slightly seedy friend. "An amazing thing happened tonight on my way home." Even more amazing than a burning racket.

Granddad wiped the lenses of his glasses on the hem of his polo shirt. "I'm glad someone had an exciting evening."

Whenever he channeled Eeyore, she pretended not to hear. "I had to stop short to avoid a jogger. Hitting the brakes hard brought back a memory. I did the same thing that night in January. Maybe the rest will come back too."

"Dwelling on the past won't change it." Granddad gestured toward the agitated Jimmy Stewart on the TV screen. "There's a man destroyed by his memories."

Val picked at loose threads on the sofa arm. "I just want to know what happened. I need the truth."

"You store a lot in your noggin. Recipe ingredients, movie plots, bits of trivia. They pop out when you need them. That night you had a concussion. It's not your fault you can't remember."

"I know." But the accident might have been her fault. With no memory of what led to it, Val didn't know if her anger had turned destructive. Could she have crashed the car deliberately, as the man riding with her claimed? That night had tested her character. After five months she still didn't know if she'd passed or failed.

"Take my advice, Val, and let it go."

Granddad squeezed her hand. "How was your game tonight? Did they pair you with a geezer again?"

The change of subject brought Val out of her funk. "This time I had a younger partner, in his thirties. He works in D.C. and is looking for a weekend place. Gunnar Swensen."

"Scandinavian?"

"Possibly, but mixed with Latin blood. Thick dark hair, bluish eyes." Plus rugged features and a crooked nose. But a megawatt smile transformed his face from almost a train wreck to almost attractive. "He's pretty buff for someone who works in an office. His tennis isn't bad, and he wants to play me in singles."

Granddad's eyebrows rose, furry white squiggles in his forehead. "Gonna whup him?"

"Gonna try. Tennis gives a short player like me a fighting chance against a taller, stronger one. That's why I like it."

"Losing to a small woman — that'll test his mettle." Granddad laughed.

"Tony couldn't handle it." Her ex-fiancé used to sulk whenever he lost to her.

Granddad covered his ears. "No more about Tony. You need to get over the past."

Ironic advice from a man nursing a grudge

against a long-dead nephew. Val stood up. "Okay, I'll focus on the future. Tomorrow evening I have to work on a catering menu. Just heat up tonight's leftovers for yourself, and I'll scrounge around for snacks."

"Leftovers. Hmph. That's the best you can do for your grandfather?"

"You can always cook up something yourself. My recipe file is your recipe file."

"If I burn the place down, it's all on you." He aimed his remote at the TV.

Early Tuesday Val parked in front of Nadia's Cape Cod, bleary-eyed from a late night. Describing and pricing the mouthwatering dishes she could prepare for the club party had taken longer than expected. She walked past Nadia's Lexus in the driveway and glanced at the bed of river rock where the racket had burned. A good rain would wash away any trace of the fire. No rain in today's forecast though. No cool breeze off the bay either. The creek behind the house had barely a ripple, and Nadia's kayak sat motionless next to her dock.

Val climbed the porch steps and rang the bell twice. She pounded on the door. No answer. Nadia wasn't the type to oversleep or forget an appointment. Unlikely a woman in her forties would have a heart attack, but maybe she'd fallen and hit her head. Val tried the knob. It turned.

She poked her head into the hall. "Nadia?" No answer. "Anybody home?" she shouted up the stairs. Again, only silence.

She walked toward the back of the house, the floorboards creaking with each step. She froze at the entrance to the kitchen.

Nadia lay on the floor. An alabaster doll with open eyes. A wood tennis racket stuck out of the base of her throat, its shaved handle like a spear, the racket head listing to one side.

CHAPTER 2

Val felt her throat close. Her knees gave way. She grabbed the door frame, breathed deeply, and tried to stay upright.

Her head cleared. She could do nothing for Nadia. The bluish skin tone, the congealed blood — Val had seen enough crime shows to know what that meant. Nadia had been dead for hours. Murdered. What if the murderer was still here? No, of course no one was here. Why would the murderer stay around waiting to be caught?

She had to get help. She rummaged in her tote bag. No cell phone. She staggered back to the hall with tears clouding her vision. A desk phone sat on the hall table, but she shouldn't touch anything at a crime scene. She used her car key to punch the Speaker button and 911.

Words caught in her throat when the dispatcher answered. She forced them out. "Val Deniston calling from 156 Creek

Road. I found Nadia Westrin dead here. Murdered."

"Murdered?" The dispatcher sounded skeptical. She barraged Val with questions and then gave advice. "You should go outside and wait for the police. Go to a neighbor's house if you'll feel safer there."

Walk away? Maybe mess up the murderer's fingerprints on the way out? Even if she turned the doorknob with a tissue in her hand, she might smudge some prints.

"Ma'am, are you still there? Can you call me back on a cell phone once you're outside?"

"I don't have a cell phone with me." She must have left it on her nightstand. "How long before the police get here?"

"They'll be there as soon as possible. Don't touch anything."

The dispatcher clicked off, leaving Val to weigh the conflicting advice. Go outside, but don't touch anything. She debated a moment. She felt safe in the house, and it didn't seem right to leave Nadia alone.

Val inched back to the kitchen doorway. If she looked no farther than Nadia's bare feet and bright red toenails, her tanned legs and black Bermuda shorts, she'd think Nadia was resting. Val closed her eyes and bowed her head. Rest in peace.

When she opened her eyes, anger surged through her like an electric current. No one should die like this. Nadia would have been just as dead if someone had stabbed her with a knife. Plenty of knives in a kitchen. Why take the time to turn a racket into a lethal weapon? To mock Nadia's passion for the game? She'd reveled in competition and fought hardest when she was behind in a match. No sign of a struggle here, nothing out of place in the kitchen and the screened porch beyond it.

Next to the doorway where Val stood, wineglasses hung from a stemware rack lined up like troops for inspection. The front two didn't pass muster. Unlike their sparkling comrades, they had water spots suggesting a hasty washing. Crumbs and smears marred the counter between the stemware rack and the fridge. Across the room, though, the granite counter near the sink gleamed. Someone had cleaned half the kitchen.

Less than a month ago, at Nadia's Memorial Day party, food and drinks covered the countertops, and guests from the club, her real estate office, and the neighborhood filled the small house. Had one of them murdered her? No stranger had killed Nadia. The weapon hinted at a grudge against her.

Val's stomach knotted. Monique had a big grudge and would be a suspect. Val had to warn her. Better for her cousin to hear about the murder from her than from the police.

She rushed to the hall and then fidgeted in front of the phone. Should she use it? The police would trace calls on this line. They'd wonder why she'd phoned her cousin from the murder scene. The call would have to wait.

She studied the jottings on the notepad near the phone. Nadia's abbreviations, cramped writing, and lack of punctuation made it hard to tell where one word ended and the next began. *ZACHARNAROVIAK* appeared at the top of the page, then a line that read *56MAPLE BRK 3BR 2BA RANCH FP FNCD YD Tues430.* A phone number followed, then a solid line halfway across the page, and six letters — *F O R S A L.*

Val knew enough real estate shorthand to decipher the notes. Someone with a long last name and a brick house on Maple Street had made an appointment with Nadia for this afternoon at four-thirty. Nadia had taken down the client's phone number and the property details. Maybe she'd started composing a For Sale ad, but something — or someone — interrupted her. Now she'd never finish that ad or meet that client.

From the hallway Val peered into the living room. Nadia's tennis trophies sat on the mantel. A tall curio cabinet held her collection of miniature buildings. One shelf had a display of houses common on Maryland's Eastern Shore, including a modest Cape Cod like Nadia's and a Queen Anne Victorian like Granddad's. Another shelf held tiny half-timbered cottages and adobe haciendas. A miniature brownstone reminded Val of the place where she and two college classmates had rented an apartment when they first arrived in New York a decade ago. Now the other two women were married with children, living in the suburbs, and she'd moved even farther from the city.

A siren wailed. Police at last. Val parked herself by the front door.

The sidelight gave her a view of a ruddy man coming up the walk — Chief Yardley, the new head of the Bayport police and her grandfather's friend. The chief reminded her of a gingerbread man, his round head on a barrel-chested frame, his neck barely visible.

He opened the door with a latex-gloved hand. "What's going on, Val? Where's — ?"

30

"The kitchen." She pointed toward the back of the house.

"Stay here. Leave the door open. The EMTs are right behind us." The chief lumbered down the hall, followed by a uniformed officer young enough to work undercover at a high school.

"Omigod!" The young cop's voice carried into the hall.

Two husky paramedics rushed in. Val waved them toward the kitchen.

Voices came from the back of the house, but only the chief's words carried. "You can't do much here, boys. I called the medical examiner. This here beats anything I ever seen."

Val wondered how many murders Earl Yardley had investigated in his career. He'd worked as a detective in various Maryland jurisdictions and only recently taken over as chief in Bayport. He probably hadn't expected a murder in a tourist town with a few thousand year-round residents.

The chief returned to the hall with the rookie cop and snapped his cell phone closed. "Nadia Westrin. Her name's on lots of real estate signs. Friend of yours, Val?"

"I know her from tennis at the club. She asked me to meet her here to talk about the menu for a club party. I rang the bell a few

31

times. With her car in the driveway, I figured she had to be home. I tried the knob, went in, and found . . ." Val relived the shock of her first glimpse of Nadia dead and felt dizzy again.

"Hey, you look shook up." The chief pointed to the staircase leading to the second story. "Sit on the steps. Put your head between your knees." He summoned the EMTs from the kitchen.

By the time they finished taking her pulse and her blood pressure, she felt steady again. They insisted she stay seated and made her drink water.

"You ready to answer some questions, Val?" At her nod, the chief pointed to the notebook in the rookie cop's hands. "What are you scribbling?"

"The details, sir. The victim is a white female, middle-aged —"

"Middle age is a moving target, son." The chief looked down at Val. "What all do you know about her? Age, marital status, anything else?"

"Early forties. Divorced. No children." As for her affair with Monique's husband, the police would have to discover that without Val's help. "Nadia's ex-husband, Joe Westrin, moved from Bayport, but he lives somewhere around here, maybe Treadwell.

He still comes to the club to work out."

The chief stroked his chin. "Hard feelings between them?"

"The few times I saw him talking to Nadia at the club, they looked civil enough." Most divorces, though, left hard feelings.

"What about the racket that's stuck in her? Does it belong to her?"

"It's not the racket she played with. She had the latest equipment. Wood rackets are antiques."

"When was the last time you saw her?"

"Sunday night." Over a burning racket. Hard not to view that ugly incident as a prelude to the murder. Val shifted her position on the step and raked the carpet with her fingers. "Let me tell you what happened that night."

Officer Wade gaped at her description of the burning racket.

The chief grimaced. "How come I didn't hear about this?"

"It wasn't much of a fire. A garden hose took care of it. And Nadia didn't want to notify the police." Not a wise decision in retrospect. "When we pulled the charred racket out of the ground, we saw that the handle had been whittled to a point turning it into a stake."

The chief gestured with his thumb toward

the kitchen. "Like the racket out there."

"I can search the premises for the burned racket, Chief," Officer Wade said.

"Folks with more crime scene experience will do that. I need you to take down Ms. Deniston's information. Val, I want you to tell Officer Wade everything that happened this morning and the night of the fire. And give him the names of the victim's pals at the racket club."

A bearded man arrived with a medical bag. The chief went back to the kitchen with him.

While Val talked to Officer Wade, people filed by. The EMTs went out. Crime scene technicians came in with cases and cameras.

The chief ambled back into the hall. "What were you doing last night, Val?"

She didn't need to ask when Nadia had died. The chief's question made that clear. "I was home with Granddad." Though they'd barely seen each other.

While she'd worked on her catering proposal upstairs, he'd watched videos and gone to bed downstairs. She could have left the house by the back staircase, and he wouldn't have missed her. Her parents could confirm she'd answered the house phone at nine. By now, though, they were sailing on the high seas, taking their boat to the Bahamas. Val didn't expect to hear from them until the weekend.

"Oh my gosh." She rubbed her temples. "I just remembered something. Nadia called yesterday around five and left a message for me."

"What about?" the chief asked.

"She confirmed our meeting this morning and asked me to call her. That's all. I'd turned off my phone to concentrate on something and didn't hear her message until late last night. I expected to see her this morning, so I didn't bother returning the call." She sighed. "I wish now I'd called her back."

"Don't beat yourself up over it. Any idea who did this?"

She shook her head. "You'd better ask people who've known her longer."

The chief checked the officer's notes, nodded his approval, and returned to the kitchen.

Officer Wade closed his notebook when she finished giving her statement and smiled at her. "You friends with the chief? He don't usually call people by their first name."

"I've known him since I was about this high." She held her hand three feet from the floor. "His father and my granddad were good friends. The chief's father died young.

35

Granddad stayed in touch with the family and did guy things with the chief — fishing, Orioles games."

"Did you grow up in Bayport?"

"No, I'm a Navy brat. We never lived long any place my father was stationed. This was the closest thing to home I had. I spent summers here with my grandparents until I was sixteen." During two of those summers, Monique had also visited Bayport. They'd come to know each other, despite the feud between two branches of the family. What adolescent can resist a forbidden friendship? "After that, I only made short visits here."

"But you live in Bayport now?"

"Only since January."

The door burst open. A man with a shaved head strutted into the hall. He had a pale and puffy face, like risen dough that needs a punch. His shaved head made his other features more prominent — eagle eyes and curiously small ears for a man with such a big head.

"Deputy Holtzman from the sheriff's office." He spoke as if introducing himself to a large gathering. "Where's your chief?"

Officer Wade squared his shoulders. "In the kitchen, sir." He nodded toward the back of the house.

Holtzman pointed at Val. "Who are you?"

She stood up. "I'm Val Deniston."

"She found the victim and called us." Officer Wade waved his notebook. "I just took her statement."

Holtzman scrutinized her from top to toe as if sizing her up for a prison jumpsuit. Somewhere she'd read that the person who reports a crime is always the initial suspect. The deputy stopped staring at her as the chief came into the hall.

"Ah, Holtzman. Glad you got here fast. I see you've met Ms. Deniston." The chief turned to Officer Wade. "Go out to the street and shoo those nosy neighbors away. I don't want them to see Ms. Deniston leaving. If folks don't know she was here, they can't pester her about what she saw. Once she's gone, you go back to the station and type up what she told you."

"Yes, sir." The officer left.

"Val, can you stop by the station later this morning? We'll go over the information you gave us and see if you want to add anything."

"I'll be there." Even if it meant closing the café for a while.

The chief hustled Val up the driveway. "Don't go around telling folks what you saw here. The story we'll give the press is that the victim died of a sharp force injury. In other words, she was stabbed, but we're not telling what the weapon was. Understand?"

"I won't say a word about the racket." Hard to believe the police could keep that detail secret. "Did you find the burned racket?"

"In the trash bin. Lucky for us the garbage collection on this street isn't until tomorrow." He hovered over her until she climbed into her car. "Give your granddaddy my regards."

"I will. Who's in charge of a case like this? The Bayport police or the sheriff's office?"

"We take the lead, but we don't have the manpower to investigate major crimes. I get resources from the sheriff's department to conduct interviews. The crime scene unit comes from the state police. We all cooperate on a big case like this."

Good. The sheriff's deputy wouldn't be taking over. Val broke the speed limit in her rush to get home.

A faint burning smell hit her when she opened the side door to the house. Nothing new. Granddad liked his toast crispy and sometimes overshot the mark. The house reeked of his blackened bread at least once a week.

She went into the front room. The former "courting parlor" now served as a study.

38

She'd brightened it up with three coats of lemon paint to set off the chocolate brown woodwork.

She called her cousin and left messages on her cell phone and landline. Monique had no reason to stay home, her husband having taken their young children to visit his parents. Val also tried to reach Bethany O'Shay, the tennis team's youngest member and Nadia's recently dumped doubles partner. Bethany didn't pick up either.

Next she phoned Tanisha, the college student who'd opened the café this morning, and coaxed her into staying until closing time. Val didn't tell her about Nadia's death, but she should tell Tanisha's mother, Althea, a member of Nadia's tennis team. Althea could break the news to her daughter. "I'd like to talk to your mom. Is she at home now or in her office?"

"She went to Cumberland today to do something for a client. She's going to spend the night there and drive back tomorrow."

Val put the phone down, glad to postpone delivering bad news. The burning smell had gotten stronger. She raced to the kitchen. No sign of Granddad. He must be in his bedroom. A mixing bowl, eggshells, and globs of batter decorated the counter near the stove. Smoke seeped from the oven door. She turned on the exhaust fan over the stove and backed away, coughing.

She snatched a dish towel from the counter and held it over her nose. It felt wet and sticky, and had a familiar sweet smell. Just what she needed — a cake batter facial. She opened the oven. The blast of heat nearly knocked her over. Smoke billowed out. Her eyes burned.

Granddad appeared in the doorway. "What are you doing, Val? You smoked up the whole place." He coughed and wheezed.

All she needed was for him to collapse gasping for breath. "Get out of the house. Now."

She put on oven mitts, reached inside the hot cavern, and pulled out a large pan crusted with a black substance, charred remains of a baking project gone awry. With the pan at arm's length, she ran out the side door and set it down on the driveway.

Back in the house, she opened the windows in the study, the sitting room, and the dining room. Luckily her grandfather's bedroom door was closed against the smoke. She left it that way, went back to the kitchen, and checked the stove. No wonder it was giving off the heat of an inferno. The oven was set to more than five hundred degrees.

She turned it off and studied the mess on

the island counter. Thick yellow liquid dripped from her mixer's blades. An empty box of cake mix and one of instant vanilla pudding, a tin of salad oil, and a bottle of rum sat on the counter — the ingredients for her Foolproof Rum Cake. Now she'd have to rename that recipe.

Her eyes stung from the smoke. She joined her grandfather on the front porch and sat next to him on the glider. "Rum cake, huh? How did the batter get the better of you?"

He peered at her over his reading glasses. "I mixed it for two minutes, just like the recipe said, and went to turn the mixer off. The danged thing zoomed into high speed. Surprised me so much, I dropped it."

"The recipe calls for a Bundt pan, not a roasting pan."

"How am I supposed to know what a Bundt pan is? I picked out a pan that looked the right size. The batter coated the bottom of it."

And the thin layer burned fast. "The recipe also says to set the oven at three hundred twenty-five, not five twenty-five."

"I couldn't tell if the first number was a three or a five."

"Next time you can't tell, go for the lower temperature. What made you bake a cake

41

this morning? You've never baked anything before."

He twiddled his thumbs and studied them. "I had to start somewhere. It's time I learned to cook for myself now. Who knows how long you'll be staying here?"

His sudden interest in cooking still struck her as odd. "I'll teach you to cook, but we do it together. Then I can explain things, like what a Bundt pan is."

"Okay, but no more than five ingredients. Otherwise, there's too much to keep track of." He patted her hand. "Sorry for the mess in the kitchen."

"Don't worry about it. It's better than the last kitchen I saw." With a murdered woman in it. "You made me forget, for a little while, something I thought I'd never get out of my mind."

She buried her head in his shoulder. The tears she'd corked up since finding the body flowed out. Between sniffs, she told him about finding Nadia stabbed to death. She could tell from his shallow breathing and his tense arm around her shoulder that the news upset him. She skipped over the gruesome details about the murder weapon.

"Poor thing." He stroked her hair. "You should take the rest of the day off."

"It's better if I keep busy. Chief Yardley

asked me to stop by the police station. I'll clean up the kitchen before I go. By the way, he sends his regards."

"Good man. He'll catch the murderer." Granddad eased himself out of the glider. "I'll help you in the kitchen."

He wasn't much help, but she was grateful for the company. Her morning would have been much worse if she'd come back to an empty house with nothing to do but brood over Nadia's murder. By putting the kitchen in order after Granddad's cooking disaster, she kept one form of chaos at bay.

Before leaving for the police station, Val tried her cousin's home and cell phone numbers. Still no answer. Had Monique found out about Nadia's death? Could she have panicked and run to avoid police questioning?

CHAPTER 3

Deputy Holtzman trained his raptor eyes on Val. "You rang the bell at Nadia Westrin's house, got no response, and walked in. You usually barge into people's homes like that?"

Was that the fourth or fifth hostile question he'd asked? Val had lost count. "She asked me to meet her there at seven. When she didn't come to the door, I thought I should check on her. I'd want someone to do the same for me."

Holtzman's interviewing technique lacked just one ingredient of a B-movie interrogation — the suspect sweating under hot lights. Val would welcome hot lights in this tiny room without a window but with a vent that blew polar winds at her. She leaned down to rub her knees and calves. Her short skirt suited the heat outdoors, but not the frigid air trapped under the table.

Holtzman flipped to a new notebook page. "This morning at the victim's house, you must have thought about who'd want to murder her. Any names come to mind?"

Translation: finger someone else and you can get out of the hot seat, or rather, the cold seat. "I just thought it was a pretty strange way to kill someone."

He sat immobile like a bird of prey ready to pounce, eyes glued on her. "Oh? How would you kill someone?"

She clamped her lips together. Some questions didn't deserve answers.

He leaned toward her. "Would you make it look like an accident?"

Val flinched as if a dentist had just hit a nerve with his metal probe. "What are you driving at?"

His eyes narrowed as he studied her. "Driving at? Good word choice. I'm thinking about a car accident that wasn't accidental."

Val stiffened and felt a tremor run through her. No one had ever blamed her for the crash that nearly killed the famous Chef Henri, no one except the great man himself. The police and even the insurance company had chalked it up to bad weather and road conditions. Yet Val didn't feel blameless, wondering if the black ice on the road reflected her anger at the chef for rebuking her publicly. Maybe she could have steered out of the skid if she hadn't wanted to get back at him. She gripped the seat of the metal chair to stop her hands from shaking.

Holtzman pinned her with his steady look. "You know anything about the hit-and-run?"

"Hit-and-run?" Her voice sounded faint as if coming from inside a tunnel.

"A month ago a man was struck by a car on a deserted road near here."

Val's fingers relaxed. She'd misunderstood. He was talking about someone else's accident not hers. "What's that got to do with Nadia's murder?"

"A suspicious death and a murder within a few weeks of each other, that's rare in this area."

"That's the only connection between the hit-and-run and Nadia's murder?"

"How's this for a connection? You find a woman you know horrifically murdered, and you don't show much emotion. Then I bring up the hit-and-run and get the strongest reaction I've seen all morning."

And you'll never know why I had it. "Are you accusing me of something? Because if you are, I want a lawyer."

"You have the right to counsel if you think you need it." Holtzman turned off the tape recorder, crossed the room, and opened the door. "Sit tight, Ms. Deniston. We want your fingerprints."

She jumped out of her chair. "Fingerprints? Why?"

"You were all over the crime scene. We need to differentiate your prints from the others we find there."

Of course. She would have realized that if he hadn't made her nervous by treating her like a suspect. Did he grill her because the murder weapon made every tennis player a suspect? She paced the small room, trying to warm up. Holtzman had intimidated her, and she had no motive for murdering Nadia. Someone with a motive would feel even more intimidated.

Fifteen minutes later, with the fingerprinting over, she left the police station and ran into the chief in the parking lot.

"You got your color back, Val. You doing okay?"

"Better than this morning. Has Nadia's family been notified?"

"I talked to her ex, Joe Westrin. Her only kin are elderly and don't live in the area. He's contacting them."

Sad. Almost no family to mourn her. "I hope you catch the killer fast. If there's anything I can do to help, let me know."

"Keep your ears open at the club. You may

hear something people won't tell us." He went inside the converted farmhouse that served as police headquarters.

Val climbed into her car and called her cousin. No answer. Her stomach felt hollow. She would fortify herself with a good meal — crab cakes on potato rolls for her and Granddad. After lunch she'd drive to her cousin's house if she hadn't heard from her by then.

On the way home she stopped in the town's historic district to buy lunch ingredients. On either side of the main drag, frame houses built by original settlers had morphed into gift shops, antique stores, and B&Bs. Val found a parking space two blocks off Main Street. Now that school was out, day-trippers ambled through the town and lined up at the Bake Shoppe — tots in sneakers with flashing lights, teens in flip-flops, grown-ups in boat moccasins or all-terrain sandals. Would a murder hinder or boost tourism in the town?

She bought a small container of crabmeat at the market and snagged the last rolls in the bakery. To avoid the crowd on Main Street, she took a different route back to the car, a side street with shops she rarely visited. The display window of Personali-Tees featured customized shirts, towels, and aprons. She detoured into the shop and ordered a bib apron personalized for her grandfather. If she chose a stock color, she could pick it up tomorrow. Perfect.

Farther along the same street, she sniffed a fried food odor so strong it made her stomach turn. She passed the diner, spotted Luke through its storefront window, waved, and walked on.

"Val, wait up," he called out from the diner entrance.

She retraced her steps. "Hey, Luke."

The last time she stood near him, by firelight on Nadia's lawn, she didn't get a good look at his face, but now she noticed how much he'd filled out since high school. Fleshy cheeks padded the bones that used to be prominent. The gaunt young man had turned solid, but he still used the same cologne. Canoe. It tickled her nose and her memory. For a moment she felt like a teen in love, more with the idea of love than with Luke.

He searched her face as if waiting for her to say something. "Lot of action at Nadia's place this morning. Cop cars from the town, the sheriff, state police. Her neighbor said you were there earlier. Is Nadia dead? That's what we heard."

Despite the chief's efforts, someone had

noticed Val there. Probably Irene Pritchard.

Val took a deep breath. "You heard right. The police should be making an announcement soon if they haven't already. They're treating it as a murder."

"Murder?" He ran a hand through his close-cropped brown hair. "Jeez. I was afraid something bad would happen to her. That fire the other night must have been a warning. I wonder if she knew it."

"If she saw it as a warning, she would have called the police."

Luke rubbed the back of his neck. "Or I could have called them instead of making racket jokes."

"Don't blame yourself. It was her place and her decision whether to call the police." Absolving Luke might help Val shake her own guilt.

He tilted his head toward the diner. "How 'bout lunch? On the house."

"Not today, thanks." She glanced through the diner's storefront window. No customers inside, only a tall, broad young man setting a table. She recognized him from Nadia's Memorial Day party. "That's Irene Pritchard's son, isn't it? Nadia bragged about getting him his first job."

"Yeah, Jeremy. I hired him on her say-so. He grew up next door to her." Luke lowered his voice. "The kid's gonna be broken up when he hears about her."

The "kid," though in his twenties, was awkward and shy like a teen. "It was nice of Nadia to help him out."

"She came across as a hardnose, but not with Jeremy. She even talked me into renting the room over my garage to him so he could cut the apron strings and learn to live on his own."

Some people might call that meddling, including the woman with the apron strings. Val held up her bakery bag. "I'd better head home with this. Granddad's waiting for lunch."

"Let's get together for a drink sometime. The dockside restaurant has a new patio overlooking the water."

"Uh . . . okay." She smiled, unsure whether he had a romantic encounter or a friendly chat in mind. Maybe he didn't know, either. "See you, Luke."

She hurried to her parking space. A blast of heat hit her when she opened the car door. She'd rather walk half a mile home than ride in an oven. The car might cool off in another hour, once the sun went behind the tree. She cracked the windows open and shut the door. On the way home she ambled along shady back streets, avoiding the diner.

Granddad greeted her from the glider on the front porch. "How did it go with the police? Where's your car? Did they impound it?"

She laughed and leaned against the porch railing. "It went okay. I left the car in town. Needed a walk to clear my head. Did Monique call while I was gone?"

He shook his head. "You look worried."

"I've been trying to reach her all morning to tell her about Nadia." An hour ago she'd feared her cousin had run away. Now a worse scenario popped into her mind. "One woman in my tennis group murdered, another one not returning phone calls. I'm more than worried."

"Don't be. Monique's out and about somewhere, taking care of Number One, just like her daddy did. She'll call you when she gets around to it."

Val always defended her cousin against Granddad's bias, a holdover from his rift with Monique's father. "She would answer her cell phone if she were out. I should go to her house, but I see myself ringing her doorbell like I rang Nadia's, turning the doorknob, going inside, and finding her on the floor —" Val broke off with a shudder.

Granddad eased himself out of the glider. "I'll drive you to her house after lunch. If anything looks suspicious when we get there, you can wait in the car while I check it out."

What if Monique had been murdered like Nadia? Val couldn't let Granddad see anything like that. He might have a heart attack. "I'll go myself later. Want to help me make crab cakes? Only five ingredients. Your first cooking lesson."

"I'll watch. I've done enough cooking for one day." He followed her into the kitchen.

She washed her hands and took an egg from the fridge. "Would you get the flour, olive oil, and Old Bay seasoning from the pantry?"

He lined up the ingredients on the counter. "While you were gone, I made a deal with a painter who's going to do the upstairs bathroom and hall. He cut his price way down. All you gotta do is make the salads and side dishes for his Fourth of July party."

"You're escalating. Last time I only had to bake a cake." She pried the top off the plastic container of crabmeat, dumped the crab into a bowl, and checked it for bits of shell. "The IRS frowns on unreported income from bartering. The painter and I should both report the value of our services as income on our tax forms."

"He's offered me a senior citizen discount. You're just doing your grandfather a favor. The IRS won't come after us for that. Loosen up, Val. Bend the rules once in a while."

Always the wheeler-dealer, he got a kick out of bending rules, bargaining, and even exploiting his own granddaughter. At least she was collecting references for her cooking services, if not money. And she could honestly tell her mother that he was fixing up the house — in his own wily way.

Val mixed the crabmeat with egg, flour, and Old Bay seasoning. She picked up a hunk and shaped it into a patty. The phone rang. She looked at the crabmeat clinging to her palms. "Would you get that? If it's Monique, I'll wash my hands and talk to her."

He left the room to answer the phone. He'd never bothered to put an extension in the kitchen. Val didn't bother either, using her cell phone more often than the landline.

She put the patties in the freezer to harden before frying, glanced into the hall, and saw her grandfather still on the phone. He'd never chat that long with Monique. Maybe he was negotiating with another contractor.

Fifteen minutes later he returned to the kitchen as she was browning the crab cakes.

"That was your tennis partner from Sunday night calling. Gunnar. He asked for you, but I told him you were up to your elbows in crabmeat."

She nearly dropped the spatula. "You talked to him all that time?"

"Figure I'd vet him while I had him on the phone. His voice reminds me of Richard Burton's but with an American accent. We talked fishing. I asked him to drive you to Monique's, told him you'd point out the good fishing spots on the way. He's coming by in half an hour."

"What?" Bad enough he offered her services for free. Now he was setting her up. Val flipped a crab cake and smacked it down so hard the oil splattered. "I told you I'd drive myself."

"Go easy on those crab cakes. Listen, I know you're worried about what you'll find at Monique's house. If there's a problem, a younger man will be more help than your grandfather. Besides, I want to take a nap after lunch."

She couldn't fault his reasoning. "Just don't take up matchmaking, okay?" She would give Gunnar a chance to back out of the mission her grandfather had given him.

"In case you're interested, he's not married. Don't turn purple, Val. I asked a casual question, if his wife enjoyed fishing too. I call that clever."

"I call it nosy." But also helpful. He'd managed to find out something Val wanted to know. Even so, his interference steamed her.

She got over it once they were seated at the table and the sweet crabmeat kissed her tongue. During lunch she and Granddad discussed the house repairs that still needed to be done.

The doorbell rang while she was washing the skillet.

"I'll get it." Granddad left the kitchen.

He came back a minute later. "Gunnar's on the porch. I tried to get rid of him when I saw who he was. He won't leave without talking to you." Granddad clutched her shoulders. "Don't go with him. He's dangerous!"

CHAPTER 4

"Calm down, Granddad." Val set the skillet in the dish drainer and dried her hands. Last night she would have laughed at the idea of any real danger in Bayport. Now she knew better. "What makes you think Gunnar's dangerous?"

"Saturday night when I left the Mentors Club dinner, I saw two lowlifes hanging around the docks together. A swarthy hulk with a big mustache like a pirate and Gunnar in tattered jeans. Mean bullies, waiting to pick on somebody. I steered clear of them."

Understandable. Gunnar's face would daunt most people even if he didn't have a pirate with him. "You can't judge a person based on appearances. I know Gunnar isn't a mean bully. I spent two hours with him on the tennis court. Mean players blame their partners. Bullies intimidate their opponents. He didn't do that. He was a good sport, win or lose."

Granddad rolled his eyes. "He was just trying to impress you. Like today when he shows up here in a suit."

"In grungy clothes he's a troublemaker. In a suit he's a phony. What can he wear to make you happy?"

"It's not just his clothes. You know a man by the company he keeps."

"You know nothing about his company on the docks beyond the man's build, complexion, and mustache. That's not enough to condemn both of them. After talking to Gunnar on the phone, you liked him enough to invite him here. Let's talk to him now." She tugged her grandfather toward the porch, where he'd left Gunnar to swelter. No stamp of approval, no air conditioning.

Gunnar sat on a wicker settee, rolling up his shirtsleeves, his jacket folded on the seat beside him. He stood up when he saw her. His smile made the rugged terrain of his face less forbidding. "Good to see you again, Val."

She shook his extended hand. "I'm glad to see you too, and surprised. I thought you were going back to D.C. for work."

"I did go, and then decided to take some time off this week. I drove here straight from a meeting."

That explained the suit. Val gave Grand-dad an I-hope-you're-satisfied look. "My grandfather saw you at the town dock Saturday night. You and a guy with a mustache."

"Right. We were supposed to go night fishing. The captain canceled the trip because of rough water."

Granddad stroked his chin. "Can't say as I blame him. He'd have to swab the deck after you weekenders upchucked into the wind." He ignored Val's glare. "What line of work you in, Gunder?"

"Gunnar. Accounting."

"Business must be slow for you to take off when you like. You got your own firm?"

"Not yet, though I may before long. For now, I have a government job and a lot of accumulated leave."

"That so?" Granddad crossed his arms and lifted his chin. "What part of the government?"

Gunnar looked amused at the inquisition. "Treasury. Internal Revenue Service."

Granddad ran his finger under his collar and stared at the porch floor. If Val were an IRS auditor, she'd take his body language as a "tell" and comb through his tax returns.

She wiped sweat from her forehead. Why was she thinking about taxes when she had a murder and a missing cousin to worry her? "Gunnar, I know my grandfather recruited you to drive me to my cousin's house, but I can drive myself."

"She doesn't want to impose on . . . I mean . . ." Granddad trailed off. He must have known he'd given Gunnar an opening and couldn't think of a way to retract it.

Gunnar smiled at Val. "You're not imposing. I can't check into my B&B yet anyway, and I'd enjoy your company."

Her spirits, in the dumps since finding Nadia dead, lifted slightly. "Thanks. Let's go then." She grabbed her bag from the hall.

Her grandfather acted as if she'd included him in her "let's go." He followed them to the curb and eyed Gunnar's red Miata. "I guess some people don't need a practical car." He glanced at his Buick parked in front of Gunnar's two-seater.

Uh-oh. Val guessed what he'd say next, suggest they all drive together in the behemoth Buick. Bad enough that he set her up with Gunnar. Now he would chaperone her too. She touched his shoulder. "I'll call you from Monique's. I know you're concerned about . . . things."

His eyes locked on hers. "Less concerned than I was, but take care."

She took his words as acceptance, though

not approval, of her leaving with Gunnar. Granddad turned back toward the house.

Gunnar held out the car keys to Val. "Why don't you drive? You know the way."

Six months ago she would have grabbed the keys to a sports car with no second thoughts. "You drive. You know your car." *And if you knew me, you wouldn't trust me with it.*

Val directed Gunnar along side streets to avoid the traffic in the historic district. She watched his right hand cup the gearshift, the dark hairs curling over his cocked wrist. Something stirred in her. While his face had rough patches, that hand looked smooth and deft.

She pointed to a row of shops at the edge of town. "You see the art gallery there? It used to be my grandfather's fish market. From seafood to seascapes, Bayport's history in a nutshell. Once upon a time the folks here built ships and caught oysters. Now they cater to weekenders decorating vacation homes."

"The shops changed, the small-town atmosphere didn't. People like your grandfather still feel at home here. By the way, I enjoyed meeting him."

She didn't hear any sarcasm in his voice. He couldn't have missed the negative vibes

Granddad had beamed at him. "You saw him in high curmudgeon mode. I wish I could tell you he isn't always like that, but I'd be lying. Turn left at the next intersection. Once we're on the peninsula, you'll have a view of the Chesapeake. Bayport, despite its name, isn't on the bay."

"But the river and creek feed into it. Close enough." Gunnar downshifted. "Why are you anxious to check on your cousin? Is she elderly?"

"No, Monique's a year older than me. She's a second cousin, and since I don't have sisters or first cousins, she stands in for them. I have to take good care of her."

He turned onto the peninsula road. "Her name sounds French."

"Her parents came from around here and moved to Canada before she was born. Monique grew up bilingual. Her mother came back to this area ten years ago to take care of a sick relative. Monique came with her, married a local man, and stayed." Val chewed her fingernails. "Monique's husband and kids are away now, and she's not answering her phone."

"Maybe she went out and doesn't have her cell phone or didn't juice it up."

"I know, or she could have switched it off for a meeting or a photo shoot. On any other day, I wouldn't worry if she didn't return my calls." Val took a deep breath. "Monique's on the tennis team with me. Another woman on the team was found murdered this morn—" She broke off as the Miata drifted right. "Watch out!"

The car edged off the pavement onto the shoulder.

Gunnar steered back onto the road. "You said a *tennis* player was murdered?"

"I did." But unlike him, she'd emphasized the crime, not the sport. She peered sideways at him.

He returned her look. "What's the dead woman's name?"

"Nadia Westrin. You met her Sunday night when we played mixed doubles. Petite with short hair."

He drummed his fingers on the wheel. "Oh, yeah. The real estate agent. She offered to sell me a house two minutes after she met me. How was she killed?"

"The police haven't released that information yet." A good answer, truthful and evasive at the same time. He'd probably ask more questions about the murder unless she changed the subject. "On the porch you talked about opening an accounting practice. Is that in the near future?"

"Sooner than I expected. My great-aunt

Gretchen died and left me some cash. When the inheritance comes through, I'll have enough to quit my job and take some risks."

"Cool. We should all have a Great-Aunt Gretchen."

"You wouldn't say that if you'd ever met Gretchen." Gunnar gave Val a crooked smile and glanced at her crossed legs. "You told me you moved here a few months ago, but didn't say where you lived before or what you did."

"I worked for a New York publisher, promoting their cookbooks. I did publicity for celebrity chefs."

"A good job for someone who's into cooking."

"I was, but the experience turned me off pretentious gourmet cuisine. I decided to write my own cookbook with recipes that don't require exotic ingredients and lots of prep. The job didn't leave me any time to do that. I came home exhausted at night." Val pointed to the cornfields flanking the road. "I missed serene sights like this. After a decade in the city, I burned out."

"I like fields of grain if they're near large bodies of water. Where I grew up in the Midwest, the fields go on and on." Gunnar slowed down and watched an osprey until it flew out of sight. "You have time to play

64

singles this week?"

"Sure." Val was glad he'd be around for a few days. She wouldn't mind seeing more of him and, judging by how often he looked at her bare legs, he wouldn't mind seeing more of her either. "The café's open for breakfast and lunch. After I close it at two, I usually hang around to clean up or prepare things for the next day. Do you want to play late in the afternoon?"

"I'll try to reserve a court for tomorrow."

"Maybe by then the police will have cleared out. Today they're probably combing the club for evidence and murder suspects."

"The club? Why there?"

Because of the weapon, which Val couldn't mention. She cracked open the car window and let in a moist breeze. "Nadia spent a lot of time playing tennis and made some enemies at the club."

"Arguments on the tennis court don't lead to murder."

"Says who? The Italian painter Caravaggio got into a fight after betting on a tennis game. He killed his opponent in a duel."

Gunnar's mouth turned down in skepticism. "You made that up."

"Did not. I OD'd on trivia games in my misspent youth. I remember a lot of random factoids." And forget important things, like how she'd nearly killed the man who'd entrusted her with his life and his vintage car.

"Okay, but that duel was over money, not tennis. Greed explains most crimes. The police will look into who benefits from Nadia's death."

"Gee, you sound like an accountant. Don't put your money on greed as the motive in this case. Nadia drove a Lexus to impress her clients, but she lived in a small house. I doubt she was rich."

Gunnar slowed down as the road narrowed and ran alongside the bay. "Rich is relative. Some people kill for running shoes or over a sports bet, like that Italian painter."

They lapsed into silence. Val expected him to show interest in the water views and the fishing prospects, but he didn't. He just stared straight ahead. Maybe news of the murder had dampened his enthusiasm for the Eastern Shore as a weekend getaway.

Monique's sprawling ranch house came into view toward the end of the peninsula.

Val's shoulders tensed at the sight of the white van in the driveway. "Her car's here." Not necessarily good news. This morning Nadia's car had sat in the driveway too.

Gunnar parked on the road next to the

mailbox. As they climbed from the Miata, Monique came around the side of her van and waved. "Hi, there."

Val waved back and spoke to Gunnar across the hood of the car. "Monique must not have heard about Nadia or she wouldn't look so carefree. I'll have to break the news." Though she'd rather not have a witness when she warned her cousin about the police.

Monique met them at the top of the driveway. She introduced herself to Gunnar and shook hands with him. "Nice to meet you. What brings the two of you out here?"

"I've been calling you since this morning," Val said. "Where have you been?"

"My French conversation group and then a sidewalk sale in Salisbury. I forgot to turn on my phone after the meeting. You won't believe the bargains I found for the kids." Monique gestured toward the back of the van stuffed with shopping bags.

Only Monique could go to a sidewalk sale in the heat and still look cucumber cool, long and slim in a green sheath dress. Her hair, golden brown like buttered toast, stayed put in its ponytail, not a wisp out of place.

Val envied those tame strands. Her own hair spiraled down, coiled out, or frizzed up, depending on weather and whim. "How come on muggy days, you're the poster girl for hair conditioner, and I'm modeling a fright wig?"

Monique grinned. "You're not even close to a fright wig."

"But if you want one," Gunnar said, "we can drive back to town with the top down." A buzz came from his shirt pocket. He pulled out his cell phone and glanced at it. "Excuse me."

He stepped away to stand under the shade of a tree and studied the display, apparently reading a text or an e-mail.

Monique turned her back to him. "In case you were wondering, but afraid to ask," she spoke in an undertone, "I didn't burn the racket at Nadia's house."

"Good." Whew. "How did you hear about the fire?"

"Chatty called me yesterday morning after talking to Nadia. You saw the whole thing. I'm surprised you didn't tell me about it. What were you doing at Nadia's place Sunday night anyway?"

Val ignored her cousin's accusatory tone. "Nadia needed a ride home from the club. She asked me to keep quiet about the burning racket. I wonder why she blabbed to Chatty." The nickname suited Chatty Ridenour's personality far better than her given name, Charity.

"Because she wants her to ferret out the culprit, and of course, I'm first on the list." Monique glanced back at Gunnar, who was pressing buttons, texting a return message. "Who is that guy? How long have you known him?"

"I met him Sunday night. We played mixed doubles. He's visiting from Washington and —" Val broke off as Gunnar approached them.

"I have to head to town now." He jotted on a scrap of paper and handed it to Val. "My cell phone number. I'll come back to pick you up. Call me when you're ready."

"Don't bother driving all the way here again," Monique said. "I can drop Val off when I run errands in town."

He nodded, agreeing more quickly than Val liked. She watched him leave with mixed emotions. Now she wouldn't have to mince words when she told Monique about Nadia's murder, but she'd looked forward to riding back with him. Who'd summoned him to town? The fishing buddy who looked like a pirate, or someone else he knew in Bayport?

The heat from the asphalt driveway penetrated the soles of Val's sandals. "My feet feel like dough baking on a pizza stone. Let's go inside and talk."

While her cousin carried shopping bags to the bedroom wing, Val phoned her grandfather from the family room adjacent to the kitchen. She told him she'd located Monique and would hitch a ride back to town with her. No hurry, Granddad told her, he was going out to dinner with a friend. She'd have pressed him for details if she hadn't been so anxious to talk to her cousin.

Monique collapsed onto the sofa next to Val, slipped off her sandals, and put her feet on the kidney-shaped coffee table. "What's up?"

"Nadia is —" Words stuck in Val's throat like muesli without milk. "She's . . . dead."

Her cousin's mouth dropped open. "Dead? A heart attack, or what?"

"She was murdered. Last night. In her house."

Monique clapped one hand over her mouth and the other over her stomach, looking as if she was fighting nausea. "Murdered in Bayport? I can't believe it. You think you're protecting your kids by keeping them out of cities, but no place is safe anymore."

Shock had narrowed her focus. A murder near her sanctuary. Her children at risk.

70

How long before Monique, the photographer, widened her lens and saw the risk to herself?

Monique stood up and wandered as if in a trance to her retro kitchen. Its knotty pine cabinets and laminated counters belonged on the set of a 1950s sitcom. Nostalgia for the past didn't interfere with her passion for the latest appliances. Her fingers danced over the surface of the espresso-latte-cappuccino maker. The contraption had enough dials, levers, and buttons for a cockpit. It might even fly. Right now it was revving up, grinding beans.

The coffee fragrance apparently woke Monique from her daze. She leaned against the counter. "It's terrible about Nadia. Too many maniacs with guns out there."

Val joined her at the kitchen counter. "Maniacs with guns aren't the only people who commit murders. You had a grudge against Nadia and made it public. You might end up a suspect."

Monique flinched as if Val had thrown ice water at her. "You think I killed Nadia?"

"Of course not. I just want to warn you that the police will have questions."

"I have nothing to hide. I'll be glad to answer their questions."

Typical Monique. Whenever they were

71

behind in a tennis match, she showed similar bravado. But Deputy Holtzman made a more formidable opponent than any they'd met on the court. "It won't be a cakewalk, Monique. The deputy who —" A chirp from the cordless phone on the counter interrupted Val.

Her cousin grabbed the phone. "Hi. . . . Val just told me. Isn't it awful?" She covered the mouthpiece and whispered, "It's Yumiko."

The club's tennis manager. The news about Nadia had obviously reached the club. While Monique listened to Yumiko, the coffeemaker hissed and burbled. Val imagined the club members hissing and whispering about Nadia's murder, exchanging theories about the culprit.

Monique nodded with the phone held to her ear. "Of course I'll play. Everything's changed now. . . . I can take over as captain next season. . . . She's here. I'll put her on." Monique handed Val the phone and drifted to the sliding glass door with its view of oak trees and the water beyond.

Val cradled the phone and braced herself for a volley of words. Unlike most second-language speakers, Yumiko talked fast. The more she had to say, the more syllables she dropped. Val had done something similar in

72

her first Spanish class, racing through her oral responses in hopes that the teacher wouldn't notice whether she'd said *las* or *los.* "Hi, Yumiko."

"I want to know is it okay to play the team match on Thursday. If we don't play, we have to forfeit, and this match decides who is league champion. Monique says she will take Nadia's place. But I don't like to play if it disrespects Nadia." Yumiko paused for a quick breath. "What is the right thing to do?"

Val could look in a dozen etiquette books without finding guidance for this situation. Her basic rule would have to suffice. "The right thing is not to tell other people what's right. Let them decide for themselves. Why don't we get the whole team together around six on Thursday? We'll meet in the café and have a little ceremony in honor of Nadia. Then anyone who wants to play can stay for the match. I'll set out some snacks for the gathering."

This morning she'd gone to Nadia's house with creative menus to showcase her catering skills. Now she would make nibbles for a somber memorial to the woman. A lump formed in Val's throat.

"Good idea to have a ceremony, Val. I will make soothing tea for it. Chatty is here at the club now. I will tell her about the ceremony. I couldn't reach Althea and Bethany."

"Leave it to me. I'll let them know what we're doing." Val hung up. She turned to her cousin, still standing motionless in front of the sliding door. "You'll join the rest of us in a toast to Nadia, won't you?"

"Of course. Once we get that out of the way, I'm sure we can coax everyone to play the match."

"Don't coax. Hang back and let the others reach a consensus on whether to play, okay?"

"Why?"

"Last week, in front of the whole team, you accused Nadia of seducing your husband and said you wouldn't play for her team anymore. You even wanted the rest of us to quit the team. Now you're talking about taking over as captain, stepping into her tennis shoes after she's dead." Not as bad as dancing on her grave, but close. "Are you listening to me?"

Her cousin gave no sign of it. She jerked the sliding door open. "What's *he* doing here?"

CHAPTER 5

Val joined Monique on the patio outside the family room. Nothing moved in the backyard thick with vegetation. "I don't see anyone out here."

"Maverick's tying up at the dock."

Through the bushes in the backyard, Val glimpsed Monique's husband on his way from the dock to the garden shed. "I thought he'd taken the children to visit his parents."

Monique pursed her lips. "He did. He must have left Mike and Mandy with his folks. He knows I hate that. They ply the kids with candy and let them stay up late. If he's there, at least the kids go to bed on time."

Her husband emerged from the shed, tossed a canvas bag into his boat, and walked up the path to the house. Lean and compact, with wavy hair falling over his forehead and curling down his neck, Maverick Mott looked more like a playboy than a family man pushing forty . . . usually. Today, though, lines of tension surrounded his mouth and eyes.

He greeted Val and his wife with a nod, the battery that powered his ever-ready smile out of juice. He must have heard about Nadia.

Monique stood planted in front of the sliding door as if barring his entry into the house. "Back so soon? I thought you were spending the week in Philadelphia."

"You didn't get my phone message? My guys are way behind schedule at the boat-yard. I drove down this morning to help them. The kids will be fine. I'll go back on the weekend to pick them up. I just zoomed over here to grab a tool." He fixed his gaze on the runabout he used for commuting between the house and his boatyard across the river.

Monique put her hands on her hips. "A tool? That's the only reason you came here?"

He stepped closer to her and studied her face like a nearsighted man who'd lost his glasses. "There's a rumor at the boatyard about Nadia. Do you know anything about it?"

Monique returned her husband's steady

gaze. "Val just told me. Nadia's dead. Murdered."

Silence as heavy as the humid air fell over them. Val felt she was watching two actors who'd lost their scripts. How did a married couple discuss the murder of "the other woman"? Preferably without an audience.

"Time for me to leave." Val reached for the door handle. "Oops. I don't have a car."

Maverick perked up. He'd heard a cue. "I can drop you off at the park dock."

Val was tempted. The water route offered a straight shot to town in contrast to the peninsula road. A five-minute walk from the park dock would take her to the street where she'd left her car. "Monique was going to drop me off when she ran errands." Val glanced at her cousin.

"Hitch a ride with him." Monique raised her chin toward Maverick. "I'll do the errands tomorrow. Right now I'd rather be alone."

Val opened the sliding door. "I'll get my bag." She slipped back inside.

The house smelled of the coffee Monique had brewed but never poured. The phone in the kitchen enticed Val even more than the coffee. She made sure Monique and Maverick couldn't see her from the patio and pushed the button on Monique's phone to access the call history. She located the number she wanted, for Maverick's parents in Philadelphia, and stored it in her own cell phone. Then she returned to the patio.

Monique stood alone, her back to the house. "Maverick's waiting for you on the dock."

Val put a hand on her cousin's shoulder. "I'll stay if you want me to."

"Thank you, but I wouldn't be good company. I need to think about Nadia. Maverick. The kids. All of it."

"Call me if you want to talk."

A minute later, Val climbed into the runabout with Maverick and sat in a molded fiberglass seat. He fired up the motor and whooshed away from the dock. Her head snapped back.

He made a wide right turn toward town. "Do you know what happened to Nadia? How she was killed?"

Val knew how to evade those questions. "I don't think the police have released that information yet."

He ran his fingers through his thick, sun-streaked hair. "What a nightmare. Monique bad-mouths Nadia at the club, and Nadia's murdered a few days later. I hope the police arrest the killer soon. Until then, Monique's in an awkward position."

Val clenched her teeth so hard she nearly broke a molar. "*You* put her in that position."

Maverick jerked the wheel. Her accusation must have rattled him. Until today, their conversations had run to the social and superficial.

He used one hand to shield his eyes from the sun. "What happened between Nadia and me meant nothing. It was over. I told Monique that last week. She forgave me."

"Really?" Val lumped him with all the cheating politicians who interpreted their wives' stoicism in front of cameras as forgiveness. "She forgave you, and that's why you left town?"

His grip tightened on the wheel as the boat rocked in the wake of a passing cruiser. He watched the horizon intently. "The kids visit my folks every year when preschool lets out. Monique couldn't come with us. She had two weddings last weekend. June's a busy month for photographers."

Val hunched forward and folded her arms, trying to shield them from the sun. "Did Nadia know your affair with her *meant nothing*?"

He gave her an are-you-nuts look. "I called her from Philadelphia yesterday and said we had to stop seeing each other."

Too much information. Why make such a point of where he'd called from and when? Val's skin prickled with sunburn and suspicion. "Nadia was okay with that?" Hard to imagine she'd go gently into jilted lover limbo.

"We both knew it was just a fling."

"When you called her *from Philadelphia yesterday,* did she tell you what happened the night before?" Val asked.

"The racket burning?" He throttled down as they approached the town dock. "Monique didn't do it. She dissed Nadia at the club and got it out of her system. No further reprisals needed."

Val cringed at "further reprisals." Maverick's supposed defense of his wife emphasized her motive for murder. "Say that to the police, and Monique might end up in handcuffs. You don't make her look innocent of revenge by explaining how she's already taken it."

Maverick ignored her in favor of the motor, the wheel, and the pier. He maneuvered the runabout alongside the town dock and dropped her off, his face grim.

Val fished out her cell phone on the way to her car. She called the number for Maverick's parents, grateful that the caller ID on her phone identified her location, but not her name. She had no reason to check on Maverick other than the belief that a man who cheats also lies. Could she catch him in a lie without lying herself?

She spoke fast when a woman answered the phone. "Mrs. Mott? You're Maverick Mott's mother, right, the man who restores boats? I have some questions for him and understood he was staying with you." Misleading, yes, but no outright lies.

"He was here earlier in the week, but left yesterday. He should be back in the boatyard today. In Bayport, Maryland. Do you want the number there?"

"I can look it up. Thanks for your help." Val clicked off.

So Maverick hadn't left Philadelphia this morning as he'd implied. Now that she'd uncovered his deceit, what should she do about it? Should she confront him and ask where he'd spent last night? Or tell Monique he'd lied? Neither action appealed to Val. She'd rather eat stinkbugs on a TV reality show than interfere in her cousin's marriage. But if Maverick lied to the police about where he'd spent the night of the murder, Val wouldn't hesitate to tell them the truth.

She opened the door to her Saturn and stepped back from its pent-up heat. The car didn't cool off until she'd driven halfway to the Cool Down Café.

Val put a pan of oatmeal energy bars in the oven and set the timer for thirty-five minutes. The bars would supplement her dwindling supply of biscotti for tomorrow's customers. She still hadn't heard from Bethany. Might as well try her again.

A cheery voice answered the call. "Hi there. This is Bethany O'Shay."

"Hey, it's Val. I'm glad I finally reached you. I tried you at home and on your cell." Bethany was the only person Val knew under the age of thirty who didn't treat her cell phone like a combination lifeline and security blanket. She probably hadn't even checked her messages.

"I was at school all day for meetings and classroom cleanup. I'm just leaving now. Tonight is our teacher-staff potluck dinner. Schools out, and we're partying." Bethany enunciated every syllable as if Val were one of her first graders.

"I can't leave the café because I just put something in the oven. I need to talk to you in person. Can you stop by here?" Val heard nothing on the line and wondered if she'd lost the connection. "Are you there?"

"Did you decide you don't want me as

82

your assistant this summer? You don't have to break it to me gently. I can handle it."

"No, that's not it. I still want you to work at the café. We can talk about your schedule this afternoon."

Fifteen minutes later, Bethany traipsed into the club in lime high-tops, a tiered skirt in jelly bean colors, and a hot pink top that bunched around her waist. The outfit emphasized her ample size and clashed with her cascade of ginger curls.

She sat on a swivel stool and peered over the snack bar at Val's mixing bowl. "What are you making?"

"A layered brunch casserole called a strata. You start with cubes of day-old bread, add meat or veggies in the next layer, then a cheese layer, and top it off with eggs and milk." Val poured the egg-and-milk mixture over the layers. "The flavors blend overnight in the fridge. You bake it the next morning."

Bethany eyed a carton of empty eggshells next to the casserole dish. "You used a lot of eggs. Aren't they bad for you?"

Not as bad as the wacky diets Bethany tried. Val covered the casserole and stored it in the fridge. "Each serving will have less than half an egg in it. It won't kill you."

"I can't eat anything like that. I'm on an all-red diet. Today I had berries for breakfast and lunch. I'm sure I'll get used to it in a few days, but right now I'm a little hungry. I miss bread and meat."

This latest diet probably wouldn't last any longer than Bethany's previous ones. Why did she try one fad diet after another? Maybe her negative body image stemmed from her long tennis partnership with tiny Nadia, eater of seeds, shoots, and leaves. A new wardrobe would help Bethany more than any diet. In simpler styles and quiet colors, she would still look robust, but not overweight.

"You want red, Bethany? I got it." Val poured her a cranberry juice spritzer and set out a bowl of veggie chips. "The orange ones are sweet potato chips, the red ones are nothing but beets." Plus fat and salt.

Bethany chewed her lower lip. "Beets are on my diet, but I'm not sure about chips."

"If you don't want the beet chips, just leave them." Fat chance. She would need the stress relief of crunchy food before long. Val walked around the counter, sat on the stool next to Bethany's, and took a deep breath. "I have some bad news. Nadia —"

"Bad news and Nadia go together. The way she treated me was just beyond belief."

Bethany had nursed those hurt feelings for more than a week. Maybe Val could apply a salve to them before giving the shock treatment. "People move on and get new tennis partners all the time. You can't take it personally."

"Nadia made it personal. She practically accused me of cheating." Bethany grabbed a handful of mostly red chips. "She claimed I made bad line calls. No one's ever said that."

But plenty of people thought it. She often called her opponents' shots out when other players would have judged them good. Val figured Bethany needed glasses, but this wasn't the time to suggest an eye exam. "None of that will matter when you hear my news. Nadia's dead."

Bethany jerked as if someone had just slapped her. Her green eyes bugged out. "Dead? What happened? An accident?"

"Definitely not an accident. She —"

"Did her house burn down?"

Odd question. "Why would you think that?"

Bethany blinked rapidly. "I heard about the racket burning, and not long ago a couple of houses around here went up in flames."

Val vaguely remembered some recent arsons. "Her house didn't burn down. She was found there this morning. The police are treating her death as a murder."

"Murder? Oh, my God." Bethany squeezed her eyes shut. Two tears escaped from between her lashes and rolled down her cheeks. She wiped them with the back of her hand and opened her eyes. "But how did it happen? Did a burglar break in and shoot her?"

"The police haven't revealed the details yet." The oven timer dinged. Val welcomed the interruption. She had responded to all the questions she cared to answer about Nadia's death. She walked around the eating bar, removed the pan with the baked oatmeal mixture from the oven, and set it on a trivet. "We're having a get-together here in memory of Nadia, Thursday at six, before the team match."

"Yes, we should do that." Bethany pulled a neatly folded tissue from her skirt pocket and blotted her eyelashes. "Poor Nadia. I just wish we'd been on better terms before she died. She never had a chance to say she was sorry. And I didn't have the chance to forgive her."

She looked so forlorn Val wanted to comfort her. "It's always bad when someone dies, especially if you have unresolved conflicts. Forgive her now. It's not too late."

"I get your point. I have to let go of my

anger." She let go of the tissue in her clenched fist.

"Don't show any anger when you talk to the police. They'll want to interview us all."

"I have to talk to the police?" Bethany knocked over her cranberry spritzer. "Should I tell them how Nadia treated me?"

Val grabbed a dishcloth and mopped up the spill. "Just answer their questions with facts. You don't have to tell them your feelings about the way she treated you." She rinsed the counter with a clean cloth and refilled Bethany's drink. "How did you hear about the racket burning?"

"Chatty told me. I bet whoever set that fire murdered Nadia."

"It's a foolish risk to take the day before committing a murder." Unless something happened in the interim to turn a vandal into a killer.

Bethany studied a beet chip. "We have to figure out who did it."

"The police are on it."

"The police here direct traffic and keep the tourists happy. What do they know about murder? Nobody ever gets murdered here. You lived in New York. They have murders there all the time."

Val reached for a knife to cut the oatmeal energy bars. "I never ran across a single dead body in New York." She couldn't say the same for Bayport.

"We're way ahead of the police because we knew Nadia. I wonder if Joe Westrin snapped and killed her." Bethany snapped a beet chip in two. "She treated him like dirt. Got rid of him like she got rid of me."

Val suppressed a laugh. Anyone who could equate switching tennis partners with divorcing a husband took the game way too seriously. No doubt the police would question Nadia's ex. A current or former spouse always made a good suspect in a murder . . . once the police ruled out the person who found the body. "I barely know Joe. He stopped by the café a couple of times. Seemed like a nice guy."

"Too nice for Nadia." Bethany gulped her cranberry drink. "She was ruthless in her real estate dealings too."

"Who told you that?"

"Common knowledge, according to Bigby."

Bethany spoke the last three words the way other people might say "according to Webster" or "according to Hoyle." Who dared to doubt her brother Bigby's real estate expertise? He could turn farmland into tract housing overnight. He also brought the personality of a bulldozer to the tennis court. Each time the ball came over the net in doubles, he bellowed "Mine!" Either his partners stayed out of his way or he mowed them down. Maybe the big man had mowed down little Nadia, his former doubles partner, and that explained the frostiness Val had noticed between them.

Val ran her knife around the edge of the baking pan. "I heard that Bigby and Nadia used to play mixed doubles together. How come they stopped?"

"You're the one who said people get new tennis partners all the time." Bethany scowled. "I hope you're not suggesting Bigby had anything to do with Nadia's death. He would never hurt her."

"I didn't suggest anything."

Easy to understand Bethany's defensive reaction. She could see Joe Westrin as a murderer, but not her brother Bigby, and Val could imagine Bigby a killer, but her cousin Monique? Never. Yet here at the club, where the mud flew as fast as the tennis balls, Monique would be the obvious suspect. Her tirade against Nadia last week guaranteed that. Val would do her best to keep that mud off her cousin.

Her knife crunched through the oatmeal pastry. Even a small blade like this would have pierced Nadia's flesh with ease. Yet someone had gone to the trouble of shaving down a racket handle instead of reaching for a kitchen knife. Why?

Bethany climbed off the stool. "It's after four. I have to go home and make baked red beans for the teacher potluck. Can I start working tomorrow morning? I've worked a few weekends so I know the routine."

"Sure." Val could think of nothing she wanted more than to sleep in tomorrow. Today felt like the longest day she'd ever lived through, and it still had hours to go. "Call me if you have a question. The breakfast casseroles bake for forty-five minutes at 325 degrees."

"Okeydoke. Thanks, Val."

Val lifted the breakfast bars from the pan with a spatula and stored them away. She had the uneasy feeling she was supposed to be somewhere else. Her watch read four-thirty. Could she have forgotten an appointment?

No, Nadia had made an appointment. She'd written *Tues430* in the notes Val had seen near the phone while waiting for the police this morning. The notes included an address on Maple Street and a long name starting with Z and ending with K. Val couldn't remember the syllables that came between those letters or the exact address. Maple Street was only a few blocks long, though, and she could probably find the house from the description in Nadia's notes — a brick ranch with a fenced yard. Someone might be waiting there for Nadia now.

If Val had a meeting scheduled with a person who would never show up, she'd want to know sooner rather than later. She grabbed her bag and rushed out of the club. She would keep Nadia's appointment.

CHAPTER 6

Val drove along Maple Street, where most of the mailboxes had names painted on them. She braked when she saw a long name beginning with Z. She parked in front of a modest one-story house, a perfect size for Granddad if she could ever talk him into giving up the big Victorian. She studied the name on the mailbox for a few seconds, silently pronouncing each syllable. The name didn't end with a K as she'd remembered from Nadia's notes, but the mailbox probably couldn't fit the full name. A window air conditioner hummed as she approached the front door.

She rapped on the door and, when a woman with permed gray curls opened it, she said, "Hi. Are you Mrs. Zach-ar-na-rov—"

"I told you to call me Mrs. Z, Nadia. Come on in."

"I'm not —" A deliciously sweet aroma

wafted toward Val and drew her inside. She followed Mrs. Z into a small, tidy living room.

The elderly woman bent herself into a straight-backed chair and gestured toward a sofa slip-covered in a worn floral fabric. "Sit down. Help yourself to some cookies and iced tea."

The coffee table held a glass pitcher of amber liquid with lemon slices and mint sprigs floating amid ice cubes. The table's centerpiece was a plate piled with golden mounds studded with brown-edged coconut flakes. They looked like macaroons but with a more intense color than usual. Val hesitated. Should she eat cookies under false pretenses? Maybe just one.

She perched on the sofa edge, took a cookie from the plate, and bit into the moist, sweet confection. "Umm. Whole eggs, not just the whites. That's why they're golden." And sinfully rich.

Mrs. Z leaned forward, the skin around her eyes crinkling. "Very good, Nadia, picking out my secret ingredient. You enjoy baking?"

Val's mouth felt suddenly dry, and the cookie stuck in her throat. "I apologize if I misled you. I'm not Nadia. She's a . . . a friend of mine. I came here to tell you she can't meet with you. She died very suddenly."

The older woman clutched the arms of her chair. "Oh, I'm sorry. Sudden death is a terrible thing, but not as bad as a prolonged, painful death." She sighed.

Val waited while Mrs. Z took off her gold-rimmed glasses and wiped away a tear. Nadia's death had apparently reminded her of someone else's passing, someone close to her. "I assume you didn't know Nadia, or you wouldn't have mistaken me for her."

"I talked to her for the first time last night. I finally decided to sell my house and called her right away. I was afraid if I waited until morning, I'd change my mind again."

Mrs. Z might have been the last person Nadia spoke with, aside from the murderer. To find out more about that call, Val would have to improvise. On the phone with Maverick's mother, she'd avoided a blatant lie. Now she saw no alternative. "I was trying to reach Nadia last night myself, but couldn't get through. She may have been on the phone with you. What time did you talk to her?"

"Around nine-thirty, but I don't understand why you didn't get through. Her phone has call waiting. She put me on hold to take another call."

"Oh, that wasn't me. I called her later than that." One lie always leads to another.

"She may have had company by the time you phoned. After she took that other call, she sounded rushed. She said she was expecting someone at her house any minute."

Val's pulse quickened. Perhaps the call interrupting Mrs. Z's conversation had come from the murderer making sure Nadia was alone. Once Val told the police what she'd just heard from Mrs. Z, they could trace that call and possibly solve the case.

Val poured herself a glass of iced tea. "I'd really like to have your recipe for the macaroons if you're willing to share it."

"Of course. Recipes are meant to be shared, and I know this one by heart."

Val pulled out the paper Gunnar had given her with his cell phone number and jotted the recipe on the back. It was simple enough she could have remembered it. It even met Granddad's criteria, only five ingredients.

She stood up and thanked Mrs. Z for the tea, the cookies, and the recipe, leaving out what she was most grateful for, the information about Nadia's phone calls.

Mrs. Z walked her to the door. "Nadia came highly recommended. Are you also a real estate agent? I sure could use one."

"Sorry, I don't work in real estate, but I'll ask my friends if they can recommend anyone."

Val climbed into her Saturn. She would, of course, tell Chief Yardley about Maverick's lie and Nadia's visitor, but why rush it? She was on a roll and might dig up even more leads. Time to focus on the murder weapon. Where would someone get an antique racket? Bayport had plenty of antique shops, most too upscale to deal in old sports equipment. Val bypassed the historic district and drove to a cluster of secondhand stores off the main drag at the edge of town.

The salesclerks at Cobweb Corner and Must Haves didn't know the stock. She spent half an hour poking through the junk in each place before concluding that both shops had plenty of cobwebs and must, but no wood rackets.

When she asked about antique rackets at Old 'N Things, the bearded owner tucked his thumbs into his red suspenders. "We don't got any. They ain't rare enough to be valuable or new enough to be useful. Folks keep 'em in garages and attics in case their grandkids wanna use 'em."

A teenaged clerk shifting crockery on a

shelf turned around. "I saw a bunch of those rackets at Darwin's Sports. Hanging up near the ceiling. Decorations, I guess. You want directions to the place?"

"Thanks. I know where it is." But she'd never noticed the décor in Darwin's store.

She knew him as the club's part-time tennis pro and the only person she'd ever met who went by a single name like a rock star. Calling himself Darwin beat using the name his parents had foisted on him, Darwin Darwin.

Val parked her car two blocks off Main Street in front of Darwin's Sports. Its business logo, an X formed by a racket and a barbell, reflected the shop's wares and its owner. Darwin had a reputation as a certified tennis pro and a certifiable dumbbell.

He was helping a customer trying on shoes when Val entered the shop. A teenage clerk at the checkout counter chatted on her cell phone while ogling Darwin. A tennis has-been in his late twenties, he'd never graduated from the satellite circuit to a major tournament, but he could still compete in the local Adonis stakes. Transport him to Southern California, and he'd have looked like the archetypal surfer, skin tanned and hair bleached.

Val studied the vintage equipment decorating the walls above the merchandise displays. Badminton rackets with small round heads, squash rackets with heads shaped like teardrops, and tennis rackets with oval heads, several made of wood. No obvious empty spots on the wall to suggest rackets removed for nefarious purposes.

"Hey, Val." Chatty Ridenour beckoned from the clothing racks beyond the shoe display.

Val joined her tennis teammate. Chatty's intricately tied scarf matched her indigo blue eye shadow and lent panache to her simple outfit, a white shirt and cropped pants. Without her flawless complexion and flair for clothes, she would go unnoticed, a woman in her late thirties with straight brown hair, average in height and weight.

She pulled a tissue from her pocket and dabbed under her nose. "I've been miserable ever since I heard Nadia was killed. The police cornered me at the club. I couldn't bear to play tennis after that. I had to shop to calm down."

"And I had to cook." To each her own medicine. "What happened with the police?"

"They asked lots of questions about Nadia, how well I knew her, things like that. I asked how she was killed, but they wouldn't tell me."

"Did you say anything about the trouble between her and Monique?"

Chatty answered Val's question by flipping through the clothes rack, caressing the fabrics. Emotions never disturbed her lineless face, emerging instead in her hands. Her agitated fingers telegraphed that she'd blabbed to the police.

Val tamped down her annoyance. "It doesn't matter. If you didn't tell them, someone else would have."

"I didn't want to, but the deputy with the shaved head wouldn't let up on me. He also kept talking about a hit-and-run a few weeks ago. What's that about?"

"Who knows? He asked me about it too. He's obsessed with that hit-and-run though I can't see what —" Val broke off as Darwin approached them.

He flashed a smile worthy of a toothpaste ad. "Can I help you, ladies?"

Val couldn't risk talking about wood rackets in front of the inquisitive Chatty. "Um, she's looking for tennis clothes."

Chatty waved to a broad-shouldered teenager entering the shop. "Hey, Kyle. You play tennis too?"

The young man sauntered toward them. "How you doing, Mrs. Ridenour? Yeah, I'm taking up the game." He clapped Darwin on the shoulder. "You got my special order, man?"

Darwin tilted his head toward the rear of the shop. "In the backroom. 'Scuse us, ladies."

Val watched two sets of massive shoulders and bulging biceps go through a door at the back. "In Granddad's video store, guys used to ask for the films stored in the backroom. He didn't carry adult videos, but everybody knows backrooms are for things you can't do in public."

Chatty touched an index finger to her lips and pointed her other index finger toward the clothes rack behind Val. The salesclerk stood at the rack, near enough to eavesdrop. If she'd heard Val's comment about backrooms, she might repeat it to Darwin.

Val searched for something bland to say. "Darwin and Kyle look like they spend a lot of time lifting weights."

"Darwin believes in survival of the fittest." Chatty winked. "He volunteers as the fitness coach for the high school football team. Kyle's the linebacker and my son's idol. I'm surprised he's picking up a special order. I thought only racket retentives like my ex-husband did that."

Val had never heard of racket retentives

though she recognized the behavior. "Adventurous eaters try new dishes. Other people only eat familiar foods. Same with rackets, I guess."

"But what if you can't buy your familiar food anymore? Do you refuse to eat? When my —" A rapper ringtone from the clerk's cell phone interrupted Chatty and sent the clerk back to the checkout counter she used as a phone booth. "When my ex broke his racket, he wouldn't even look at new ones. He wanted that obsolete model and nothing else. Darwin managed to find some used ones, restrung them, and sold them as a special order at a megaprice."

Ironic of Chatty to talk about megaprices. "He charged what the market would bear. I'm sure you do the same with the cosmetics you sell."

Chatty stood up tall, growing two inches in her indignation. "I charge less than high-end department stores."

Oops. "Sorry. I was talking basic economics, nothing personal. I don't know anything about cosmetic prices."

"Obviously." Chatty gave Val a forehead-to-chin appraisal and turned back to the clothes rack. She held up a pink dress trimmed in lace. "This is too small for me, but you'd look cute in it."

"I don't do cute. As a kid I threw tantrums whenever people called me 'cute,' just to prove them wrong. Besides, I have all the tennis clothes I need." Two pairs of shorts and a bunch of T-shirts.

Val glanced at the door to the backroom. Still closed. She wandered toward a display where dozens of shiny rackets hung at different heights and angles, some with brightly colored strings. They looked like giant lollipops. She took down a lime green one and went through the motions of serving.

Chatty reached for the racket. "Let's see that thing. Hmm. Head heavy. You gotta be careful buying a new racket. It might ruin your game."

"You're just trying to turn me into a racket retentive." Val took the racket back from Chatty and hung it up. "Anyway, I'm not rushing into buying new gear. I'm here to pick Darwin's brain."

"That won't take long. Be sure to use words of one syllable, and talk about sports and cars. That's all he knows. But with a bod like that, who needs a mind?"

Val laughed. "He must have something going for him if he's running a shop at his age."

"Absolutely. A rich daddy who sold the family estate to a developer and moved south. He gave his tennis bum the money to open this shop."

Val looked behind Chatty and saw Darwin maneuver through the weight equipment aisles. The football star followed, carrying his special order in a vinyl racket cover. Now why couldn't Darwin have just fetched the racket and brought it to the sales floor?

"Earth to Val." Chatty waved her hand in front of Val's face. "Listen, I have a theory that I want to share with you. About the arson."

"Arson?" The two men glanced at Val. She lowered her voice. "What arson?"

"The racket at Nadia's." Chatty matched Val's quiet tones. "I think I know who did it and why, but it's a long story, and I can't talk now."

"How about tomorrow?"

"I'm taking my son to Ocean City for a beach day. Can we get together Thursday, after you close the café? I'll drop by and give you a facial."

A package deal. No facial, no gossip. Val remembered Monique's warning about Chatty: "Don't let her near your door with her creams and oils. She spikes them with truth serum. She'll coax you into telling her things you've never told anyone else." Val had laughed, but heeded the advice and resisted Chatty's offers of a facial . . . until now.

"Okay. Meet me at the café at two."

Chatty took her clothing purchase to the checkout counter as the high school football star left the shop.

Darwin joined Val at the racket display. He selected a wide-bodied orange racket. "You can try these rackets, you know. Take 'em out for a test drive."

Val hefted the racket he held out. "It looks like it could —" Val almost said kill somebody. "It looks heavy, but it feels lighter than most rackets. What's it made of?"

"Fiberglass and graphite." He took down a banana yellow racket and held it up for Val's inspection. "This one's made of Kevlar and hypercarbon. Space-age materials."

Chatty called out from the shop door. "See you Thursday, Val."

Val glanced at two teenage boys who'd just entered the shop. She'd better get to the point fast before Darwin abandoned her for other customers. "I heard you fill special orders for older rackets. Do you ever get requests for wood rackets?"

Darwin frowned. "There's a wood core racket with graphite —"

"I meant an all-wood racket, the kind people used to play with."

Darwin looked like a decorator whose client demanded an avocado shag rug. "Wood rackets are heavy. The head size is too small. Even the best players wouldn't be competitive with that kind of racket." And you, lady, are not the best, his intonation said.

"So no one's asked you to order one?" He shook his head, and she continued. "Where could someone buy a wood racket? Where did you get the ones hanging on the wall?"

He put back the high-tech model he'd tried to sell her. "Flea markets. Garage sales."

Perfect places to pay in cash and leave no paper trail. Her hope of finding the source of the racket used in the murder dimmed. "I'll have to think about what racket to buy. Thanks."

She left the shop. The humid air outside carried aromas of fresh bread, tomato sauce, and garlic. She glanced at her watch. Seven-thirty. No wonder her stomach was growling. For the first time in months, she didn't have to go home and make dinner for her grandfather. He was eating out. Why shouldn't she? She followed her nose to Bayport's newest restaurant, the Tuscan Eaterie, half a block away.

The restaurant had no free tables and a long waiting line. She snagged a seat at the bar, which offered the full menu. She studied it and ordered a risotto. The bronze-toned mirror behind the bar gave her an oblique view of the restaurant door, patrons leaving, others coming in. She glimpsed a couple as they exited, an older man in a white shirt shepherding a woman with a short gray pixie hairdo. From the back, the man resembled Granddad. Val swiveled to look directly at the door, but by then the couple had disappeared. The older guy couldn't have been her grandfather. He wore white dress shirts only to funerals. Tonight he'd probably gone to the diner in his overalls to eat with his friend, Ned.

Val had to wait so long for her meal she was tempted to walk out. The noise in the bar gave her a headache. Her food, when it finally arrived, covered barely a third of a square white plate. Three brown commas of salad dressing punctuated the arugula sprigs decorating a corner of the plate. Finding the morsels of seafood in her rice would have required a magnifying glass. She ate slowly, trying to identify the ingredients in the risotto.

Midway through dinner she heard her cell phone ringing but didn't bother climbing off the bar stool to fish it out of her bag. She couldn't have heard the caller over the din anyway, and the ring was muffled enough that no one else at the bar noticed it. It rang again as she was wiping her plate clean with a piece of bread, and again she ignored it. By the time she left the restaurant, it was almost nine and darker than usual because of a thick cloud cover.

She retrieved her phone messages.

"Val, it's Monique. Call me. It's important. I'll try you at home." Click.

"Where are you, Val? I have to talk to you. I need your help." Click.

Her cousin's voice bordered on frantic. What could be wrong? She dialed Monique's number. Maverick answered and told her that Monique was lying down.

"Is she sick?"

"No, she's in shock. Can you come right away? She won't talk to anyone but you."

Val's phone beeped a warning that the battery was low. "I'm leaving now." What on earth had happened?

She rushed to her car parked in front of Darwin's Sports. As she climbed in, she noticed Darwin locking the shop doors. She drove with the window open, her hair ruffled by the damp air. The peninsula road was even more deserted than when Gunnar had driven on it with her this afternoon. Deserted, except for the SUV looming behind her, its headlights in her rearview mirror like enormous penetrating eyes. She hated tailgaters.

She took her foot off the accelerator and steered as far to the right as she could on the road. The SUV made no move to pass.

She slowed to a crawl. The SUV slowed as well.

Maybe the tailgater was afraid to pass her on this road.

She pressed the accelerator and drove as fast as she dared. Her pursuer sped up as well. She slowed down again. The SUV did the same.

A pang of fear gripped her. She pressed the buttons to roll up her windows. How long before she'd see some houses, any sign of life? Nothing for miles except empty fish and tackle shops.

She reached for her cell phone, but dropped it in her lap when the SUV pulled out to pass her. Neck and neck on a narrow road. She glanced sideways. Too dark to see the driver. Her palms damp with sweat slid on the steering wheel. Her heart hammered against her rib cage.

The SUV edged closer. She eased the Saturn to the right. The car bucked on the rough shoulder. It scraped the bushes at the side of the road. She was dizzy, losing control, as she had on the icy highway.

No. She could manage the car this time. The road wasn't slick. She just had to keep her head.

But a second later the Saturn lost the road and Val slammed on the brakes.

CHAPTER 7

Val's car stopped with a bump, her seat belt harness tight across her chest. She'd hit something, an obstacle not visible in her headlight beams. She restarted the stalled car. The wheels resisted going forward. She reversed and touched the gas pedal lightly. The car limped back, hard to steer. Something was out of whack.

Up ahead, the SUV's brake lights flashed on and the taillights moved to the right. It was pulling to the side of the road. She grabbed her cell phone, and fumbled to unlock the keyboard. As soon as she did, it shut off. No juice left.

Would the SUV driver come after her? Would she be raped, beaten, left for dead? Suppose the SUV driver was the murderer? Serial killers had targeted nurses and prostitutes, so why not tennis players? Should she run?

No. Better to stay in the car and try to attract attention. She leaned on her horn. Was anyone around to hear?

On the other side of the road, headlights lit up the darkness.

Val blew the horn again. The oncoming pickup truck slowed and pulled over near Val's car. Seconds later, the SUV's taillights grew smaller and disappeared. Gone, at least for the moment.

The pickup driver tapped on her window. "You need help?"

She nodded and flung open the car door. "Thank you for stopping. The SUV you just passed ran me off the road."

The man stroked his grizzled whiskers. "He was probably just trying to get in front of you. You didn't have to get off the road. There was plenty of room for both of you."

The matter-of-fact tone and slow speech of the man exasperated her. "You don't understand. He was trying to — I don't know what he was trying, but —"

"Calm down, lady. Are you hurt?"

"No, but I think I have a flat." She had changed a flat before, but never in the dark.

He took a flashlight from his pickup and walked around the front of her car. "I see what happened. You hit a fuse box that some idiot pitched on the side of the road. It split the sidewall on your right front tire. Long as you got a spare, I'll fix ya up in no time."

While the man jacked up her car, Val searched the dark road ahead. Suppose the SUV driver turned around and rammed her car? Would she have time to warn the man helping her? Only a motorcycle and a pickup passed by during the tire change. The bully with the SUV might be waiting for her between here and Monique's house.

She watched the Good Samaritan load the flat tire into her trunk. "Do you live nearby?"

"Coupla miles back the way you came, there's a turnoff. That's my road."

She could U-turn and follow him, but once he turned off, he'd leave her on a road as deserted as this one. "I'm only going a mile or two farther on this road. Could you drive behind me until I reach my cousin's house? Just to make sure everything's all right." And the SUV wasn't waiting for her around the next bend.

The man picked up his tools. "I gotta get home to the missus. She'll call the Coast Guard if I don't show up soon. Your spare tire's good, but don't drive real far on it. It's one of them small ones."

Val thanked him and offered him twenty dollars, which he refused. She pulled out on the empty road toward Monique's house, her hands clammy on the wheel.

After a mile, headlights appeared in her mirror. They'd come from nowhere. Had the driver lurked off the road, waiting for her car to pass? She turned into Monique's driveway and watched in the rearview mirror as the vehicle behind her slowed down and drove past. At least it didn't follow her into the driveway. She ran to the house door and pounded on it.

Maverick opened it. "Glad you finally got here."

"Me too." Val stumbled into the hall. The air-conditioned house felt cold as a tomb. She shivered. "An SUV just ran me off the road. A few more feet, I'd have been in the water."

"Probably a teenager. No driving experience."

Those road maneuvers didn't strike Val as the work of a novice. "I wish I'd gotten a look at the driver or the license number. I want to call the police."

"Don't do that." Maverick blocked her from going beyond the hallway. "If they show up here, Monique will freak out. She's had all she can take of the police for one day."

Uh-oh. "What's going on?"

"The police came here and questioned us.

Monique's worried they suspect her of the murder. They knew about her harangue against Nadia at the club. The sheriff's deputy, Holtzman, really leaned on her."

"He leaned on me too, and all I did was find Nadia dead." Oops. Val bit her lip as Monique emerged from the bedroom wing.

"You found Nadia?" Monique's eyes and nose were red from crying, her face puffy, her long hair tangled. "Then you must know — how was she killed? Was it with a hatchet?"

"A hatchet?" Val shook her head. "Look, I can't talk about how she was killed. The police put a gag on me."

"Please, Val. They think I did it." Her voice rose to a hysterical wail.

"Take it easy, Monique." Maverick put his hand on her arm.

Monique jerked away from him. "Don't tell me what to do. You put me in this mess." She stumbled to the window seat in the living room, plunked down, and twisted herself into a pretzel, arms and legs crossed in front of her.

Val squeezed next to her cousin. "What happened with the police?"

"They came by, asked some questions about Nadia, and wanted to look in our shed. We said sure, we have nothing to hide." Monique's chin trembled. "Then they found our hatchet and took it away."

Not good. The police don't just willy-nilly remove tools. "Did they say why they wanted the hatchet?" When Monique didn't respond, Val gestured with her palm up toward Maverick.

He wet his lips. "A hatchet can leave identifying marks on wood like a rifle leaves on a bullet. Ours has a flaw in the blade. The police ran some tests, came back here, and said our hatchet was used to shave the handle of the racket burned at Nadia's." He gestured toward his wife as if turning the mike over to a co-anchor. "Monique?"

Val didn't need the words. Her cousin's sagging face told her the bad news. "You burned the racket? God, I hope you didn't lie to the police." *The way you lied to me.* "What did you say to them?"

Monique huddled in the window seat and twirled her hair, tying it in knots. "At first I denied setting the racket on fire. Then I admitted it. I figured, what's the big deal? I didn't damage anything at Nadia's, not even a blade of grass. I'm not a vandal."

The police weren't looking for a vandal. "What happened after that?"

"They treated me like a criminal. They asked me the same questions over and over."

Val knew how it felt. Holtzman had used the same technique on her. "What questions?"

"When did I last see Nadia? Where was I on Monday night? I was home by myself. I can't prove it, so they think I murdered Nadia."

Who could blame them? Monique had a motive, no alibi, and a prior act of aggression with a wood racket. Val struggled to reassure her cousin. "Look at the bright side. The police haven't arrested you." Yet. They probably would have arrested her if they could have connected her to the murder weapon.

Maverick loomed above his wife. "You should have called a lawyer as soon as you heard Nadia was murdered."

Monique aimed her index fingers at him like a pair of six-shooters. "You should have kept it in your pants."

He rolled his eyes. "How many times do I have to say I'm sorry?"

His wife glared at him. She usually passed for younger than she was, especially with her hair in a ponytail, but now fear etched lines in her forehead and hollowed out her cheeks.

Val spoke quietly to Monique. "If I'd known you set the racket on fire, I'd have suggested you tell the police or get a lawyer. Why did you lie to me?"

A tear rolled down Monique's cheek. "I didn't want you to know. You thought I was wrong to stop playing on Nadia's team. And here I'd done something much worse, something totally stupid and childish." Monique uncurled her body. She covered her face with her hands, her shoulders heaving as she sobbed.

"I'll make some coffee." Maverick retreated into the kitchen.

Monique looked up. "He can't stand it when I cry."

"A lot of men can't stand to see a woman cry," Val said. But most of them try to console the woman. They don't just leave the room.

"I didn't kill Nadia." Monique clutched Val's arm. "You believe me, don't you?"

"Of course." Val's inner skeptic reminded her that she'd fallen for Monique's lie about the burned racket. Yet she gave her cousin the benefit of the doubt. She empathized with any woman whose partner cheated on her. She also felt bad about the way her grandfather had cut himself off from Monique's parents. Despite the family feud, she and Monique had found each other years ago. They'd forged a secret friendship, two young teens dropped off with relatives in Bayport, where neither had any friends. Those summers meant enough to Val that she would treat her cousin as innocent until proven guilty and stand by her if she were guilty.

Monique gnawed on her knuckles. "I feel like a spider in a web. Someone's trying to make it look like I did it."

And doing a darn good job of it. "I wonder if anyone watched you set the fire. When I drove Nadia home from the club Sunday night, I saw a jogger in a hoodie near her house."

"That was me. I set up the racket and waited until I saw headlights on the road from the club. When the car turned into Nadia's neighborhood, I lit the fire, ran off, and then backtracked through the woods to my car."

Val stood up, leaving the window seat to Monique. "Where did you get the racket you burned?"

"From the garage. It was Maverick's old racket from when he was a kid." Monique twisted her wedding ring. "That's why I burned it. It was this phallic thing that represented him."

Val understood, recalling her own outrage at her fiancé for cheating. In one symbolic act, Monique had vented her anger at both Maverick and Nadia.

Maverick returned and strode to the liquor cabinet. "There's coffee in the kitchen if you want some. I think I need something stronger." He gripped a bottle of bourbon.

Monique stood up and rubbed her forehead. "I've got a splitting headache. I'm going to bed. You can sleep in the den, Maverick." She turned away from him. "Thanks for coming by, Val."

"Why don't I spend the night here? In case you can't sleep and need someone to talk to." Besides that jerk of a husband.

Monique's eyes glistened. "Thank you. Mandy's bed has clean sheets on it. I'll bring you towels and a nightgown."

As she left the living room, Maverick poured amber liquid into a tumbler. "How about it, Val?"

"Not for me. I have to call my grandfather and tell him I'm staying here."

Maverick pulled a phone from a pocket in his cargo shorts. "You can use this."

She told Granddad she was spending the night at her cousin's and cut him off before he could ask why. Cradling the phone in her hand, she watched Maverick getting his fix. He swirled the bourbon, sipped, and held his glass up, as if gazing through alcohol would bring him enlightenment. Had he ever before faced a crisis? On the tennis court, he anticipated shots so well, he never had to run. The ball gravitated to the sweet spot of his racket. Things just naturally went Maverick's way, on and off the court, at least until his wife discovered his affair and his lover was murdered.

She handed him the phone and went into Mandy's room. The bed's ruffled spread and puffy shams reminded her of the girly décor she'd banished from her own room as a child, replacing the bedspread with a sleeping bag to her mother's annoyance.

Her cousin came into the room, carrying embroidered towels and a lace-trimmed nightgown nothing like the sleep shirts Val usually wore.

Monique sprawled on a pink beanbag lounger. "I was just thinking about the fun we had those two summers. Your grandparents and my aunt had no clue when we went to the library, or the movies, or the town dock that we were meeting each other."

Val sat on the edge of the bed. "My grandmother knew, but she never told Granddad."

"I've been meaning to ask you, are you

120

still planning to move back to New York?"

Did that question stem from the fear that Val would leave her alone to face a murder charge? "I'm not going to pick up and move in the near future. But part of me wants to go back to redeem myself after Chef Henri trashed my reputation."

Monique shifted from lying on the bean-bag to sitting on it. "If the other part of you wants to stay here and you go back there because of what he did, you're letting him control your life."

"That's not the only reason to go back. I miss the museums, theaters, restaurants." Yet she had more friends and family in Bay-port than in the city where she'd lived for a decade, and she would miss them if she left. "What about you? Are you staying with Maverick?"

Monique fiddled with her wedding ring. "My father died when I was seven. My mother raised two kids on her own. I don't want Mike and Mandy growing up without a father. Maverick and I will stay together until the kids are old enough to live on their own. Then, if he doesn't change . . ." She stood up and gave the beanbag the kick that she probably wanted to give her husband.

"Kids make a difference." Val counted herself lucky to have discovered Tony's cheating before they were married and had children. Six months ago when she broke off their engagement, she'd faced the pain of knowing that their five years together meant nothing to him. If they'd had children, though, she'd have attempted to repair their relationship, and her pain might have become chronic.

Monique stifled a yawn and crossed the room toward the door. "How's the cookbook coming?"

"I'm still working my way through Grandma's recipes, trimming the fat and switching to fresh instead of canned ingredients. My own recipes are all organized. Now I have to write them up so someone besides me can understand them. Then I'll need people to test them."

"I'll help. I can suggest things to jazz up your recipes and give them more edge."

Val cringed inside. Her cousin's exotic variations rarely improved any dish and often ruined it. "Thanks. You look exhausted, Monique."

Her cousin nodded. "I am. See you in the morning." She closed the door behind her.

Val had trouble falling asleep. A lot had changed in the last hour. Earlier today, she'd assumed the police would find Nadia's murderer. Now she wasn't sure. She liked

Chief Yardley as a family friend, but for all she knew, he'd risen through the ranks because of management skills, not investigative work. And Deputy Holtzman had treated Monique like a criminal. With her as the perfect suspect, the police might not bother investigating further. But if Val found evidence implicating someone else, they couldn't ignore it.

She didn't see herself as competing with the police, just pursuing a different goal. They wanted to close the case fast. She wanted to keep it open. Tomorrow she'd try to wangle information from the chief about the murder investigation. She now had an excuse to stop by the police station — to file a report about the SUV that ran her off the road.

That road incident faded in importance compared to her cousin's predicament. Val went to sleep almost convinced it was a random act of aggression.

She woke up believing otherwise. An image stuck in her mind — Darwin locking his shop door while she climbed into her car to drive to Monique's. Easy for him to follow her onto the peninsula. But why would he try to force her off the road? Maybe her offhand comment about under-the-table transactions had gotten back to him through his eavesdropping salesclerk. That comment would have made him nervous if he peddled porn or drugs from his backroom. Alternately, her talk about wood rackets would have spooked him if he'd murdered Nadia. He had a perfect opportunity and two possible motives to put Val out of commission. The key question: Did he own a light SUV?

CHAPTER 8

Val sat at the breakfast bar in her cousin's kitchen, sipping coffee and eating waffles, while Monique pried cooked batter from her "nonstick" waffle iron. They both twisted toward the wall-mounted television in the adjacent family room to watch a local newscaster.

"This is Junie May Jussup standing outside Bayport police headquarters. The police are treating the death of town resident Nadia Westrin as suspicious. She was found early yesterday morning in her home on Creek Road, some eight to ten hours after her death. The police are asking anyone in the vicinity of Creek Road on Monday night between nine and midnight to contact them. No information yet about the cause of her death or the progress of the police investigation. Stay tuned for breaking news about this case and for interviews with Nadia Westrin's neighbors and friends. Now back to the studio and the weather report."

Monique pressed a button on the remote and shut off the TV. "Not much new about Nadia's murder." She glanced at Val's half-empty plate. "I'm glad you're enjoying my spiced waffles. Can you guess what's in them?"

Enjoying wasn't the word that came to mind as Val chewed the waffle. "I taste whole wheat flour, molasses, allspice, and crystallized ginger."

Her cousin often made comfort food with a twist that took it out of the comfort zone. Tradition warred with offbeat urges in her cooking and her life.

Monique put her mixing bowl in the dishwasher. "My kids didn't like these waffles. They wanted 'regular' waffles."

"Regular, as in crispy outside, fluffy inside, and maple syrup instead of agave nectar? What's wrong with kids these days?"

Her cousin waved a dish towel like a white flag. "I surrender. I'll ditch the recipe."

Val ditched the rest of her waffle and put her empty plate in the dishwasher. Fortified with coffee, she could broach sensitive topics. "How did you find out Maverick and Nadia were having an affair?"

Monique rolled her eyes. "An anonymous note. It came in the mail on Thursday."

She'd wasted no time before acting on it, confronting Nadia that evening at the club. "Do you still have the letter?"

"I'll get it." Monique left the room.

So far this morning, she hadn't given in to the despair she'd shown last night. The tension level had also decreased from last night, in part because Maverick had left for work before either woman woke up.

Monique returned to the kitchen and handed Val a home decorating magazine. "The note's tucked between the pages. I didn't want Maverick to find it. I'd rather let him believe I figured out he was sleeping with Nadia. He'll think twice before he cheats on me again."

He might think twice and still cheat. Val flipped through the magazine and found a folded page of lined, yellow paper. She unfolded it and read a penciled message in large letters: FIND OUT WHAT NADIA'S DOING WITH YOUR HUSBAND. MAYBE YOU CAN LEARN ENOUGH TO KEEP HIM HOME NIGHTS.

Nasty note. Not only did it tell Monique about her husband's affair, it insulted her as well. It also provoked her to actions that made her a murder suspect. The busybody who'd sent it had a lot to answer for.

Monique stared at it over Val's shoulder.

"I didn't even rate a proper anonymous note, letters cut from a newspaper and stuck on the page."

Val smiled at her cousin's attempt at humor. "Do you have the envelope it came in?"

"I threw it out. Take that letter with you. I don't want it in the house anymore."

Val slipped the note back in the magazine. "You need a lawyer, Monique. Fortunately, we have one on our tennis team. Call Althea." She pointed to the phone.

"She does family law. Divorces. Custody cases. I don't need that kind of lawyer."

"Althea has contacts. Ask her to give you the names of the best criminal defense attorneys in southern Maryland. Set up an appointment with one of them ASAP, and don't talk to the police again without a lawyer sitting next to you."

"Aye, aye, ma'am." Monique saluted.

On her way out, Val hugged her cousin. "I'll call you if I find out anything important. Otherwise I'll see you tomorrow at six at the club. After the little ceremony for Nadia, let the others decide whether to play the match. We'll go with the flow, okay?"

Monique nodded. She stood at the door as Val backed out onto the road.

Val stopped at home to shower and change

128

clothes. Granddad wasn't in his usual chair facing the TV and the fireplace. Instead he sat at the mahogany dining table strewn with papers, clippings, and index cards. Maybe he'd finally gotten around to sorting through one of his catchall drawers.

"Hey, Granddad," she called from the sitting room.

He looked startled, his furry eyebrows shooting up. "Don't sneak up on me like that." He slipped the page in front of him under a pile of papers.

What was he hiding from her? She went through the archway to the dining room. Her jaw dropped. Those weren't his papers. "You dumped my recipes on the table. I had them all organized, and now look at them."

"I'm reorganizing them." He picked up an index card and put it on top of a pile. "What's the problem? Sunday night you said, 'My recipe file is your recipe file.' That's an exact quote."

"I meant you could use them, not completely destroy my system." She'd grouped the recipes by the chapters in her cookbook. Now she'd have to put them back in order. She suppressed the anger boiling inside and flipped through the first few cards in the pile in front of him. Two soups, three desserts, and a main course. "This is a random bunch of recipes."

"They look random to you. Like most women, you're not geared toward numbers. I'm sorting the recipes by how many ingredients they have. The ones in that pile all have seven. I figure when I run out of the ones with five ingredients, I can just cross out two lines in these recipes." He beamed at her like a teacher who'd just explained subtraction to a second grader.

She counted to five before replying. "I would have located some simple recipes for you. We could have cooked them together. You didn't give me the chance."

"You've been gallivanting for the last twenty-four hours. I couldn't wait any longer."

True. She'd left him on his own since yesterday morning. "You haven't cooked anything for seventy-odd years, and now you want to start yesterday. What's the rush?"

"Well, I'm not getting any younger."

"Don't play the age card with me. You have something up your sleeve." Possibly to do with that paper he'd hidden under a pile when she came in. Today she couldn't spare the time to find out what he was up to, not with a murder charge hanging over Monique. Val walked behind his chair toward the kitchen and the back staircase. "Any calls for me while I was gallivanting?"

Granddad pointed to a stack of recipes on index cards. "You know why I put that pile of recipes aside? They all have stuff in them I don't recognize. Sofrito. Tempeh. Kofta. What kind of food is that?"

Changing the subject wouldn't work with her. "Did I get any calls, Granddad?"

He sniffed. "Yeah. Gunnar. He reserved a tennis court for four-thirty today."

Granddad wouldn't have even mentioned that call without her pressing him on it. He was still poring over her recipe collection when she left the house.

She drove to the Bayport police station. The chief could see her in half an hour. While waiting for him, she reported on last night's road incident. The gray-haired officer who took down her information wanted to know as much about her actions as the other driver's. Had she perhaps cut off the SUV, blown her horn, or gestured? The officer concluded the interview by giving her a handout with tips on dealing with road bullies.

Chief Yardley fetched her from the reception area. "Let's go outside. I was about to take a break anyway." He led her out a back door to a small yard enclosed by a chain link fence.

She followed him to a bench shaded by a white oak. "I saw my cousin last night. She told me she'd burned the racket at Nadia's house." Val leaned against the back of the wood bench.

He took out his pipe and sat down next to her. "She tell you anything else?"

"That she didn't kill Nadia. Monique is a good person, Chief. Right now she's under a lot of stress, which explains why she set that fire."

He opened a leather pouch containing tobacco. "Doing something under stress is okay. Lying to the police about it two days later isn't."

"She's ashamed of what she did. That's why she didn't tell me or the police at first. That doesn't mean she's a murderer. Is she a suspect?"

"She's guilty of starting a fire on someone's property. That much we know." The chief filled his pipe. "We're still gathering evidence about the murder."

Val could guess what evidence they'd like to find to clinch the case against Monique. "Correct me if I'm wrong, but the racket at the murder scene wasn't shaved with the hatchet you found at Monique's, was it?"

"It was carved exactly the same way as

the burned racket, but with a sharper tool."

"Doesn't that mean someone else did it? She'd have used the same hatchet."

The chief drew on his pipe. "Not necessarily. Maybe she had a hard time carving the first racket. Her hatchet was old and dull, so she bought a new one."

She raised her index finger like a student with a question. "Where's the new tool now? I bet you didn't find it at Monique's place."

"Would you keep a tool you used to make a murder weapon?"

"You can't have it both ways. If Monique realized the new hatchet could connect her to the murder weapon, she must have known the old hatchet could connect her to the burning racket. Why would she chuck one and keep the other?"

He pulled the pipe from his mouth. "Her husband might notice a new hatchet and wonder why she bought it. And he'd notice if the old hatchet was gone."

"So what if it was gone? Tools are always disappearing. Like socks."

"A hatchet isn't the only thing that leaves a mark. The person wielding it does too. Suppose I give a wood racket and a hatchet to ten different people and tell them to taper the handle. One person might whack it from the throat down to the butt in a single stroke." He demonstrated the technique on the stem of his pipe. "Another might chip away at the last two inches of the handle. I guarantee no two rackets would look the same at the end."

"But what if you show your carvers a tapered racket before they start working and tell them their task is to duplicate it? Or suppose you describe the results you want? You wouldn't see a lot of variations."

"I'll concede that someone who saw that racket could have carved another one the same way, but not based just on a description."

"We could run an experiment." Val caught the chief scowling at her. "I mean, you could run it."

"I run with the facts. I don't need experiments."

"Luckily, I have a few facts. Monique's husband, who heard about the burned racket from Nadia, was cagey about where he was the night of the murder. He led Monique to believe he stayed in Philadelphia Monday night, but I know he left earlier that day. Grandma Mott told me." Val tried to make it sound as if she knew Monique's mother-in-law well.

The chief glowered. "Checking on alibis is

our job, not yours."

"I can't help it if people tell me things. I discovered something else. Nadia was on the phone with a real estate client on Monday night around nine-thirty when another call came in. Nadia put her client on hold."

The pipe moved up and down in the chief's mouth. "How did you find that out?"

Val described the note she'd seen next to Nadia's phone and the reasoning that led her to visit Mrs. Z. "When Nadia came back on the line after taking another call, she told Mrs. Z she was expecting someone. That other call could have been the murderer setting up a meeting with Nadia. If you could trace that call . . ."

"We did. It came from a prepaid burner phone. No way to find out who made the call." The chief peered inside the bowl of his pipe. "I like the way you pick up on details and look at all the angles. You could teach my rookies a thing or two. But they could teach you the first rule of investigation — the simplest solution is usually the right one."

And Monique fit the bill, with her motive, her history of intimidating the victim, and no alibi. After years of watching *Law & Order* reruns, Val could guess what the police would do next — try to place the suspect at the crime scene. "If you find Monique's DNA at Nadia's house, it won't prove anything. Nadia threw a party on Memorial Day. She invited the racket club crowd and her neighbors. We all have strands of hair caught in her rugs."

"That DNA stuff takes time and costs money." He tapped his pipe against his heel. "Shoe leather does the job faster. The sheriff's deputies and every officer I can spare are out interviewing. Someone must have seen something that night."

Val breathed in the pipe smoke that hung like a haze in the still air, an entrancing woodsy scent with traces of almond and vanilla. She'd said what she could to convince the chief of Monique's innocence. Now for another matter. "Last night someone forced my car off the road."

The chief sat up straighter and scrutinized her face. "Did you get hurt?"

"No injuries except to my tire." She repeated what she'd told the gray-haired officer earlier. "Right before that happened, my car was parked in front of Darwin's Sports. Darwin saw me drive off and could have followed me from there to the peninsula. Can you check if he has a light-colored SUV?"

"I can check, but I can't do anything about it. Unless you actually saw him behind the wheel, we don't have cause to investigate him. Why would he run you off the road?"

"I don't know. Maybe something I said at the shop annoyed him." She debated whether to tell him she'd asked about wood rackets.

The chief stood up, a signal that she'd occupied enough of his time. "Darwin has a quick temper. He used to settle scores with his fists. If you annoyed him, you'd best stay clear of him."

"He teaches tennis at the club. I can't totally avoid him, but I'll try."

"Don't repeat anything I told you about those rackets, the burned one or the weapon. That information's under embargo. I don't want anyone convicted by the media."

She walked with him back into the building. "I'll keep quiet. Monique's life will be hell if word gets out about the racket burning."

"That should have crossed her mind before she did it. Your granddaddy doesn't think much of her side of the family, says they always act without thinking."

Val pressed her lips together to cork an

angry retort. "Monique's father moved to Canada during the Vietnam War. I'm sure he didn't exile himself without thinking long and hard about it. And the way Granddad treated 'her side of the family' gives me more reason to stand by her."

The chief escorted Val out of the building. "But how well do you know her? You may be seeing what you want to see, not what's really there."

Could Val have missed a violent streak in her cousin? A week ago, she would have said no. Since then, Monique had set a racket on fire. An act of revenge, yes, but one that caused no physical harm. Killing someone, though, was in another league. "If Monique confesses to the murder, Chief, I'll admit I really didn't know her." But not until then.

Meanwhile, Val would need an excuse to find out more about Nadia. What had she done in the days before the murder? Had she argued with anyone? Who could have seen the charred racket in the twenty-four hours between when it burned and when Nadia was murdered? Answering those questions might lead to murder suspects other than Monique.

Val drove from the police station to the club. She expected to find Bethany frantic for help with the lunch crowd. Apparently, though, Bethany's experience with six-year-olds gave her the skills to handle hungry customers. Val left her to it and waylaid the club manager. She gave him the catering menus and prices, explaining that Nadia had requested them for the tennis team party. He glanced at them and said he'd give Val a catering contract.

Val owed Nadia for that, but how do you pay a debt to a dead woman? She convinced the manager that the club newsletter should run an article about Nadia and offered to write it. He accepted her offer.

Now that she had a license to snoop, she would talk to real estate developer Bigby O'Shay, Nadia's former mixed doubles partner and Bethany's brother. Val had seen the hostility between him and Nadia. Though Bethany had insisted her brother would never hurt Nadia, Val wanted to judge that for herself.

CHAPTER 9

Outside the town limits, Val drove past billboards announcing the opening of a new gated community, Bigby O'Shay's latest venture. Bethany's brother used his own initials when he named his developments — Bay Overlook, Broad Outlands, and now Bayport Oaks. Club members called him B.O. behind his back, but not to his face.

The woman in the sales trailer at Bayport Oaks told Val to follow the construction noise to find Bigby and warned her that he might be too busy to talk.

Val would take up less of his time if he'd answer her key questions: What caused the friction between him and Nadia? When was the last time he saw her? Did he know what the charred racket looked like? She had good reasons not to ask that last question. The chief had barred her from mentioning the racket. Bigby wouldn't tell the truth if he had anything to hide, and she might be putting herself in danger if he was the murderer. She'd have to treat the interview more like risotto than instant rice, adding ingredients gradually while stirring gently.

She spotted a husky man on a dirt path, got out of the car, and waved.

Bigby strutted toward her, a clipboard under his arm. His dusty shirt clung to his sweaty body. "What can I do for you, Val?" he bellowed over the roar of an earthmover.

"I wanted to talk to you about Nadia."

"I heard you were at her house yesterday morning with the police. Did you find out how she was killed?"

"The police aren't telling anyone. I'm here because I'm writing an article about Nadia for the club newsletter."

"What kind of article?"

"A short tribute. You know, what was special about her, that sort of thing." Val fished props from her bag, a pen and a small scratchpad. "As her mixed doubles partner, you must have known her pretty well."

"Look at those guys." Bigby gestured toward a bulldozer driver who'd just idled the engine and climbed out of the cab. "Taking another break. It's a miracle I get any houses built. What do you want from me, Val?"

"Tennis was an important part of Nadia's

life. I want your perspective on her as a doubles partner."

"We had a good run, won a few tournaments. Nadia had a great forehand and went after every ball."

With both of them going after every ball, they must have collided on the court. Val looked up from jotting notes. "Yet you stopped playing together."

"Yeah, she was a great tennis player, but not the best partner for me. We couldn't agree on strategy, not even who should play which side of the court."

Val tucked her notepad away to encourage him to speak more freely. "Tennis at the club won't be the same without Nadia. I keep thinking about the last time I talked to her, Sunday night after mixed doubles. When did you last see her?"

Drills whined and hammers banged. Bigby studied the partially finished house where the noises originated, scratched his neck, and looked back at Val. "Can't remember."

A lie for sure, but his hesitation made him look innocent of murder. If he'd killed Nadia, he'd have answered more quickly with the story he intended to tell the police if they asked the same question. But some guilty people don't prepare for police interviews, never expecting to get caught.

Val still had no idea what caused the antagonism between him and Nadia. "You must have dealt with Nadia outside the club. With both of you in real estate —"

"Different ends of the business."

"Did Nadia enjoy a good reputation in the real estate community?"

His face grew redder. "Sounds like you're trying to dig up dirt on her."

Val glanced around at the denuded landscape. Nothing but dirt here. "I need to understand Nadia to write the newsletter article."

"I said all I got to say about her. If you want more intimate details, go see Maverick Mott." Bigby turned away.

No surprise that he knew about Nadia's affair after Monique's tirade at the club, but why the sneering tone? The affair must have bugged him, or he wouldn't have mentioned it.

Bigby pointed at an idle bulldozer, and yelled, "Hey, Luis. What's going on over there? Why ain't you working?" He swung around and thrust his clipboard under Val's nose. "Know what this is? A list of what I have to do today. I'm building houses here. I got no time to talk."

She glanced at the clipboard. Heck, his

to-do list wasn't all that long. He just wrote big. Big man, big mouth, big writing. Val felt a jolt like an electric charge. Monique's anonymous note had similar large letters on the same type of lined, yellow paper.

If Val ever hoped to extract information from him, she had to leave on good terms. "Sorry I bothered you when you're busy."

His eyes narrowed as if he doubted her sincerity, but just for a moment. Then his face relaxed. "You hear anything about a service for Nadia?"

Val detected a genuine emotion behind the question. "Not yet."

"Let Bethany know when you do. She'll tell me."

Bigby left her, stomped toward an idle bulldozer, and yelled at the idle man beside it.

On her way back to the car, Val spotted a sheet of yellow paper crumpled near a ditch. She turned around to make sure Bigby couldn't see her, grabbed the page, and thrust it into her handbag. Back in the car, she unfolded it. It listed names and assigned tasks, a work roster in Bigby's characteristic large print. She compared the page to Monique's anonymous note. To the untrained eye, the writing looked the same.

Val left Bayport Oaks with her questions

unanswered about Bigby's rift with Nadia and his access to the charred racket, but at least she now knew he'd sent the anonymous note. Somehow he'd uncovered Nadia's affair with Maverick and done his best to break it up. Why? A grudge or jealousy? Either made a good motive for murder.

Val couldn't think of anyone she'd rather cast as a murderer than Bigby. Even before watching him browbeat his workers today, she'd disliked him for his tennis court behavior. When he shoved his partner aside, argued over close points, and hurled his racket to the ground, he showed how selfish, overbearing, and uncontrolled he was. But few court bullies resorted to murder. Before bringing up Bigby's name with the chief, Val needed to know more about his relationship with Nadia. Clearly, he hadn't wanted to talk about it, but his sister might, given a little coaxing.

Val drove back to the café. By the time she arrived, Bethany had already gone, leaving crumbs on the bistro tables and smears on the eating bar. Val wiped down the surfaces and inventoried the fridge contents. Plenty of yogurt and juice for smoothies, not many fruits and vegetables. A trip to the roadside stand would take care of that problem. But first, she needed to eat.

Between talking to the police and to Bigby, she'd forgotten lunch. She made a turkey sandwich with garlic cheese spread and dried cranberries. As she sat at the counter eating, Bethany dashed in.

The splotches on her face matched her pink top. "I came back to clean the tables. I was in such a rush I forgot to do it." Her voice crackled with tension.

"Relax. I took care of it." Val peered at Bethany's red-rimmed eyes. "You look like you've been crying. Where have you been?"

"The police station. After what you said yesterday, I decided to tell them what happened between me and Nadia. Then they couldn't accuse me of hiding anything. While I was talking about her, I started crying. I'm going to miss her. The policeman who was with me was so nice. He brought me a box of tissues, and some coffee and a doughnut."

"Which policeman?"

"The one with the shaved head."

Val nearly choked on her sandwich. She washed it down with iced tea. "Deputy Holtzman? He was nice to you?"

"Uh-huh. Too bad he was wearing a wedding ring. All the attractive men are already married."

Val now had proof of what she'd previously only suspected — that Bethany needed her eyes examined. Far from being attractive, Holtzman could take the blue ribbon in the county fair's Ugly Dude contest. His personality had matched his looks yesterday, but not today. What had changed him? His first day on the case, he'd grilled everyone as a potential suspect. By the time Bethany walked into the police station, though, he already had his suspect. Would Val's defense of her cousin carry any weight with the chief if his helper from the sheriff's office built a case against Monique? Not unless Val could build a case against someone else. First at bat, Bigby O'Shay.

She patted the stool next to hers at the counter. "Sit down. I want to talk to you."

Bethany eyed the seat as if it were electrified. "I can't stay long."

Val couldn't fathom Bethany's skittishness. "This won't take long. I'm writing an article about Nadia for the club newsletter, and I need your help."

"In that case . . ." Bethany slid onto the seat.

"I want to mention Nadia's work as a real estate agent in my article, but only if she has a good reputation. Yesterday you told me that Bigby called her ruthless. What made him say that?"

Bethany pressed her lips together. "I don't like to speak ill of the dead."

Which is what people say when they're about to do just that. "And I don't intend to write anything bad about her, but we all know she had her faults."

Bethany looked down at her hands, her fingers tightly interlaced. "I asked Bigby why he wasn't playing with her anymore. He said she kept nagging him to put her in charge of sales at his new development. But of course, he couldn't do that. He always works with the same agent. So Nadia got mad at him."

"And that's why she dropped him as a doubles partner."

"It was the other way around. He dropped her when he realized what she was really after."

"That doesn't make sense. Why should Bigby resent Nadia just because she wanted a job in his company?" And why would Nadia want to sit in a sales trailer? Maybe she had problems at the realty office where she worked. Val made a mental note to go by Nadia's office tomorrow.

"She was coming on to Bigby, acting like she was attracted to him, but all she wanted was to advance her career. Wouldn't you resent someone who did that to you?"

"I'd especially resent it if I found that person attractive." So would Bigby. With his hopes of a romance with Nadia dashed, he might have written that anonymous letter out of spite.

Bethany gnawed on her thumb. "Can I still work here even though I didn't clean up before I left?"

Ah. She was worried about being fired. The wound from being "fired" as Nadia's tennis partner hadn't yet healed. Bethany needed to be needed. Val had felt the same way after her car crash led to a career crash.

She squeezed Bethany's arm. "I can't manage without you, and I should have given you a checklist for closing. In fact, I could use your help tomorrow if you can work."

"I have a dentist appointment first thing in the morning. I can work after that."

"Good. I'll open the café for breakfast. Come in when you can."

"Okeydoke. See you then." Bethany slid off the counter stool.

A minute after she left the café, her physical opposite came in — Althea Johnson, svelte, dark-skinned, and twice Bethany's age. She was the tennis team member most likely to grieve for Nadia. Always serious, she looked downright grim today with deep vertical lines scoring her forehead.

Val embraced her. "I'm sorry. You were close to Nadia. This must be hard on you."

Althea adjusted her tortoiseshell glasses. "I can't believe she's gone. Do you have any idea how she was killed?"

"The police aren't saying. Sit down." Val led her to one of the four bistro tables in the café. "Do you want something to eat or drink?"

Althea shook her head. "I'm about to get on the treadmill and run until I drop. Otherwise I won't sleep tonight." She took off her glasses and cleaned them with the hem of her T-shirt. "I remember the day I met Nadia five years ago. The first thing she asked was if my parents named me after the great Althea Gibson."

"Did they?"

"Uh-huh, and they put a racket in my hand at an early age. Too bad I wasn't as talented as my namesake." Althea's frown lines softened. "Were you named after anybody?"

"The patron saint of chocolate. I was born on February 14th and named Valentine. You got a racket to go with your name, and I got velvet and lace dresses."

"I bet you rebelled against that."

Val nodded. "Tomboy since preschool.

150

Did you rebel?"

"I gave up tennis for decades." Althea tightened the laces of her running shoes. "Nadia got me back into the game. She coaxed me to join the club and the tennis team."

Val understood Althea's soft spot for the person who made her feel welcome. "Monique did the same for me. I think she put in a good word with the club manager so I'd get the café job."

"Really? I know Nadia did. The manager was going to give the café contract to Nadia's neighbor, Irene Pritchard, until Nadia convinced him you'd do a better job."

Val could scarcely believe it. "Nadia never told me that."

"She didn't want it to get back to Irene. I wasn't supposed to tell anyone. Keep it to yourself."

"I will. Why would she prefer me to Irene? She barely knew me." But Nadia may have known her neighbor too well. Irene's tea shop had gone under, possibly because of bad management or mediocre food.

"Nadia liked to exert her influence. Some people call that meddling. I'd give a more positive spin to her interference in this case. She gave you a chance to prove yourself."

Or she seized a chance to stick it to Irene

for whatever reason. Val couldn't slough off her opinion of Nadia as self-serving. For the first time, though, she felt bad about leaving her out of the dinner party she'd thrown for the team's other unmarried women. Val had invited Bethany and Chatty because she wanted to know them better. She couldn't say the same for Nadia.

"Thanks for telling me, Althea." Thanks for the guilt trip. "We're meeting here for a farewell toast to Nadia tomorrow at six. Before the team match."

"I'll come for the toast, but I don't think we should play a match so soon after Nadia died." She stood up. "I'm off to the tread-mill. See you tomorrow."

Val left the café to run errands. She drove into town to pick up the apron she'd ordered for Granddad and stopped at a road-side stand. Usually she spent a lot of time picking out fresh produce. Today she'd have to hurry to get back before Gunnar showed up for their tennis date.

An hour after leaving the club, she returned. As she toted vegetables and fruit from her car, she spotted Darwin on his way out of the club. He didn't make eye contact with her. She stood inside the club's glass doors until she saw Darwin pull out of the parking lot. He drove a light SUV, proof enough for her, if not the police, that he'd tried to force her off the road last night. She would take the chief's advice and avoid Darwin from now on.

She stowed her produce in the fridge and headed for the locker room. She always kept shorts, shoes, and a racket there in case a tennis opportunity arose. She changed and returned to the club's reception area to wait for Gunnar.

Luke Forsa strode in. He wore a navy T-shirt that emphasized his muscular build and advertised his mom's diner.

She raised her racket by way of greeting. "Hey, Luke. What brings you here?" She'd never before seen him at the club.

"Thinking of joining. From what I hear, the club has a lot to offer." He gazed at her as if she were the club feature he liked best. "I was hoping to check out your café too. Unless you're dishing out food with a racket, it looks like I'm out of luck."

"The café closes at two. You play tennis?"

"I never got into it." He nodded toward the room full of exercise equipment. "The weights and indoor track are more my speed. I'm glad I ran into you. Someone at the diner told Mom that you were at the police station today. Is everything okay?"

"Everything's good." As long as she didn't

153

mind the complete loss of privacy that came with living in a small town. "Who ratted on me?"

He grinned. "Mom didn't say. Did you find out anything about the murder investigation?"

"Not really." She tucked her racket under one arm. "I went to the police to report that someone forced me off the road last night."

He frowned. "Who?"

"I didn't get a look at the driver. He was in a light SUV."

"Probably a tourist who's used to wider roads. You gotta watch out for them. I hope you didn't get banged up."

"I'm fine. My car hit a few bumps." While waiting for Gunnar, she could pick Luke's brain. He might have a different perspective on Nadia than the club members did. "By the way, I'm writing an article about Nadia for the club newsletter. Maybe you can help me out. How well did you know her?"

"Hardly at all. When I moved back here two years ago, she sold me my house in Cove Acres."

"Cove Acres? On the road between here and her house?" At his nod, Val conjured a vision of aluminum-sided tract mansions like mushrooms on bare flat land. Not as appealing as the modest old houses shaded by tall trees in Nadia's neighborhood. "Did she stay in touch after the sale went through?"

He tilted his head from side to side. "Not with me, though she'd drop by the diner once in a while."

The weight-conscious Nadia couldn't have found much to her liking on the diner menu. "I've never seen her eat anything but seeds and leaves."

"We serve salads at the diner, you know."

Val still doubted the food had attracted Nadia. She might have gone there to troll for clients, senior citizens who wanted to sell their houses or tourists looking for weekend places. "I suppose she also wanted to check on Irene Pritchard's boy. How's Jeremy doing?"

"Nadia's death hit him hard, but he still managed to come to work today. He's a dependable worker. She did a good deed when she talked me into hiring him."

"I'll be sure to mention in the article that she helped young people." Nadia's good deeds, while perfect for the newsletter article, wouldn't help Val find the murderer.

Gunnar came through the club entrance, an athletic bag slung over his shoulder.

"Here's my tennis opponent." Val motioned for him to join them.

She introduced the two men. They eyed each other warily and shook hands with taut forearms as if trying to crack each other's bones. Neither cracked a smile. Were they engaging in the alpha male greeting ritual, or did they view themselves as rivals for her?

Gunnar touched Val's shoulder. "Ready to play?"

"More than ready." Tennis was exactly what she needed to take her mind off murder — if only for a short while. "See you, Luke."

"Don't forget you promised to meet me for a drink."

Luke's parting shot hit its mark. Annoyance flitted across Gunnar's face for a split second before he adjusted it to bland as vanilla pudding. Val had made no promises to Luke, but why tell Gunnar that? A bit of jealousy could stoke the fires of attraction. She'd learned a little about Gunnar's character while playing with him as his mixed doubles partner. She'd know even more about him after playing against him.

CHAPTER 10

Val and Gunnar stopped for a break before the third set, with the score tied at one set for each of them.

Val refilled her water bottle at the cooler while Gunnar toweled off and sat on the bench alongside the court.

She approached the bench. "I have a theory that people reveal their true selves on the tennis court. In the heat of competition, their inhibitions fall away."

Gunnar switched from sitting to lying on the bench. "Okay, Frau Doctor Freud. I'm ready for your analysis. How did I do in the tennis personality test?"

She gave him a mock sympathetic look. "Sadly, the test revealed you're very deceptive. At the beginning of our match, you weren't really trying to win. Then, after you lulled me into complacency, you brought out the big guns."

"My ego likes your theory. I didn't play

badly. I just held back to gain a competitive advantage."

"You're also totally unpredictable. You kept changing tactics, even when you were ahead. That's unusual. Most tennis players have their game and stick to it."

"Better unpredictable than boring." He sat up and patted the bench next to him. "Your turn on the analyst's couch."

She didn't have enough room to lie on the bench unless she put her head in his lap, which might destroy his concentration for the third set . . . or hers. She sat upright. "What do you know about me as a competitor?"

"You're way better looking than most of my opponents. That's why I had trouble concentrating on the game."

"So far, so good. What else?"

"You don't give up. The more behind you fell, the harder you played. And you're a good loser."

"Ha. I'm a much better winner than loser, as you'll see when we play the next set. The third set isn't about superior tactics or good strokes. It's about stamina." She stood up to show she was ready to play.

He fixed her with his aquamarine eyes. "My stamina will surprise you."

Her face grew warm. With any luck,

exercising in the heat had turned it pink enough that he wouldn't notice her blush. "I'd love to put your stamina to the test." Nice that she hadn't forgotten how to flirt though years had passed since the last time she'd done it.

He tugged at her hand. "Sit down, and tell me how you're doing. Better than yesterday?"

Val parked herself on the bench. Yesterday in the car with him, she'd worried about a murderer targeting Monique. Now, the police were targeting Monique as the murderer, and Val had someone gunning for her too. "Better in some ways, worse in others. Last night, I drove to my cousin's house. On the way there, an SUV driver stalked me and ran me off the road."

He drummed his fingers on the bench slats and peppered her with questions. No, she didn't know the make or even the color of the SUV, other than that it was light. She hadn't glimpsed either the driver or the license plate.

"Anything distinctive about the SUV, a dent or something dangling from the rearview mirror?"

She shook her head. "I was too terrified to notice anything. I focused on controlling the car."

"I'm glad you weren't hurt." He squeezed her hand gently.

She squeezed back, though she wanted to hug him instead. "You're the first person to take this seriously. Everyone else brushed it off or gave me driving tips." That included the man who changed her tire, the cop who took her statement, Maverick, and even Luke.

A chirp came from Gunnar's athletic bag. He pulled out a cell phone and glanced at the display. "I gotta take this call. Excuse me."

He put the phone to his ear and walked to the far end of the court. The instincts of a man who guards against eavesdroppers?

A minute later, he tucked the phone into a pocket in his shorts and returned to the bench. "I'm sorry. I have to leave. Something came up."

Val said nothing for a moment, hoping for details about that "something," whether it related to family, job, or another woman. No matter. She'd make the best of it. "So you're forfeiting? I'll take the win any way I can get it." She thrust out her hand for the end-of-match handshake.

"You're a good sport." He shook her hand and then held it a few seconds longer than usual. "Can I make it up to you by taking you to dinner Friday night? You pick the restaurant."

A real date, unlike Luke's let's-get-together-for-a-drink-sometime. "I'd like that. How about the crab house on the waterfront?"

"Sounds good. Pick you up around seven?"

"Perfect." She could make sure that her grandfather ate a good meal before she left with Gunnar.

She showered in the locker room, drove home, and found her grandfather in the kitchen. He stood over a pan with butter sizzling in it.

She turned the flame off under the pan. "Hi, Granddad. What are you doing?"

"Melting butter. What are you doing?"

"Keeping the butter from burning."

"About time you came home. Everything's almost ready."

She spotted six white potatoes turning brown on the counter, their peelings mounded in the sink except for errant ones clinging to the backsplash, faucet, and dish drainer. "That's a lot of potatoes for two of us."

"I know that, Smarty Pants. Ned went fishing this morning, caught rockfish, and brought us one. I asked him to join us for dinner. He needs a break from institutional food."

"Great. I haven't seen much of him since he moved to the senior village." She eyed the potatoes. "That's still a lot of potatoes for three people."

Granddad held up an index card. "Your recipe here calls for six spuds and five ingredients. It tasted pretty good when you made it. I don't want to mess with it."

Val messed with the recipe herself whenever she made it for him, substituting olive oil for half the butter to reduce the cholesterol. He didn't know that, of course. "How about I make the potatoes, and you deal with the rockfish?"

"After a beer." He took a bottle from the refrigerator, poured the beer into a glass, and sat at the small kitchen table.

She cut the potatoes into quarters. "Why didn't you go fishing with Ned?"

"Let's just say I had other fish to fry today. What have you been doing?"

Whenever she asked a question he didn't want to answer, he countered with a question of his own. He wouldn't tell her anything about his day, but she had lots to tell about hers.

She explained Monique's predicament without mentioning the burned racket or

162

the murder weapon. As she coated the potatoes with flour and Parmesan cheese, she summarized what Bethany and the chief had told her and outlined her suspicions of Bigby.

By the time she stopped talking, the potatoes were roasting in the oven, she was assembling salad ingredients, and her grandfather had finished his beer.

"Don't start on the fish yet, Granddad. I want to show you something." She fetched the Personali-Tees shopping bag from the vestibule and handed it to him. "There's a gift for you inside."

Granddad's face lit up like a small boy's on Christmas morning. He pulled out a khaki apron with CODGER COOK printed in red across the front. He grinned, put the apron on, and tied it in the back. "It fits real good. Thank you."

"It fits in every way." Except maybe the "Cook" part. "You're welcome."

"I want to look at myself in the mirror." He returned a minute later without the apron.

Did he only pretend to like it? "Why aren't you wearing your gift?"

"I'd rather get fish guts on my old clothes than a nice clean apron. I'm saving that for a special occasion." He took the rockfish from the refrigerator.

"If I buy you another apron, I'll prestain it to make sure you wear it."

Granddad unwrapped the fish and set it on a large cutting board. "Getting back to business, you'd like to pin the murder on Bigby, the big cheese, but he doesn't even have a whiff of a motive."

She wrinkled her nose and sniffed. "Freshly caught fish has no smell either, but that doesn't mean it isn't fish. Despite what Bethany said, I think Nadia dumped Bigby as a partner."

"Didn't you say Nadia dumped Bethany as a partner too? You don't think she's guilty."

"She doesn't have the courage to commit a murder. Bigby has the personality to eliminate anyone in his way. I compared his handwriting with the anonymous note Monique received. Bigby sent that note."

Granddad pointed his knife at her. "Why would he bother doing that if he was gonna kill Nadia?"

"I guess he wasn't planning to murder her when he wrote it."

"You're talking about a man who buys up land years before he starts building on it, and you're saying he's not a planner?"

"Business sense doesn't apply to emotional matters. Two different parts of the brain at work." She whirled the lettuce in a salad dryer. "He dodged my questions about Nadia. I'm always suspicious when people don't give straight answers. Monique's husband, for example, misled her about where he was the night of the murder. He could have killed Nadia."

"Why?"

"To get rid of a demanding mistress and frame his wife."

Granddad sliced deftly into the fish. "Let's dissect that motive. If Monique's arrested and convicted, where does that leave him? With two brats to raise on his own."

"Depending on how Monique and Maverick set up their finances, he might get control of the fortune she inherited from her mother's uncle. That leaves him with two brats and a lot of money."

"Not after she pays her legal team. With a high-priced lawyer, she could even beat the rap, but how much of the money would be left? Maverick's better off now with a joint checking account than he would be with the cockamamie scheme you thought up."

Val bristled at his criticism. "Why wouldn't he tell Monique where he was the night of the murder?"

Granddad cleaned out the insides of the

fish. "Because he was with another woman."

Val leaned against the counter and watched her grandfather handle the knife. He'd gutted her murder theories as thoroughly as he'd gutted the fish. "You have any better ideas?"

"The way I see it, there are five obvious suspects, and you missed four of them."

"At least I got one right."

"Half right. Let's start with the two that have the strongest motives. Hell hath no fury like a woman scorned, as the saying goes." He scraped the fish and sent its translucent scales flipping in all directions. "Monique's husband scorned her for Nadia, and Nadia scorned Bethany as a tennis partner."

Val moved the salad bowl out of the range of flying fish scales. "If you knew Bethany better, you'd realize she couldn't pull off a murder." Especially a murder like Nadia's, which required careful planning and execution, not to mention a strong stomach. "And you're prejudiced against Monique."

"Well, you're biased in favor of women. Long as you have a male to accuse of murder, you won't even consider a female." He scraped scales rhythmically without missing a beat. "You'll be happy to know I got a few men for you. The usual suspect is the victim's ex. He's number three on my list."

"Joe Westrin." The police might not investigate the usual suspect if they were convinced Monique committed the murder. "I saw him with Nadia at the club. They looked more like old friends than bitter exes."

Granddad examined the fish under the lengthwise slit he'd just made. "You never know what's festering inside."

"You have a point. I'll try to reach Joe tomorrow and sound out some club members about the Westrins' marriage and divorce."

Granddad put his knife down and faced her. "Stay out of this, Val. It's okay for us to talk about it, but I don't want you getting in the way of a murderer. Leave it to the police."

"I'm not going to confront anybody. I'll poke around the edges and tell Chief Yardley what I find out."

"I once poked around the edges of a sweater your grandmother knitted and unraveled the whole thing. She wanted to kill me, and she wasn't a murderer. What do you think happens when you start unraveling a murderer's sweater?"

"I'll keep my knitting needles handy." Val

sliced tomatoes for the salad. "Who's your next candidate?"

"Maverick. You had the right man for the wrong reason. He's sitting pretty with a rich wife and a mistress on the side. When the mistress tells him she's pregnant, she's toast." Granddad rinsed the fish. "Mind you, she might not have been pregnant. She only had to say she was for Maverick's motive to kick in."

Unfortunately, that latest scenario gave Monique another reason to kill Nadia. Val didn't like any of her grandfather's theories. She clung to the hope that his fifth suspect would serve as the magic bullet shattering the police case against her cousin. "Who's the last person on your list?"

He put the fish down and caught her eye. "Gunnar."

CHAPTER 11

Val dropped her tomato knife, faced her grandfather, and thunked herself on the forehead. "So that's who did Nadia in. Did he act alone or in cahoots with the pirate?"

"I'm serious, Val. Gunnar no sooner shows up in town than there's a murder. That's just plain fishy. And he looks like a hit man."

"The movie version of a hit man. Real hit men look average and leave town as soon as the job is done. Gunnar didn't go away after the murder. He came back."

Granddad rinsed his knife under the faucet. "If he isn't a hit man, he mighta had a personal reason to kill Nadia."

"They didn't know each other. They met for the first time Sunday at the club."

"Did she tell you that?"

Val tamped down her growing annoyance. "He told me."

"There you go. The only one who could say otherwise is dead. It worries me how you're defending him." The creases in Granddad's forehead deepened. "Face it, Val, your taste in men stinks."

"Thanks for reminding me." Her sarcasm masked her niggling doubts about Gunnar. She didn't suspect him of murder, but of selecting what and what not to tell her. He gave more details about the inheritance he expected than about the phone calls that made him rush away, as if he'd followed a script about Great-Aunt Gretchen. The calls, though, had taken him by surprise.

The doorbell rang. Granddad wiped his hands on a paper towel. "That's Ned. Let's not talk murder over dinner. He's a worry-wart."

Halfway through dinner, Granddad looked ready to murder his buddy. Ned regaled Val with her grandfather's recent doings — taking computer classes at the community center, spending this afternoon there printing pages he wouldn't show anyone, and "courting" the youngest and most attractive widow at the senior village. All news to Val. The man she'd glimpsed from behind at the Tuscan Eaterie might have been Granddad leaving the restaurant with the widow he'd invited to dinner. Val refrained from asking her grandfather about his date. Maybe if she didn't inquire into his private life, he'd butt out of hers.

As soon as Ned left, Granddad disappeared into his bedroom, and Val phoned Joe Westrin, Nadia's ex. The voice on his answering machine reported that Jackie and Joe weren't available. Apparently, Joe had a new wife or a live-in girlfriend. Val left a message for him, her usual request for help with the newsletter article on Nadia.

She cleaned up the kitchen, climbed into bed exhausted, and closed her eyes.

She was driving, elated that Nadia sat in the passenger seat. She wasn't dead after all. The steering wheel came off in Val's hands, and Nadia screamed. If only Val could force the steering wheel back on the post, she could keep them both alive. The car veered off a bridge and plummeted toward the water.

Val awoke in a sweat, her heart racing. She had recurring car-crash nightmares. A passenger always sat next to her, her former fiancé or Chef Henri or Granddad. Never before had a dead person sat in the doomed car. Maybe her subconscious was telling her she'd gone off the road in her pursuit of Nadia's killer. How could she get back on track?

Wide-awake now, Val crept downstairs for crackers and warm milk, her mother's remedy for sleeplessness. As she passed through the sitting room on her way to the kitchen, she heard bushes rustling under the side windows near the driveway. Maybe deer, though they usually didn't come close to the house.

She looked out the dining room window and could barely see the shape of her car. The light over the side door was off. She went into the vestibule at the side entrance and flipped the switch. Still dark in the driveway. The bulb must have burned out.

Two nights ago, she would have fetched a flashlight and gone outside to investigate the noise and replace the bulb. But now, with a murderer at large, she was taking no chances. She could at least turn on the inside lights. She flipped all the switches from the study to the back porch. The glow from the windows should keep deer from coming close. It would also create the illusion of alert occupants to discourage any human prowlers.

She gave up on sleeping and went to the shelves flanking the fireplace in the sitting room. Some books stood upright, others lay piled sideways, their colorful spines creating a quilt pattern. No one had shifted the books in decades. When she wanted to reread a classic, she knew where to find it.

She took down *Memoirs of Sherlock Holmes,* nestled on the sofa, and read only a few pages of the first story, "Silver Blaze," before her eyes closed.

At dawn on Thursday, Val abandoned the sofa where she'd spent most of the night and made coffee. After dressing, she went outside and walked all around the house. No sign of anything amiss. She didn't need to change the lightbulb near the side door, only tighten it in the socket. Probably Granddad hadn't screwed it in all the way, and vibration had worked it loose.

Val left the café at ten when Bethany arrived to relieve her. She drove to the Bayport Properties office in town to find out what she could about Nadia's professional life and reputation.

The receptionist in the office greeted her. "Hello, I'm Mavis. How can I help you?"

"Hi. I'm Val Deniston, a friend of Nadia's from the Bayport Racket and Fitness Club. I'm writing an article about her for the club newsletter. I was hoping her colleagues here could give me some information or anecdotes about her that I can work into the article."

Mavis frowned and chewed her lip. "Our agents are fairly busy this morning. I'll let them know what you want and, if you leave your phone number, I'm sure one of them will call you."

In other words, get lost. Val would have to convince Mavis that she wasn't a snoopy reporter, but a pal — or better yet, a client — of Nadia's. "Nadia called me from here Monday, and I didn't get a chance to return the call. I have no idea why she phoned me. If I could talk to someone who works with her, we might figure out why she called, and I won't feel so bad about not getting back to her." A lame story, but at least it didn't prompt the receptionist to escort her to the door.

"Are you interested in buying or selling a house? That's probably why she called."

"She knew I was fixing up my grand-father's house, but it's not ready for sale yet."

Mavis smiled at the mention of a potential sale. "Nadia was mentoring a new agent, Kimberly. She might be able to help you. I'll let her know you're writing an article about Nadia."

Thirty seconds later Kimberly met Val in the reception area. The real estate agent looked like a high school cheerleader in a business suit. "So you were like one of Nadia's friends? We're all totally bummed out by what happened to her. She was such an aggressive agent, and what a great body she had for a woman her age."

The receptionist, a woman about Nadia's age, rolled her eyes. "*Aggressive* isn't the right word. She knew how to follow up with clients and close a deal. Maybe she found a client for the house you're fixing up, Val, and that's why she called you."

"Maybe. Was she working with any new clients the last few days?"

"We can check the master schedule." Kimberly led her from the reception area to a corridor with a huge whiteboard calendar on its wall. "Her appointments are in orange marker. We each have our own color."

Val studied the orange entries on the board. "Why did she write 'STONED' under Friday?"

Kimberly giggled. "Stone is the last name. The 'D' is the person's first initial. The squares on the calendar are so small you have to use abbreviations or else write real tiny."

Val gave Kimberly a thumbs-up. "Got it. I see Nadia worked with D. Stone on Friday and with N. Singh on Saturday."

Kimberly tapped the board with a long purple fingernail. "Mr. Singh was looking for waterfront property. She spent the whole day with him, and the next day she held an open house."

"Thank you for taking the time to explain this to me, Kimberly."

"No problem." Her voice barely rose over a whisper. "I'm glad to talk to someone who's like young. Most everyone here has gray hair."

Fortunately, Val had recently plucked her three gray hairs. "Nadia didn't list any names for Monday. Did she take the day off?"

"She was in the office most of the day Monday except right in the middle when she borrowed my car. Hers had a dead battery."

"She borrowed your car to go meet a client?"

Kimberly shook her head. "She'd have put the client's name on the schedule. She was gone a couple of hours, like eleven to one-thirty. After she returned my car keys, she went out to lunch. When she came back, she handled some drop-in clients. Then she asked me to run her by the club to pick up her car. A mechanic had gone out there and installed a new battery."

"Would you say she had an ordinary day on Monday?"

"Not really." Kimberly glanced at a nearby

room where a man was on the phone. She leaned toward Val. "I didn't mention this to anyone in the office. I went out for lunch around noon that day. Since Nadia took my car, I had to walk. On my way back, I saw my car on Main Street, driven by a woman with long black hair."

Val scratched her head. "Nadia lent your car to someone else?"

"That's what I thought at first. Then I saw the driver had on the same red top Nadia wore that day. It was her wearing a wig."

Val felt her blood pumping faster. "Can we talk somewhere private?" She followed Kimberly to a miniscule office. "Did you see anyone in the car with Nadia?"

"She was alone. I asked her about the wig later. She said it was a joke. To see if an old friend would recognize her in disguise."

If Nadia had told the truth, the police should find out who that old friend was. If she'd lied, they should investigate the reason for her disguise. "Did Nadia ever borrow a car or wear a wig before Monday?"

"Not that I know. Is it important? Should I tell the police?"

"Call Chief Yardley and tell him."

"I'll do that." Kimberly reached into her desk drawer and pulled out a small spiral notebook. "I found this in my car this morning, stuck between the two front seats. It must have slid down when Nadia drove my car. It's her writing. Nothing to do with business, though. Backhands, serves, tennis stuff. Do you think I should give it to the police?"

"Can I see it?" Val opened the spiral and skimmed the first ten pages. They contained notes in Nadia's printing style, back-slanted capital letters. "I doubt the police need this. Nadia was our tennis team captain. These are her records of our matches, who played for the opposing team, what their strengths and weaknesses were. She must have thought it would help us the next time we played against them." Though that wouldn't happen until next season, and Nadia wouldn't be there to benefit from what she'd written.

"I get it. Scouting out the competition. You want to keep the notebook?"

"Sure. I'll give it to whoever takes Nadia's place as team captain." Val tucked it in her bag. Nothing she'd heard yet supported Bethany's claim that other agents resented Nadia's tactics. Kimberly might need a push to talk about that subject. "Did Nadia ever complain about another agent or a developer?" Like Bigby O'Shay.

"Not to me."

"A few months ago, I moved here from New York, where real estate agents are very ruthless. They'll do anything for a sale. Is that the way it is here?"

"We hang on to our own clients, but that's not like ruthless or anything."

"You said earlier that Nadia was aggressive."

"I meant it in a good way. Once she had a prospect, she never let go. But she wasn't mean or anything. I'm going to miss her." Kimberly slumped, her cheery demeanor gone. "She like helped me a lot, and she really didn't have to."

"How did she help you?"

"With sales tips and advice. Like a few weeks ago, she heard me calling a new client by his first name and told me to address everyone as Mr. or Ms. She said older people get turned off when younger people use their first names. I never thought of that. Everyone I know uses first names. It's like friendlier, you know. She also said she'd help me get better at finding and keeping clients."

Val knew of one client Nadia's protégée might enlist. She asked Kimberly for a business card and wrote "Zacharnaroviak" on the back of it. "Here's the name of a client Nadia never had a chance to see. If you contact her, maybe this woman will list her house with you. She lives on Maple Street and likes to be called Mrs. Z."

"Wow. I really appreciate this."

Not as much as Val appreciated what the agent had told her about Nadia's actions on Monday. Wearing a wig on a sweltering day made no sense unless Nadia had to disguise herself. Had she ever done that before the day of the murder? If anyone could answer that, Chatty could.

Val looked forward to this afternoon's facial-and-gossip session, though she'd have to stay on her guard. Chatty would want to get as much information as she gave.

CHAPTER 12

Chatty arrived twenty minutes after the café closed, toting a campstool and a black case for her products. Thanks to tinted contact lenses, her irises matched her violet smock and her eye shadow. Her lipstick matched her hot pink scarf. She pointed to an armless settee in the far corner of the café. "You can lie there while I give you a facial."

Val tried to get comfortable on the narrow settee. She looked up at Chatty. "I feel like I'm at the dentist's."

"Trust me. You'll love this." Chatty unfolded the stool, extracted three bottles from her suitcase, and unscrewed the caps. "What's your theory on who set the racket on fire?"

"I don't have a theory." Instead, Val knew the disturbing facts and wished she didn't.

Chatty dotted pink lotion on Val's forehead, cheeks, nose, and chin. "Well, I think it was Bigby. I heard him talking about it at the club on Monday. He pretended to be outraged that someone would do that to Nadia. But how would he know about it unless he did it himself?"

"Maybe he heard it from Bethany. You told her and Monique." But how much did she tell them? "Did you actually see the burned racket?"

"Uh-huh. Nadia showed it to me when I picked her up Monday morning. Her car was on the fritz, and she needed a ride to work."

"Where was the racket when you saw it?"

"She pulled it from the trash bin outside her house." Chatty spread liquid silk from Val's jaw to her forehead. "She wanted me to sound out Monique and Bethany. She thought one of them burned it and might come clean with me."

"But you think Bigby did it. Why?"

Chatty massaged Val's cheekbones. "Because of what happened between him and Nadia. When she told me, I was speechless."

"I hope you'll make up for that now."

Chatty tapped Val's cheek in a mock slap. She looked toward the café entrance. "Here comes Irene Pritchard."

A tall, pale woman with gray hair like corrugated metal approached them. Nadia's next-door neighbor reminded Val of her fifth grade teacher, the aptly named Mrs. Stern, whose steely gaze could make even the schoolyard bully cringe.

Chatty took her hands off Val's face and massaged her own fingers.

Irene looked down at Val. "I came in for a cup of tea, but there's no one behind the counter."

Val had never before seen Irene at the club, much less at the café they'd both applied to manage. "We're closed now. The hours are posted at the entrance to the alcove."

"Closed in the middle of the afternoon? What time do you reopen?"

"Not until tomorrow." Val felt as if she'd missed a homework assignment. "We're open every day from eight to two."

"Hmm." Irene squinted at the slacker, pivoted, and left.

Something besides tea must have brought her here. Val shrugged. Back to more important things. "You were about to tell me what happened between Nadia and Bigby."

"They were all business when they started playing mixed doubles. They talked strategy and dissected their opponents' games. Then Bigby got friendlier. He'd give Nadia a pat on the rump after a good point and a big hug after winning a set."

"Was she okay with that?" Val closed her eyes, enjoying the gentle pressure of Chatty's fingers.

"She tried to wiggle away, but he didn't seem to notice. When he invited her out, Nadia had her excuses ready. She said she was busy, maybe they could do it some other time. She figured if she said 'no' often enough, Bigby would catch on."

"That probably didn't work. Bigby doesn't do subtle."

"No kidding." Chatty's palms pressed against Val's forehead from her eyebrows to her hairline. "He showed up on her doorstep one night, a bouquet in his hand and a gleam in his eye. As soon as she let him in — and what else could she do? — he started pawing her."

Val's eyes flew open. "And then what?"

"When she backed away, he said, 'Hey, Nadia, wouldn't you like to be the agent for my new development? Get commissions on all those houses?' Like she should sleep with him to get commissions? She threw him out of course."

A new take on Nadia and the sales job at Bigby's development. Bethany's version of the story had obviously come from Bigby. "No wonder Nadia stopped playing tennis with him."

"And, after that night, she would see Bigby now and again parked across the street, sitting there watching her house."

Val bolted upright. "He stalked her? Did she tell the police?"

"No. She wasn't positive it was him. The car looked like his, but it had tinted windows. She couldn't see the driver." Chatty wrung her greased hands. "Maybe Bigby went from harassing Nadia, to burning the racket, to . . . killing her."

"You have to tell the police what Nadia said." If Chief Yardley had known about a stalker, maybe he wouldn't have been so hard on Monique.

"I hate to cross Bigby. He has a lot of influence in this town."

"A stalker makes a damned good murder suspect, whether it was Bigby or not. In any case, the police won't tell him where their information came from. Call Chief Yardley."

"Later. Lie back down. The facial isn't over." She reached for a bottle of milky lotion.

"Good." Val liked the massage more than she expected.

Chatty's eyes half closed as she resumed the facial, a ghost of a smile and a look of contentment on her face. She obviously enjoyed her work. While Bethany needed to be needed, Chatty apparently needed to knead — bread and pasta dough, faces, fabrics, whatever she could get her fingers on. Sometimes she massaged her own muscles and even the air around her, her hands in constant motion. Did she also massage the truth?

Val didn't know Chatty well enough to answer that question. "Tell me about Nadia's divorce. When did she break up with Joe?"

"A year and a half ago."

"Did she ever explain why they broke up?"

"I could never get anything out of her about that. It was a really private thing with her." Chatty tapped even faster on Val's skin as if the desire for privacy agitated her. "Nadia had a tendency to clam up about certain things. Like the day she exchanged cars with me. Not that I minded driving a Lexus instead of a Honda."

Val opened her eyes. "When did you switch cars with her?"

"Wednesday of last week. My guess is she was going someplace she didn't want to drive a flashy car." Chatty's thumbs traced circles around Val's eyes. "After she climbed into my car, she tied a scarf around her head and put on huge sunglasses, even though it was cloudy."

A scarf and sunglasses, not much of a disguise at close range, but from a distance in a moving car, they might do quite well. By Monday of this week, when she drove Kimberly's car, she had a better disguise, a dark wig. Nadia owned the right vehicle for chauffeuring people looking at property, but not the right one for . . . what? Watching someone? Evading a stalker?

Chatty massaged Val's temples. "How's Monique taking all this? Must be tough for her. First she finds out her husband's cheating on her with Nadia, and then Nadia gets murdered. That looks bad."

"I wish you wouldn't say that. You know Monique better than to think —"

"Stop frowning. You'll undo all my hard work. Of course, I don't think Monique did it. Bigby's the culprit. I hope the police arrest him soon."

Val hated to put all her hopes on Bigby as the murderer. Darwin made a good backup, the tennis pro with an SUV and a short fuse. "Did anything go on between Nadia and Darwin?"

"Are you kidding? His tastes don't run to older women. He likes 'em young with long legs and big boobs."

The opposite of Nadia's body type. "Did she ever talk about him or his shop?"

"She took a tennis lesson from him once and didn't think much of him as a teacher. She bought the occasional outfit at his shop. Other wise, she had nothing to do with him, far as I know. You think he murdered her? Is that why you're asking?"

"I have no reason to think that." Val barely had a reason to think Darwin had followed her and run her off the road, and absolutely no proof of it.

Chatty took a moist towelette from a packet and wiped her hands. "All done."

"Where's the mirror? I want to make sure I really look more beautiful." Val sat up, took the hand mirror Chatty held out, and studied her face. She couldn't see much difference except for a slight sheen.

Chatty gestured to the bottles on the table. "Now can I interest you in buying any of these wonderful products?"

The bill for Chatty's information had come due. "I might go for that pink silky stuff."

Chatty took out a pad to write up a sales slip. "I have a two-ounce travel size and a four-ounce size for home use. You can have both for forty dollars, a savings of ten dollars over the individual prices."

Val liked Chatty's gossip, but not that much. Did an itinerant cosmetologist negotiate like a used car salesman? Val picked up the pink-tinged bottle from the coffee table and sniffed. "I don't like anything with a strong scent, but this isn't bad. You know, it reminds me of the stuff I buy in the beauty aisle at the drugstore. Of course, this is pink, and that's white."

Chatty snatched the bottle from Val's hand. "You don't have to buy anything."

Val was too stunned to respond quickly. "Sorry. I didn't mean to offend you, and I was going to buy —"

"No offense taken, and no need to buy." She stowed the bottles in her case and stood up. "I'll see you back here at six for the team get-together."

What had gotten into her? She usually wasn't so touchy. Val walked her to the exit. "Thanks again for the facial. Don't forget to call the chief."

Chatty waved, the gesture more dismissive than friendly.

If she didn't tell Chief Yardley about Nadia's stalker by tomorrow, Val would do it. This evening, when the tennis team gathered for the first time since Nadia's murder, even more information might crop up that she could pass on to him.

189

CHAPTER 13

Val pulled into the club parking lot at five forty-five. Odd that only one of the six courts had a game in progress. Three others had signs of occupation — floppy athletic bags on the ground, towels flung over the net, rackets propped against the fence — but no players on them. They must have joined the crowd clustered around a camera crew near the club entrance. A van identified the crew as belonging to a Salisbury, Maryland, television station.

Val spotted Althea on the fringes of the crowd and joined her. "Is this local news covering Nadia's murder?"

"What else?" Althea put a hand on Val's shoulder. "Squeeze in front of me so you can see Chatty's get-up."

Val slipped into the space Althea made for her. Chatty wore black from her headband to her socks and shoes. She stood out among the tennis players in white or bright colors.

A newscaster spoke into a microphone. "This is Junie May Jussup at the Bayport Racket and Fitness Club. The local women's tennis team is gathering here to honor real estate agent and avid tennis player Nadia Westrin, murdered three nights ago in her Bayport home. Let's talk to one of her teammates, Chatty Ridenour." She tilted the microphone toward Chatty.

Chatty blinked her black-shadowed eyelids. "We're just devastated about Nadia. She was active in the USTA league and set up the Bayport women's tennis teams. She was our star player. Our team is a big family. We feel like we've lost not just a friend, but a close relative."

"She's laying it on as thick as her makeup," Althea muttered.

The newscaster angled the microphone toward her own mouth. "I understand Nadia was competitive on the court and off."

Chatty tilted her head toward the mike. "Nadia worked in real estate, a business where your colleagues are your rivals, everyone vying for commissions. She came to the club to take a break from all that. Tennis is competitive, of course, but it's healthy competition."

191

The newscaster gave a grim smile appropriate for a wake. "Did you see any sign of fear or anxiety from Nadia before this awful tragedy?"

Val held her breath. Chatty could double her airtime by mentioning Nadia's affair, Monique's rage, and the burned racket. Would she resist that temptation?

Chatty's head rocked from side to side. "You should ask that at her real estate office and in her neighborhood. Nadia relaxed here and put her anxieties aside."

Val wanted to applaud Chatty. Nice try at sending the news team elsewhere.

Althea leaned down to whisper in Val's ear. "The way Chatty's dodging questions, she may have a future in politics."

Val caught sight of her cousin approaching from the parking lot. "I can't let Monique walk into this, Althea. I'll take her around to the back door near the locker room. Can you open it from the inside and let us in?"

"Meet you there." Althea maneuvered around the crowd at the club entrance.

Val waylaid her cousin. "We're steering clear of a TV news crew. Let's go in the back way. The hedges will hide us."

Monique rubbed her eyes, the dark circles underneath making them look sunken. "I can't avoid the media forever."

"Practice saying two words until they roll off your tongue: *No comment.*"

"That's what guilty people say."

"And innocent people who have lawyers." Val scanned the bushes to make sure no reporters were hiding there. "By the way, did you contact a lawyer?"

"I have an appointment tomorrow with an attorney in Annapolis. But the only thing that's really going to help me is for the murderer to be caught."

True, and Val would do her best to make it happen. She had plenty to tell Chief Yardley tomorrow.

Monique helped her set out snacks at the café. The tennis team gathered there for hugs, tears, and a Perrier toast to Nadia. Althea announced a memorial service would be held at the Faith Fellowship Chapel, Saturday at eleven, followed by lunch at her house. They then took their drinks and snacks to the veranda overlooking the courts. The team's youngest members, high school and college players, had arranged to start their matches early and were already on two courts.

Val studied the women who sat at the veranda table with her. They'd welcomed her when she moved to Bayport and now formed the nucleus of her social life. Would rifts form among them under the pressure of murder or would they stick together?

Bethany bit her lower lip and sent speculative glances toward Monique. Had she decided that Monique made a more obvious suspect than her previous choice, Nadia's ex?

Monique looked toward the courts, the parking lot, and the club doors, avoiding eye contact with her teammates. The tightness around her mouth betrayed the strain of acting nonchalant while being a murder suspect.

Chatty leaned back in her chair and watched Monique. Whatever her suspicions now, she'd shown her loyalty to the team in front of the camera, trying to shift media attention from the club to Nadia's office and neighborhood.

Althea contemplated the bubbles rising in her glass of mineral water. "You know how I met Nadia? She sold me a house. At the settlement, she gave us a bottle of wine and told us to save it for a special occasion. I went to buy another bottle so I'd have enough for a dinner party, and found out it cost eighty dollars. Can you believe that?"

Chatty swirled her Diet Coke. "Nadia had a weakness for expensive wine. I could never see spending a lot of money on something to drink."

Given a choice between pricey wine and the pricey lotions Chatty sold, Val would go for the drink. "How was the wine, Althea? Worth the cost?"

"I'm no connoisseur. I invited Nadia over to share it with us, and she raved about it."

Yumiko scurried toward them from the courts, carrying a clipboard. She had a round face and a wide mouth like a smiley. "The two matches that started early are going well. Our girls are winning on both courts. We just need to win one more tonight, and then we go to the district finals."

Althea tapped her fingernails on her glass. "Give it up, Yumiko. No one wants to play."

Yumiko's mouth went from upturned to straight. "I believe Nadia would want us to play. She got the team into the league. We should play to honor her."

Bethany nodded vigorously, her ginger curls bouncing. "I don't think that would be wrong. And it would be therapy for our grief to get out there and really try to win for her. What do the rest of you think?"

Val answered before the others had a chance. "I don't favor that, but if everyone else is going to play, Monique and I will too."

After five minutes of debate, the argument "to win one for Nadia" prevailed.

Easier said than done. In the first set Val and Monique played erratically and lost quickly. They kept pace with their opponents in the second set until Val noticed a man on the veranda watching them. He wore rumpled street clothes instead of the athletic wear common at the club. He might as well have worn a sandwich board that said REPORTER on it. A minute later, Chatty and Althea grimly shook hands with their smiling opponents. One match lost. If that wasn't depressing enough, the reporter intercepted Chatty as she left the court.

Val and Monique lost their momentum and the match. Val glanced at the third court, where Bethany and Yumiko looked worn-out and dispirited. They weren't winning either. Unless their match turned around, the team wouldn't go to the district finals this year.

Val stopped by the locker room. Althea stood in shorts and a bra beside an open locker, her tennis clothes and a damp towel heaped at her feet.

She pulled a folded T-shirt from her locker. "Why did we play tonight? How could anyone concentrate on a game?"

Althea often couched her opinions in questions she didn't expect anyone to answer.

Val parked herself on the wooden bench between two rows of lockers and loosened the laces on her shoes. "Did Chatty go home already?"

"She left with a reporter from the *Treadwell Gazette.*" Althea's voice was muffled as she pulled a shirt over her head. "It won't take him long to find out what happened here last week. Not that Chatty would intentionally hurt Monique, but she just can't stop her mouth, can she? And Monique couldn't stop her jealousy."

Val sprang to her cousin's defense. "What about Nadia? She couldn't stop her lust."

Althea banged the locker door shut, startling Val. "Maybe you'd call it lust. I call it loneliness."

"Lots of women are lonely, but they don't go after married men."

"From what I know of Maverick, he went after her, not vice versa. When I first joined the club, he started flirting with me and then, before long, he was coming on pretty strong. I didn't dare tell my husband. He'd have wrung Maverick's neck."

"What did you do?"

Althea folded her arms and leaned against the lockers. "I told him that, contrary to his expectations, not all black women are loose. He was shocked to be accused of racism. I was wrong, of course. He doesn't discriminate. He thinks all women are his for the asking."

Maverick didn't discriminate based on age either. Althea and Nadia both had a few years on him. Maybe he figured an older woman would be grateful for his attentions. "No wonder Monique went ballistic."

"But why did she do it now? He's had other affairs. She must have known."

Not necessarily. Easy enough to overlook signs of cheating if you don't want to see them, as Val had done with her fiancé. "If Monique knew about those other affairs, she may have reached a breaking point. And Nadia was her friend. Monique felt betrayed by her."

Althea dropped her athletic bag on the bench next to Val. "She expected more fidelity from her friends than from her husband. What does that say about their marriage?"

"Okay, the Motts don't have a great marriage. Nadia still shouldn't have done it."

"Agreed, but Maverick hit on her when she was vulnerable."

"Nadia vulnerable? How did I miss that?"

Val kept the sarcasm out of her voice, but only with great effort.

"You haven't lived here long. You didn't take the time — have the time to get to know her." Althea sat on the bench opposite Val. "I can't believe Bethany pushed us into playing tonight. Yumiko too. They didn't want to think about Nadia any longer than necessary."

"Well, Nadia treated Bethany pretty roughly."

"Are you kidding? She put up with her longer than the rest of us would have. Yet Bethany got more sympathy when Nadia ended the partnership than Nadia got for sticking with her."

"Nobody blamed Nadia for breaking up the partnership, only for the way she did it."

Althea's dark eyes studied Val. "What do you know about the way she did it?"

"Bethany told me —" Val broke off. "Of course, she's not an unbiased source." Yet Val had accepted Bethany's version of the incident.

"I'll tell you what really happened. I overheard the whole thing. It was after our team practice last week. Nadia and Bethany were in the locker room here, and I was toweling off in there." Althea pointed her thumb toward the shower room. "Nadia said what most people say when they want to end a partnership — 'we're not playing as well together as we used to.' What's the socially correct response to that?"

"You shake hands and say good-bye?"

"But that's not what Bethany did. Oh no, she said, they were playing as well as they ever had. She told Nadia to check their match record. When the gentle approach didn't work, Nadia got more blunt." Althea shoved her foot into her tennis shoe.

Blunt or cruel? "She accused Bethany of making questionable line calls."

"That's the truth, and someone needed to say it. When Bethany joined the club two years ago, Nadia took her on as a partner to ease her into team tennis." Althea propped her foot up on the bench and tied her shoe slowly and deliberately, as she might tie up an argument in court. "Bethany wouldn't leave the nest without a push."

A gentler push might have done the trick. Futile to argue the point with Althea. She wouldn't admit Nadia's faults any more than she would a client's guilt in court. She acted like a defense attorney, making a case to counter Bethany's prosecution case. Each side shaded the facts.

Althea packed up her athletic gear.

Val had yet to hear Althea's take on the murder. "Who do you think hated Nadia enough to kill her?"

"Are you sure that's the right question? Hate isn't the only reason to kill." Althea retied her shoe as if she hadn't gotten it right the first time. "Mind you, that was a general statement. I'm not going to speculate on who killed Nadia or why."

A lawyerly response. Perhaps Val could get her to respond to a yes-no question. "Do you know why Nadia divorced Joe?"

"You're on a roll with the wrong questions. I represented Nadia in the divorce, and it went smoothly." The locker room door squeaked. Two women entered, flushed and sweaty from a workout, towels slung over their shoulders. End of private conversation. Althea stood up. "See you Saturday at the memorial service, Val."

"Bye."

Val didn't move from the bench, weighed down by sadness. Maybe grief was infectious, and she'd caught it from Althea. Adding to her shock over Nadia's death and her concern for Monique, Val now felt a sense of loss. If a murderer hadn't struck, she might have come to know Nadia and seen a better side of her. Val blamed herself for rushing to judgment based on a brief acquaintance. She'd accepted Monique's view of Nadia as predatory and Bethany's view of Nadia as heartless because they reinforced her own opinions. And Althea had called her on it.

Val pressed her palms down on the bench and hoisted herself up. From now on, she would do better. She'd have to give up her own biases and reserve judgment until she knew the facts. That much she owed Nadia.

She left the locker room and went out to the parking lot. Climbing into the car reminded her of the last time she'd driven home from the club in darkness Sunday night, Nadia sitting next to her. Would a phone call to the police about the burning racket have changed anything? Would returning Nadia's call the following day have made any difference? Without knowing the answers, Val couldn't shake her guilt.

Fifteen minutes later, she turned into her grandfather's driveway and climbed out of the car. Beams from the headlights of a slow-moving vehicle lit up the street. She bolted into the house by the side door. A dollop of paranoia on a slice of guilt pie — a recipe for a bad night's sleep.

Granddad paused the movie he was watching as she rushed by his easy chair to look out the front window. No cars. No headlights. No movement.

"What's going on, Val?"

"Nothing. What are you watching?" She joined him in the sitting room.

"*Rebecca*. It's the inquest scene." He turned away from the TV's frozen image. "You find any new suspects today?"

She lounged on the sofa. "No, but I have a new victim, or at least one with different traits than the one I had yesterday."

She told him how Althea had undermined her assumptions about Nadia.

Granddad took off his glasses, cleaned them, and put them back on. "Sounds like Althea's grieving. Grief has made her angry at anyone who runs down Nadia. But her view of Nadia is no more valid than anyone else's." Granddad pointed his remote at the TV. "The dead Rebecca is a different person depending on who's talking about her. The widower, his young bride, the housekeeper."

Val remembered enough of the film to understand his point. "But facts come out that clarify what Rebecca's really like."

"Life doesn't tie up loose ends as well as the movies do."

He went back to watching the movie. She took *Memoirs of Sherlock Holmes* and the *Treadwell Gazette* upstairs to read in bed. Usually the local newspaper put her to sleep. Tonight, though, she devoured the articles on Nadia's murder. They contained nothing she didn't already know and left out things she knew that the media didn't.

She turned to the Thursday food section. An article about the opening of the Tuscan Eaterie and an interview with a local farmer took second billing to the feature article — Beloved Recipe Columnist Hangs Up Her Apron. The nostalgic farewell from the retiring columnist ended with her most popular recipes — Southern fried chicken, corn pudding, and whipped cream pound cake, a legendary favorite with Elvis Presley, who used to down the entire cake at one sitting and ask for seconds.

Val scanned the dessert recipe. Its ingredients included two sticks of butter, seven eggs, and a cup of heavy cream. Between the calorie counter in her brain and the calculator on her phone, she estimated the cake at 6,500 calories. If she ate only one slice, she'd have to make up for it by skipping a meal. Elvis would have been better off with a food guilt complex like hers.

A sidebar on the page noted that the deadline had passed to enter the contest for the new recipe columnist. The newspaper would announce the winner in the weekend food section. Darn. If she'd known about the contest, she'd have entered it. Though writing for the local newspaper wouldn't pay much, a column could lead to bigger things, even a contract for a cookbook.

She finished the Sherlock story she'd started last night, yawned, and turned off the light. Thirty minutes later she still hadn't fallen asleep. A change of scenery might help. She went downstairs and curled up on the sofa. The darkness magnified even the slightest noise. The refrigerator hummed two rooms away. The air-conditioner fan kicked on. A muffled click came from the driveway near where she'd parked.

Had she locked the car door before running into the house tonight? She couldn't remember. Might as well lock it now. She fetched her key ring, aimed her fob at the driveway, and pressed the lock button. From the window she could see her headlights blinking in response.

Then she heard a clatter from behind the house.

CHAPTER 14

Val stood in the side vestibule, clutching her keys so tightly they dug into her palm. She heard no more noises from the backyard, but silence worried her more than sound. If she called 911, how long would it take for the police to respond? Right now, she'd settle for getting rid of whatever was out there, and she had the perfect tool to do that fast.

She pressed the alarm button on her car remote. The car horn blared in the driveway. Beep. Beep. Beep. Obnoxious noise. Val covered her ears with her hands. After thirty seconds she hit the button again to silence the car.

The phone rang. Harvey, the neighbor on the other side of the driveway, complained about the alarm. She apologized without explaining why it had gone off.

She tiptoed to her grandfather's closed door. She cracked it open and heard him snoring. At least the horn hadn't disturbed him. A little hearing loss contributed to a good night's sleep.

Had it woken anyone else? Val peeked out the front window. A police car pulled up to the curb. She grabbed a light coat from the closet, put it on over her nightshirt, and opened the door to a man in uniform. He made a reassuring presence with broad shoulders and a fortyish weathered face. He'd heard the alarm while on patrol. Someone on the street had called the police to report a possible car theft at Val's address.

She explained about the noises in the driveway and the backyard. His head bobbed up and down in sympathy until she got to the part about the alarm.

"You purposely set off a car alarm at two in the morning? I could give you a citation for that. We have noise ordinances in this town."

His words stunned her into silence — for three seconds. "You're going to ticket me for protecting myself? What was I supposed to do? Let someone break into my house?"

"You got a problem, you call 911."

Her car alarm had summoned the police faster than the 911 call she'd made to report the murder. Best not to mention that.

Instead, apply the rules of a routine traffic stop. The cop is always right. A spoonful of humility makes the fine go away. "Sorry. I should have called 911. I was half asleep, not thinking straight."

The weather report from the officer's face switched from thunderous to partly cloudy. "Okay. I'll call for backup and make sure no one's lurking in the neighborhood."

Another patrol car arrived within five minutes. The two officers spent a quarter of an hour checking behind her house and along the street. Nothing unusual, aside from an overturned metal watering can and a bike on its side. From their description, Val identified the bike as hers. The officers concluded she'd probably heard a raccoon knocking into things while trying to get into the trash.

The officer with the weathered face said, "By the way, if noises make you nervous at night, you should have more light fixtures around the sides and the back of the house. The bulb was loose in the one on the driveway side. I tightened it."

Val pointed to herself. "I tightened that bulb this morning, and I'm pretty sure a raccoon didn't loosen it."

He laughed. "Nope, can't pin that on the

coon. You probably didn't turn it all the way."

The other officer frowned. "We'll patrol the neighborhood for the next few hours, just in case. Good night, ma'am."

Knowing that the police would keep an eye out tonight calmed Val and helped her sleep.

On her way to the club the next morning, she turned down Creek Road, Nadia's street. Did the murderer park here on Monday night or walk to Nadia's? Val stared at the creek, barely visible through the shrubbery around Nadia's house. The road wasn't the only way here.

All along the Eastern Shore, peninsulas jutted into the Chesapeake, splayed fingers of land gnarled by coves and wrinkled with creeks. A boat launched from any of those interconnected waterways around Bayport could have brought the murderer here. Easy to glide to Nadia's dock by the light of Monday's crescent moon. No one on the street would have seen the killer arriving by water and going into Nadia's house through the back porch.

Val slid two quiches into the café oven. They should be ready before Bethany arrived at eleven to take over serving lunch. Val closed the oven and turned around.

A big-boned woman in a calf-length denim skirt stood at the entrance to the café alcove. Irene Pritchard had returned, probably with the same goal in mind as she'd had yesterday when she showed up after the café closed. She approached the counter at a funereal pace and sat on a stool, adding another few inches to her height.

Val nodded. "Good morning, Irene. I want to offer my condolences. It's hard losing a neighbor."

Irene donned the half-moon glasses dangling from her corded necklace and peered at Val over them. "I didn't lose her. The good Lord took her back home."

With help from a murderer.

Val would have to get over her awkwardness at talking to the woman who would have managed the café if Nadia hadn't interfered. Not only could Irene provide a neighbor's perspective on Nadia, she might have seen something the night of the murder.

Irene scrutinized the café's short menu. "Interesting. There's almost nothing on your menu like what I served in my tea shop. We had scones, meat pies, sausage rolls, and cucumber sandwiches on crustless bread."

Hard to imagine the gym rats laying down their barbells to lunch on cucumber sandwiches. "Can I get you some coffee, Irene? Iced tea? A smoothie?"

"How about a cup of herbal tea?"

Val reached in the back of a drawer, feeling around for the herbal tea bags she'd stashed away. "The club members usually order high octane black tea on ice, but I should have some herbals, peppermint or chamomile, in my tea bag collection."

"Tea bags? Not loose tea? I'll have decaf iced coffee instead."

"Coming up." Val didn't need tea leaves to tell her she faced a tough cookie. She filled a glass with ice.

"By the way, did you enter the contest for the *Treadwell Gazette*'s new food columnist?"

Ah. That explained Irene's visit. She must have entered the contest. She'd come here to find out if Val was competing with her again for a job.

Val looked her in the eye. "I didn't even know about the contest until it was too late to enter." She hoped her answer would clear the air between them. She poured the decaf coffee over the ice and set the drink in front of Irene. "How long were you and Nadia neighbors?"

"More than fifteen years. She moved next door just about when Jeremy was starting school. He was crazy about her."

Val heard the warmth in Irene's voice when she mentioned her son. "Nadia thought the world of him. Tell me why he liked her so much."

"She spent time with him. She used to read him stories and think up games that would help him learn his letters and numbers. School was hard for him."

Chalk up another point for Nadia the Good, catching up fast to Nadia the Evil. "I heard she helped Jeremy get a job at the diner too."

Irene stirred sugar into her iced coffee. "She practically dragged him there. He was too shy to go on his own. Now he's real happy at his work."

Val poured herself a hot coffee and walked around the counter to sit next to Irene. "Where did Nadia live before she moved next door to you?"

"Virginia Beach. She met Joe when he was on vacation there. He's from this area. After they got married, they settled here."

"Does she still have family in Virginia?"

Irene sipped the iced coffee. "Not anymore. Her parents are dead. She was an only child. There's an aunt and uncle up in

New England, but they're getting on. She always said that the folks at the club were like family to her."

A family that might include a murderer. "I can't believe someone could go into Nadia's house and kill her without anyone in the neighborhood noticing. Did you see or hear anything unusual the night she died?"

"The houses aren't that close. We were watching television. It's always on real loud because Roger's hard of hearing."

"What about the neighbors on the other side? Could they have heard anything?"

"The Marshalls have been in Europe the last few weeks. Not due back 'til after Fourth of July. As for Mr. Grant, across the way from Nadia, he was probably drunk as usual and passed out. Most nights everybody's inside minding their own business. That's why someone could get away with setting fire to that racket."

"Did you tell anybody about the fire?"

"Just Roger."

Val had tried conversing with Irene's husband, Roger, at Nadia's party, and found it rough going, possibly because of his hearing problem. Calling him taciturn was like calling an anorexic slender. Roger probably hadn't spread the story of the burned racket. "How's Jeremy coping with Nadia's death?"

"He offered to move back in, to protect us in case someone came to murder us in our beds. You could see he was pretty scared too, but he wanted to defend his folks."

"That's sweet of him. Would you like him to move back?"

"I had mixed feelings when Luke offered him the apartment. Roger and I are getting on. We have to think about the future."

Val couldn't tell if Irene wanted Jeremy to practice living independently, which he'd have to do eventually, or if she wanted him home to help as she aged. "How did Nadia feel about Jeremy leaving home?"

"I talked it over with her. She said she'd miss having him around, but she couldn't see any harm in Jeremy giving it a try if he wanted."

Val had assumed Nadia had a larger role in Jeremy's move away from home than Irene said. "Living next to Nadia, you must have seen who her friends were and who came over to visit her." Maybe even who was lurking in a car across the street, watching Nadia's house.

"She didn't have a lot of friends. Nadia was real lonely after Joe moved out. Of course, she was holding up better than when the baby died."

Val's head jerked up. "What baby?"

"Nadia had a hard pregnancy eleven or twelve years ago. She had to stay in bed for months. Her poor little boy didn't live long after birth. She kept trying to have another baby, but the Lord didn't bless her with one. I think that's why she took such an interest in my boy."

Did Nadia, in her early forties, still hope for a child, if not with her husband, then with another man? Granddad's scenario of Maverick killing his pregnant lover didn't sound as farfetched as it had yesterday.

Val hadn't learned anything from Irene about the night of the murder, but at least she now had a new piece in the jigsaw puzzle of Nadia's life. Irene had put a face on the vulnerability that Althea had insisted was just beneath Nadia's façade. Losing a child left a wound that never completely healed.

A trio of women in body-hugging aerobic togs came into the café and sat at a bistro table.

Val jumped down from the counter stool. "Excuse me. I have to take care of these customers."

The three women all ordered the smoothie special of the day: strawberries, crushed

215

pineapple, banana, yogurt, and OJ. While Val made the smoothies and took the quiche pans from the oven, she felt Irene watching her like an old pro grading an amateur's performance.

Irene refused a refill on her coffee. "I used to make quiche at the tea shop."

Val guessed Irene wanted to compare her own quiche with these. She pointed to the veggie one. "This is a sundried tomato and spinach quiche. The other one's artichoke and prosciutto. Would you like to try a piece when they cool down?"

"Not necessary." Irene glanced at the table where the young women chatted. She leaned toward Val. "I know something other people don't know about Nadia's death."

An overlooked detail or a new suspect? Val felt a tingle of excitement and a bit of apprehension. People who know secrets about murders usually end up murdered too, at least in books and movies.

"The best thing you can do is tell your secret to the police." Val kept her voice low, taking a cue from Irene's tones.

"They already know, and so do you. Most people think you got to Nadia's house after the police. I know you were there first. Why are the police hiding that and not saying how Nadia died?"

Val stiffened. Irene's whisper, full of *s* sounds, reminded her of a hissing serpent. "The police often withhold details about crimes to help them trap the culprit."

"I live right next door. I have a right to know if there's a danger in the neighborhood."

What did she fear? A biohazard? A serial killer? "I don't think Nadia's death was related to any neighborhood threat."

"How . . . did . . . she . . . die?" The words barely escaped from behind Irene's clenched teeth.

Val sympathized with her. The police ought to release enough details to calm the neighbors. "I'm sorry. I can't help you. You'll have to ask the police."

Irene left without paying for the iced coffee.

Val took the half-empty glass from the eating bar. The more she thought about Irene's behavior, the less odd it appeared. People reacted to Nadia's demise based on their own concerns. Irene fretted about the neighborhood, Mrs. Z recalled someone else's death, and Monique worried about the safety of her children.

The three women finished their smoothies and left the café. As Val cleared their table, Bethany arrived to relieve her.

"I hope the lunch menu doesn't include strawberries, tomatoes, or beets. That red diet was murder." Bethany covered her mouth. "I shouldn't use that word lightly."

With the café empty, Val seized her chance to ask Bethany a few questions. "When Chatty told you about the burned racket, did she say where she'd seen it?"

Bethany donned an apron over her sundress printed with tropical flowers. "In the trash container at Nadia's house. Why are you asking?"

"Just curiosity." About whether Bethany could have passed that information to her brother. Val moved the blender to the sink and took it apart to wash it. "Did you tell anybody about the burned racket?"

"Just Bigby. I called him when I got off the phone with Chatty. Wasn't I supposed to tell?" Bethany sounded defensive. "Nadia didn't care. She treated it like a big joke."

"I didn't know you talked to her about it. When was that?"

"Monday afternoon."

Val's grip tightened on the blender as she washed it. "You saw her on Monday? Where?"

"The diner. I went there to pick up a sub after our teacher's meeting ran late. She'd already eaten. I stopped at her table to prove

I didn't hold a grudge about how she ditched me. When I mentioned the racket burning, she said she didn't take it seriously."

Or pretended she didn't, to show that the incident hadn't intimidated her. Val wished she knew what else Nadia had said in the diner. "Nadia tried to reach me later that afternoon. I never got back to her. Maybe she talked to you about what was on her mind."

"Nope. The busboy, Jeremy, came to clear her table, and I went to the counter to wait for my order. Nadia talked to him for a while. He went back to the kitchen. Then Luke came out to see her."

"Did she talk to anyone else at the diner?"

"She waved to Darwin when he came in, but they didn't talk while I was there." Bethany put on an apron. "I know why you're asking all these questions. You're helping the police figure out who murdered her. Do they suspect anyone we know?"

"Please don't go around saying I'm helping the police identify the murderer. That could put me in danger."

Bethany's hand flew to her mouth. "I never thought of that. I won't repeat anything you tell me. Promise."

"I have nothing to say. The police aren't

giving out information about their suspects." Val hung up her apron. "See you tomorrow at the memorial service."

She hurried out. Next stop: the diner. If anything had troubled Nadia in the hours before her murder, she might have told Jeremy or Luke about it while eating her final lunch at the diner.

CHAPTER 15

Val opened the door to the diner. Its AC circulated batter-fried air, as appetizing as cold French fries. A young couple and a toddler occupied a booth. An older couple sat at a table near the window, and two men in work boots perched on stools at the counter.

A stout, pink-haired woman bustled toward Val — Luke's mother. "A booth okay with you, hon?" Without waiting for an answer, she conducted Val to a booth with red vinyl bench seats.

Val slid into the booth. The gray laminated table came equipped with a bottle of ketchup, a glass sugar pourer with a screw-on metal top, and salt and pepper shakers of the same style. "It's good to see you again, Mrs. Forsa. I'm Val Deniston. Luke and I used to hang out as teenagers."

"Call me Rosie." She stared at Val and then snapped her fingers. "You must be

Don Myer's granddaughter. We don't see him here much anymore. How's he doing?"

"He's well, thank you." With lower blood pressure than when he frequented the diner. "I'll let him know you asked after him."

"Luke told me about you. You came back after years away. Just like him. He moved down here from Baltimore when his daddy passed." Rosie set out a paper place mat, a napkin with utensils rolled inside, and a glass of ice water. "Want to try our special today? It's one of your granddaddy's favorites — Southern fried chicken, batter fries, sweet slaw, and fried okra."

"Just a light lunch for me. How about a BLT on toast?" No one could mess up a bacon, lettuce, and tomato sandwich, not even Granddad. Not that he'd ever get the chance. His new healthy diet didn't include bacon. "And iced tea please."

Rosie wrote down the order, but made no move toward the kitchen. "You heard what happened to Nadia Westrin, didn't you? Mark my words. Someone from that club killed her. Sports rage, that's what it was."

"Sports rage?"

"It's like road rage. She did something to set somebody off in a tennis game, and they let her have it. That's what happens at hockey games." Rosie tucked the pen and pad in her apron pocket. "She shoulda asked the police for protection after somebody burned a racket on her lawn. Good thing Luke was there to put out the fire."

Val choked on her water. Luke had told his mother — and how many others? — about the racket burning. Did he cast himself as the hero of the story or did his mom assign him that role?

Rosie leaned down and cupped a hand at the side of her mouth. "Luke just broke up with his girlfriend in Baltimore, and I'm glad. I'd like to see him settle down here with a hometown gal. You married, hon?"

"No." Better change the subject or Rosie might interview her as a potential bride. Val tilted her head toward the TV on a high shelf behind the counter. On the screen two women slugged a tennis ball back and forth across the net. "Wimbledon. Are you a tennis fan, Rosie?"

"Not me, but my hubby always had sports on the TV here. When he was young, he played most everything except golf. Luke is big on sports too. He only ever played baseball, but you can't tear him away from football and basketball games on TV."

Val took advantage of the break in Rosie's word stream. "By any chance, were you here at lunchtime on Monday?"

"Most days I work breakfast and dinner. Luke does lunch. I'm only here today because the waitress called in sick." Rosie glanced toward the swinging door to the kitchen. "I better give Luke your order."

"I'd like to talk to him if he's not too busy."

"Don't worry, hon. He'll make time for you." Rosie winked.

While Val waited for her lunch, she watched the TV. With a seeded player struggling against an upstart, the match had more drama than most early rounds of tennis tournaments.

Luke delivered her BLT with chips and pickles. His dark green T-shirt clung to him, emphasizing his toned biceps and his slight paunch. A barbells and beer body. He pointed to the TV. "My money's on the Russian gal even if she's behind now."

"I always root for the underdog." Val eyed her sandwich. Mayo blobs and limp bacon overhung a burnt crust. You could, after all, mess up a BLT. "A friend of mine picked up a sub here on Monday and raved about it. She said Nadia was here talking to you."

"Yeah, Nadia was hustling as usual. Wanted me to invest in more property. It wasn't enough she sold me one house."

"Did she say anything about the racket

that burned?"

"I teased her about it. Told her she should stop hanging out with the lowlifes at the club. She didn't appreciate it."

She hadn't cared for his humor Sunday night either when he'd joked about her cremating her racket.

Val unwrapped the utensils rolled in her napkin. "Your mother knew about the burned racket."

"I told her." He leaned down as if fearing his mother might hear him. "I know Nadia wanted to keep it quiet, but stuff like that gets around. Mom would have heard it somewhere and reamed me out for not telling her."

"Did you mention it to anyone else?"

"Just Mom. Why?"

Luke told Rosie, Rosie told — how many people? As many as possible, but she'd focus on her son as a hero, not details about the charred racket.

"It's not important. Your mother's looking well. Is she still living in the house where you grew up?"

"I tried to convince her to move to a condo. No dice. The house is too much for her now that my father's gone, but she never lets go of anything."

"And she'd probably miss her friends

from the neighborhood. By the way, is Jeremy working today?"

"Making deliveries. He should be back soon." He touched her shoulder. "Enjoy your lunch."

Val scraped off mayo globs and nibbled on her sandwich while watching the street through the diner's storefront window. When a van pulled up and Jeremy climbed from it, she left the money for her lunch on the table, rushed out the door, and called to him.

Tall and broad, with an awkward gait, he'd make an intimidating hulk in a dark alley. During the day, though, he looked like an overgrown kid.

He squinted through thick lenses at Val. "Hi."

"I saw your mother this morning. She told me you were really sad about Nadia. I'm sorry. It must be hard on you."

Jeremy nodded. "I already miss Nadia."

"We'll also miss her at the racket club, where I work. I'm writing an article about her for the club newsletter, and I think you knew her really well."

"She was my friend."

"I heard you talked to her on Monday when she had lunch in the diner."

"That was the last time I saw her. I didn't

226

even have a chance to —" He looked down at his high-tops. "To say I was sorry."

"For what?" Val waited for an answer that didn't come. She spoke more gently. "Did you have a disagreement with her?"

"She asked me to do something, but I didn't want to. Mom and Dad said I shouldn't."

What could she have asked him to do that his parents advised against? Maybe they were so protective of him that they ruled out his doing anything even slightly risky, like cleaning the gutters on Nadia's steep roof.

"Hey, Jeremy." Luke called out from the door of the diner. "We got some more deliveries."

Jeremy brushed past Val. "I need to work."

Val stood in his path. "Wait, Jeremy. I'd like to talk to you about Nadia sometime when you aren't working."

"I'm off Sunday afternoon, but I always watch baseball."

"How about I stop by your apartment then?"

"Okay. I live over the garage at Luke's house. Bye." He fled into the diner.

Val went back to her car, disappointed. Stopping at the diner had given her no new information about the murder. She still had a few things to tell the chief and hoped he would return the favor.

As she drove to the police station, she had to press the brake pedal harder than usual. It felt spongy. She'd better take the car to a garage after talking to the chief. The large garage in Treadwell had several mechanics. She hoped one of them had time this afternoon to diagnose her brake problem and fix her flat tire. She'd already driven far enough on the undersized spare.

The chief couldn't see her immediately, so she settled on a wood bench in the reception area. She wouldn't leave until she talked to him about Bigby, who'd risen to the top of her suspect list, and Maverick, second on the list. Maybe by now the police knew where Maverick had spent Monday night.

She rubbed her arms. Police headquarters felt like a walk-in cooler. She looked up and saw Deputy Holtzman watching her and drinking something steaming from a Styrofoam cup. She could use some hot coffee.

He approached her. "I understand you had some trouble at your house last night. You'd better watch out. The Bayport police confirm that a raccoon is operating in your neighborhood." The sneer on his face matched his tone of voice. "And that road incident you reported two days ago? The police haven't had time to investigate that yet, but I have some advice for you. The next time someone wants to pass your car, slow down. Don't feel you have to race him."

She stood up. If she were a man, she'd be tempted to clock him. She folded her arms. "You've been hostile to me since we met. Care to tell me why?"

"Not hostile. Surprised." He sipped his coffee. "When I met you, you'd just found the body of a woman murdered in a gruesome way. Dead bodies upset most people, even when they don't know the victim. You knew her, and yet you were all business."

She'd managed to stay calm and rational only with great effort, and he was holding that against her. "I was trying to be helpful, telling you what I saw and what I did. I figured the police would want facts, not feelings."

"Just the facts, eh? That worked fine as long as you were talking about the murder. But I hit a mother lode of feelings when I brought up the hit-and-run? Care to tell me why?"

She locked on his protruding eyes. "I'm here to talk to the chief."

"Friends in high places, eh?" He walked away.

She now understood what she'd done wrong in Tuesday morning's interview. She'd been too coherent for his tastes. The harder he'd pushed to get a reaction from her, the more she'd tightened the reins on her emotions. Exactly the wrong thing to do. Bethany, on the other hand, had met his expectations and evoked his sympathy, probably by sniveling and batting her teary eyelashes at him.

Val could do without his sympathy, but she expected common courtesy. He'd mocked her for reporting two incidents to the police. When the investigation into Nadia's murder was over, when Holtzman no longer had power over her or Monique, she'd lodge a complaint with his boss at the sheriff's office. He had no right to belittle any citizen's fears.

She asked the woman at the reception desk if she could use the restroom. The receptionist pointed to a hallway and told her to follow it to the end. Offices lined both sides of the hall. The door marked CHIEF was closed.

On her way back from the restroom, she heard voices coming from an office with an open door. She caught the words "preliminary report." She slowed down and inched closer to the doorway.

"Blood sample . . . alcohol and barbiturates . . . made her drowsy or dizzy . . . not enough to kill her . . . couldn't fight back . . ."

The gray-haired officer who'd interviewed her about the road incident emerged from a room down the corridor. Val hustled to the reception area. She'd overheard enough to convince her that the murderer had drugged Nadia before killing her with the racket. With a large enough dose of alcohol and barbiturates, she would have slipped quietly away. Instead, her killer had given her the drug as an appetizer to a grisly main course. Why go to such lengths? Out of hatred or anger? Or to send a message to someone else? If so, that message hadn't yet gone out, thanks to the chief's gag order on the weapon.

The chief met Val in the reception area and led her to his office. He gestured to a straight-backed metal chair facing his desk. "Take a seat, Val. You might be able to help me, but if you're gonna balk at speaking ill of the dead, tell me now."

She perched on the hard seat that discouraged lingering. "I'm just as willing to abuse

231

the dead as the living. What do you want to know?"

He peered at her over the top of his reading glasses. "You ever see Nadia Westrin pop pills or act spacey?"

"Never. If Nadia had a headache, she went for a yoga timeout rather than swallow an aspirin. She avoided diet drinks because of the chemicals in them. Does that sound like a drug abuser to you?"

"What about alcohol?"

"She drank good wine, but not more than she could handle." An image of the wine rack in Nadia's kitchen popped into Val's mind. "The morning I found Nadia dead, I noticed two water-spotted wineglasses hanging on a rack in her kitchen. The other glasses were sparkling clean. She might have drunk wine with her killer." Wine tainted with a barbiturate.

"Good observation. You didn't come here just to tell me that."

"Chatty Ridenour had some information about Bigby O'Shea. Did she call you?"

The chief shook his head. Apparently, Chatty's tongue loosened only when her fingers massaged a face.

Val summarized Chatty's story about Nadia rejecting Bigby and later seeing him parked across from her house. The chief laced a rubber band through his fingers while she talked, his face expressionless. For all the reaction she got from him, she could have been relating a fairy tale, rather than presenting him with a murder suspect.

He flicked the rubber band into a desk drawer. "There's a lady in town who thinks the boyfriend she jilted fifty years ago parks outside her house and follows her around. She calls us once or twice a month."

"If that woman turned up murdered, wouldn't you check on that old boyfriend?"

"Okay, okay. I'll check if Mr. O'Shay has an alibi for the night of the murder."

Mr. O'Shay. More like Mr. Almighty. As a major land developer, Bigby probably had influence over the town council and the police budget. "Bigby's sister told him about the burned racket. She knew it was in Nadia's trash bin. He could have raided the trash while Nadia was working Monday and studied how the handle was tapered."

"You're speculating with no evidence at all." The chief jotted something on a pad. "I heard from Nadia's coworker, Kimberly. You did right telling her to call me, but what her information has to do with the murder, I don't know."

"That wasn't the only time Nadia borrowed a car and disguised herself. She also switched cars with Chatty, covered her hair, and wore big sunglasses. She might have been trying to elude Bigby . . . or someone else stalking her." Val threw in the last phrase so the chief couldn't accuse her of waging a campaign against Bigby.

"Wearing sunglasses and even a wig isn't proof she was stalked. Why wouldn't she have contacted us if someone was harassing her?" The chief shifted papers on his desk. "Anything else, Val?"

"Maverick's alibi?"

"Solid. We've got him on surveillance cameras in New Jersey and a paper trail. There's no way he could have driven back here and killed Nadia."

Why would he conceal his whereabouts from his wife? Maybe a hotel surveillance camera caught him checking in with another woman. Val knew the chief wouldn't give her any details about Maverick's alibi. She might as well move on to the next question. "What about Nadia's ex? Does he have an alibi?"

"An acceptable alibi and no motive."

Another potential suspect off the list.

The phone on the desk rang. The chief answered it, grunted a few times, and said, "I'll be there shortly."

"Thanks for listening to me, Chief. I

won't take up any more of your time."

"Stay out of police business, Val, or I'll report you to your granddaddy." He picked up the phone.

She left the police station and climbed into her car, going from freezer to oven without defrosting. She couldn't shake the chill from what she'd just heard. Finding out that both Maverick and Nadia's ex had alibis disheartened her. What if Bigby too came up with an alibi? She needed a backup suspect, someone who had the knowledge to duplicate the shaved racket, easy access to Nadia's house, and a motive.

One person nearly fit that profile. Irene Pritchard saw the burned racket and could have crept through the bushes to Nadia's house without anyone noticing her. Why would she kill Nadia? She didn't seem to resent her son's affection for the next-door neighbor, but Nadia may have meddled too much, pushing Jeremy into a job and supporting his move away from his parents. Recently, they'd kept him from doing something Nadia urged on him. A signal that she'd gone too far? What if Irene found out she'd lost the chance to manage the Cool Down Café because of Nadia? A minor matter in itself, but possibly the tipping point.

Val would need more than guesswork

about a motive to convince the chief to investigate Irene. Two other people had seen the prototype of the weapon — Luke and Chatty. Neither had an apparent motive. Val felt queasy about poking into their private lives in search of a motive, but she'd do it if necessary to help Monique. By the time this murder investigation ended, she might not have any friends left in Bayport. That would making leaving here easier.

She pulled out on the road and tested her brakes. They felt even spongier than before. She should have taken her car to the garage sooner, but she'd had no free time ever since finding Nadia's body. She hoped the brakes would last until she reached the garage in Treadwell.

Traffic picked up as she approached the strip mall with the largest supermarket in the area. She approached the four-way stop near the Midway Shopping Plaza and braked. Nothing happened.

She pumped the brakes. No response. She pressed the pedal to the floor. Still nothing. She barreled toward the intersection.

The road was clear ahead of her, but cars were approaching the intersection from the side roads. They would arrive first and have the right of way.

She sounded the horn. A Jeep that had

nosed into the intersection from the right stopped abruptly. Holding her breath, Val flew past the stop sign and veered around the Jeep — into the path of a tractor trailer.

The truck's air brakes whined. Its grille loomed larger and larger as the rig bore down on her.

Chapter 16

Val swerved back into her lane, just missing the tractor trailer.

She saw a crossroads with a stoplight up ahead. The light turned from green to yellow. Better to speed through the yellow light than coast to the intersection after it turned red. She hit the accelerator and leaned on the horn to make her intentions clear.

She sailed through the intersection without hitting anything.

Her luck couldn't last. She flipped on the emergency lights and jerked on the parking brake. The car shuddered but didn't stop.

She turned the wheel gently. The right tires slid off the pavement and onto the rough shoulder. The car bumped along, one set of tires on the road, the other off. As it slowed, Val eased the left tires onto the shoulder. Friction did its work, and the car finally crawled to a halt.

She released her breath and put her head

down on the steering wheel. Sweat covered her whole body. She felt clammy and quivery.

Tap, tap, tap. The noise came from the side window. Val lifted her head.

A man sporting a motorcycle helmet, a muscle shirt, and a lot of tattooed skin stared at her. "Need any help?"

Val cracked the door open. "My brakes just went out. If you're heading into Treadwell, would you stop at the first garage and ask them to send a tow truck? I'd call but I don't have their number stored in my phone."

"My phone will find nearby garages." He whipped out a smart phone, pressed some buttons, and called a number. He handed her the phone.

The garage's tow truck was on its way by the time the motorcyclist roared off.

Val rode in the truck's cab to the garage and told the burly middle-aged driver what had happened on the road.

"Your brakes been giving you trouble?" he asked.

"Not 'til today." Could someone have messed with her brakes? She felt a pang and wrapped her arms around her middle.

"It's a really old model. You have to expect problems."

A college graduation gift from her parents, the car had given her little trouble for a decade. She'd like to think its age explained her brake trouble, less frightening than the other explanation.

A mechanic at the garage said no one there would have time to diagnose her car problem today. If she wanted to wait until closing time, he'd give her a lift. She told him she'd try to find someone to pick her up.

She was about to call Granddad and remembered he was driving Ned to Baltimore for an Orioles game.

She tried Monique. No answer. Maybe she was still meeting with the lawyer in Annapolis. Val left a brief message. "My car was towed to a garage in Treadwell. I was hoping you could pick me up. If I don't call you back, assume I've gotten a ride from someone else."

Val left the same message for Althea and Bethany. She reached Chatty, who was giving facials to the guests at a waterfront estate and wouldn't finish for at least an hour.

Val searched her handbag for the scrap of paper Gunnar had given her with his cell phone number. When he answered, she told him where she was and asked him to pick her up without giving any explanation beyond "car trouble."

She paced outside the garage, too keyed up to sit in the garage's air-conditioned waiting area. Loud noises came from the bay where two mechanics worked on cars — banging, shouting, drilling. She scarcely noticed. Her memory replayed the scene on the road in slow motion. Vehicles coming at her from all sides, a truck aiming straight for her. And yet, she hadn't lost her nerve. She'd maneuvered around every obstacle and avoided an accident. How cool was that?

Her instincts had saved her. They must have worked the night of the crash in January. Ever since then, with Chef Henri claiming she'd smashed his car deliberately, she'd felt guilty until proven innocent. She couldn't prove anything, even to herself, unless her memory of what happened that night returned. But she must have done everything possible to avoid a crash just as she had this afternoon. For a change she felt innocent until proven guilty. Who knew that bad brakes could have a silver lining?

Gunnar pulled into the service station and lowered the window of his Miata. "Hop in." When she did, he said, "What happened to your car?"

"A problem with my brakes." She fastened her seat belt. "They stopped working when I was rocketing toward a stop sign by the supermarket."

He jerked in the driver's seat like a puppet with suddenly taut strings. "They didn't work at all? Did you have an accident?"

"I was lucky not to." As she described riding brakeless through two intersections and easing the car off the road, his expression changed from concern to respect.

He steered onto the road to Bayport. "You did everything right. You're one hell of a driver."

Really? Her cheeks grew warm. "Chalk it up to survival instinct."

"Everyone wants to survive. Not everyone can control a car like that."

"Thank you. I needed that." She'd remember it the next time her brakes gave out or someone ran her off the road.

Two near accidents in one week. Fear gnawed at her insides. One person could have engineered both mishaps. She already suspected Darwin of following her from his sports shop and running her off the road Tuesday night. According to Chatty, he knew all about cars. He could have messed with her brakes. The noises she'd heard late last night, the soft sound from the driveway

242

and the clatters from the backyard, suggested someone near her car, tripping in his haste to leave.

Gunnar approached the intersection Val had zoomed through without brakes. She crossed her arms to hold in a shiver.

"You look pale." Gunnar slowed down. "I can pull over if you want some fresh air."

"Can we stop by the supermarket instead?" Focusing on food would banish her willies faster than anything else. "We're having a potluck after Nadia's memorial service tomorrow. I need to pick up ingredients for a salad."

She was delighted to find four ripe avocados instead of the hard-as-rock ones the store normally carried. She also bought grape tomatoes, lemons, and two jars of hearts of palm. She added shredded coconut to her basket. If she had time, she'd make a batch of Mrs. Z's macaroons.

Val carried her purchases back to the Miata, where Gunnar was waiting for her, a cell phone at his ear.

He clicked his phone off and backed out of his parking space. "When you get home, we should check where you usually park to see if there's brake fluid on the ground."

"Good idea." The street near the diner and the police visitor spot where she'd parked might also have a pool of fluid. She pulled out her cell phone to cut off further talk about her brakes. "Excuse me while I call the college gal who's supposed to manage the café this weekend. I'd like to catch her before she heads out for Friday night fun. She may have questions for me."

By the time Val ended her call, Gunnar was turning into her street. He parked in front of the house. "I don't see your grandfather's Buick."

"He went to an Orioles game and is spending the night in Baltimore."

Gunnar's brows rose a fraction. He checked the driveway and found a spot where some fluid had leaked, a few drops not a puddle. She surveyed the ground there and behind the house, hoping to find something left behind by the person who'd tampered with her car. No luck.

"Are you still up for dinner at the crab house?" Gunnar asked.

"Looking forward to it. I have to shower first. Come back for me in about an hour."

"See you then." He watched her go inside.

When she came downstairs after showering, he was on the front porch and his car exactly where he'd parked it earlier. He hadn't left. The sky, though, had changed dramatically.

She pointed to the gray clouds rolling in. "I was going to suggest we walk, but we'd better drive to the restaurant instead. It looks like rain."

Though they arrived before seven, a line had already formed at the crab house. Most people opted to sit indoors, probably fearing rain. After a short wait, Val and Gunnar snagged a table on the outside deck. The large umbrella over it would keep them dry enough if it started raining. The deck's piers allowed boaters to tie up and eat at the restaurant, but with a storm brewing, no boats bobbed in the water. The odor of fuel competed with the aroma of seafood and suggested some boats had recently left.

Gunnar fingered the brown wrapping paper covering the wood picnic table. "This is the tablecloth?"

"Some crab houses cover the tables with newspaper. This is way more elegant." She pointed to a roll of paper towels in the center of the table. "Our dinner napkins. And don't expect forks. Have you eaten crabs before?"

He looked toward the next table where a man hammered a crab leg with a wood mallet and a woman pried meat from a claw with a knife. "Crab cakes, not ones like that."

"You had the lazy man's version. With these, you have to dig out the meat yourself. It's not for the faint of heart."

He flashed a smile. "I heard your subtext. Only a wimp would refuse the challenge of excavating a crab shell."

"I'll order a dozen." The painstaking task of digging out the crabmeat should give her time to ask him about himself. Maybe tonight she'd even crack Gunnar's shell.

The waiter brought them a pitcher of beer and dumped a steaming mound of orange, pepper-encrusted crabs on their table.

Val demonstrated how to remove the apron flap on the underside of the crab. "You flip this piece off like a pop top. Then lift off the shell." She tossed the shell and transparent membrane into a discard pile.

He grabbed a crab and copied her technique. He studied the crab's innards. "These long spongy things must be gills."

"Also known as dead man's fingers. They're a throwaway." She plucked the gills from the crab. "These wormy-looking things are intestines. Toss them out too."

"So far, we've thrown away everything we've touched. What's this greenish-yellow gunk?"

"You probably don't want to know, but it's edible. Some people use it as sauce for the crabmeat."

"I'll take mine plain. Sauces are overrated anyway." He wiped the thick paste from his fingers on the paper tablecloth.

For the next fifteen minutes, they concentrated on eating enough crab to take the edge off their hunger. The water lapping against the piers served as soothing mood music.

He refilled their beers and reached for his third crab. "About your brakes. I —"

"Let's talk about it tomorrow. I just want to relax now." And ignore the anxiety nibbling at her. She gazed at the water. "Bayport was the closest thing to a permanent home I ever had. With my father in the Navy, we moved every few years, but I always spent my summers here. What brought you to the Eastern Shore?"

"I like being near the water. If I go into business for myself, I might as well do it somewhere I like."

If he went into business for himself? Was he having second thoughts about quitting his job? "There are a lot of new businesses here, mostly restaurants, antique stores, and B&Bs."

"Yup, and not many accountants in the town. Small businesses need accountants."

Val wiped her hands on a paper towel. "So

you found a niche you want to fill here."

"And then I found other reasons to stay." He broke a claw in two, exposed a chunk of meat, and held it out to her.

She leaned toward him and nibbled on it while he held the shell. The lower half of her body tingled. Could he read her thoughts? She felt a blush creep up her face, grabbed her mallet, and pounded on a crab shell. "When I moved in with Granddad, I hoped Bayport would act like a mind-enhancing drug to tell me what should come next in my life. It's been more like an anesthetic."

"Whatever works." Gunnar tapped a claw with his mallet. "Why did you leave New York?"

"My life there revolved around my fiancé, Tony, and my job. That changed in one weekend last winter. A lawyer from Tony's firm threw a party. While we were there, a woman Tony worked with sat on the sofa next to him. Their thighs touched, and they looked at each other in a smug, secretive way." Val held up a crab claw and studied it from all angles. "I had an aha moment. All those late nights he said he was doing legal work, he was actually doing his paralegal."

"On the plus side, you found out before you married him."

"At the time, it was hard to notice the plus. Tony asked me not to make a stink and jeopardize his chance at becoming a partner." She'd never been as furious as when she realized his career mattered more to him than their engagement, but she didn't make a scene. "I spent that night on a friend's sofa. I didn't sleep, of course. The next day I had to help Chef Henri Lafarge with a cooking demo and book signing party on Long Island."

Thunder rumbled. Gunnar looked up at the dark sky. "The party didn't go well?"

"The proverbial train wreck, which ended with a real car wreck. Before the cooking demo, I broke two of the prep bowls from the chef's matching set of eighteen. When I suggested he get by with sixteen bowls by combining some ingredients in one bowl, he exploded, screaming that I knew nothing about cooking."

"Nice guy. I hope no one bought his cookbook."

"Sales were low, which he blamed on me. It started sleeting during the party. The people hosting it suggested we stay overnight, but Henri insisted on driving back to the city, though he'd had too much to drink. I called his editor, who convinced Henri to let me drive instead. There I was in a vintage

Mustang on an icy road with Henri berating me about my driving." Val gazed into her cup, swirling around what was left of the beer. "If I hadn't been upset about Tony and Henri, I might have seen the patch of ice in time and not lost control of the car."

"What happened?"

"We spun around, a car sideswiped us on the passenger side, and we hit a tree, or so I'm told. I don't remember because I had a concussion. Apparently, Henri whammed into me when the car hit us. I was wearing a seat belt, but he'd unbuckled his along the way. He ended up in the hospital with assorted broken bones. I still feel bad about that."

Gunnar reached across the table for her hand. "It wasn't your fault. He made the choice not to wear a seat belt."

"When he woke up from anesthesia, he insisted the publisher fire me. I was taken off cookbook publicity and shunted to a corner to do something that didn't interest me. I quit and came here." She tossed the remnants of a crab on the pile of shells. "I've talked enough about myself. What's your story? How did you get into accounting?"

"Boring, not worth telling."

She wouldn't let him off that easily. "Try me."

"My father was an accountant at a big company. He always said that when I got certified and had some experience, he'd leave the company and we'd open a business together. When I was in college, I took accounting courses to appease him though I was still deciding on a career. He died before my senior year. My sister needed college tuition. My mother wanted to finish her degree too. I went with accounting. Safe job, steady income."

A boring story, yes, but it showed he put his family's needs ahead of his own wishes. "How are your sister and mother doing?"

"Good. My mother's teaching, my sister's a nurse. She has two little boys."

Because of him, two women had jobs helping other people, but had he reconciled himself to accounting?

Lightning flashed, followed seconds later by a loud clap of thunder. Gunnar signaled the waiter for the check.

Val gave the sky a dirty look. How annoying that the storm arrived now when she'd finally coaxed him into talking about himself.

As he signed the credit card receipt, lightning forked across the sky over the water. "We're leaving just in time."

Raindrops hit them before they reached

the Miata. By the time Gunnar pulled up in front of the Victorian, the downpour had started. They sat in the car waiting for it to let up.

He leaned over and put his right arm around her. His left hand caressed her face and drew it closer. His lips teased around her mouth. A chaste kiss on the right corner, a small nip on her lower lip, followed by one on the upper lip. She smelled his shaving cream, the laundry soap in his shirt, the salt spray in his hair. Their mouths came together. He tasted like sweet crab, spicy Old Bay seasoning, bitter beer, and something else, soft and moist. He tasted of Gunnar.

The rain pounded on the car. She was swimming, or maybe drowning. Long time since she'd felt like that. She pulled away, surfaced, then sank again as he enfolded her in his arms. Was crab an aphrodisiac? No, that was oysters. Whatever.

"Let's go in," he said after a long deep kiss.

She knew what would happen if they went in, and she didn't want it to happen yet. If they had any future together, her first time with him should be special, a choice she made because she knew him and knew herself, not because she'd drunk half a pitcher of beer and stuffed herself with crab. She needed time. To understand him better. To weigh again Granddad's warnings about him. And to figure out how she felt about him.

She shook her head. "I can't do this now. Not tonight."

He leaned back in his seat and shut his eyes.

She felt his frustration. "I'm sorry. I just —"

"The brakes." He opened his eyes and reached for her hand. "I understand. You've had a tough day."

The brakes. Yes. But not the ones on her car.

CHAPTER 17

Vroom . . . sputter . . . vroooom.

Val groaned and put her head under the pillow. Good old Harvey next door was using his chain saw first thing Saturday morning. Either some limbs had come down during last night's storm, or he was retaliating for her car alarm waking him in the middle of the night.

She rolled out of bed and put on a T-shirt and cutoff jeans. The hall phone rang as she came down the stairs. She answered it and heard her father's voice. Her parents hadn't called since taking their cabin cruiser from its berth in Florida to the Bahamas. Her father gave her the highlights of their crossing.

Her mother took over the phone after two minutes. "Is the café doing a good business? How's your grandfather? When is he going to sell the house?"

The triple whammy. Her mother's interrogation techniques gave new meaning to the term *multiple-choice questions.* Val resorted to a tactic from her school years — answer the easy questions first and hope the clock runs out on the hard ones. "The café is doing well. I've even hired a couple of assistants. Granddad went to a baseball game in Baltimore yesterday and stayed over. He isn't back yet."

"Tell me what's going on with the house. You don't need to mince words since he's not there listening in."

"He's lining up contractors to work on the house."

"That's progress. Did Dad tell you we're extending our trip until the end of July? Will the house be fixed up by then?"

"It'll take longer than —" The doorbell chimed. "Hold on, Mom. Someone's at the door."

Val peeked out the sidelight near the front door. Gunnar stood on the porch. Her heart did a jig. She opened the door wide. "Come on in. I'm on the phone. I'll be right with you."

He carried a bakery bag in each hand and a newspaper under his arm. He must have picked up the paper from the porch where the delivery boy always threw it.

She put the phone to her ear. "I can't talk

long, Mom. A friend just came in."

Gunnar leaned against the banister a few feet away from her. He didn't look his usual spruce self. His clothes were rumpled, and his face not yet shaved. Well, Tony often skipped shaving on the weekend, and who was she to talk? She certainly looked like she'd just climbed out of bed. Gunnar's light blue shirt had a spot of yellow and reddish flecks, remnants of last night's crab feast. She'd never seen him wear the same shirt twice. Maybe he'd packed too few for the trip and run out of clean ones.

She caught the tail end of her mother's latest question and responded. "My car? Still running okay. It's getting some minor repairs."

Gunnar turned his mouth into a big O. Val grinned at his pose of disbelief.

"Tell your grandfather we'll call him later today," her mother said.

"I'll do that." She'd also tell him to keep quiet about the murder and especially about suspicions surrounding Monique. No need to worry her parents. "Have a great trip, Mom. Love to both of you."

She hung up and eyed the bags Gunnar held. "It looks like you bought out the bakery." She kissed him briefly. "I'll make coffee. How about breakfast on the front

256

porch? Last night's rain must have swept in cooler air."

"The weather's good, but your neighbor's disturbing the peace with his chain saw."

"Then let's eat in the kitchen. Granddad's taken over the dining room table." She gestured toward the piles of her recipes on the table.

Gunnar put the bakery bags on the kitchen counter.

She started the coffeemaker and arranged his purchases on a platter — muffins, croissants, and cheese Danish. "I was on the phone with my folks when you came to the door. They're in the Bahamas. They're having such a good time, they decided to stay longer."

He took the newspaper and the pastry platter to the glass-topped breakfast table. "Why not join them? Take your grandfather. Fly to the Bahamas."

Huh? Last night he hadn't acted as if he wanted to get rid of her. "What, you want to house-sit for us?"

The corners of his mouth turned up. "Listen, I'm serious. It's not safe here. In the last few days, someone you know was murdered, you were run off the road, and your brakes failed."

"Bad week." Not as bad as her final

weekend in New York. "Dibs on the blue-berry muffin. How do you like your coffee?"

"Black, please." He sat at the table. His feet tapped a muted rhythm on the floor. "I called the garage while you were showering yesterday. Your car had no brake fluid left in it. A dashboard light is supposed to tell you when the fluid's low."

She set two coffees on the table and sat across from him. "I didn't notice a warning light."

"It wasn't working. Brakes and warning lights fail, but" — he leaned forward, eye to eye with her over the small table — "it's possible someone tampered with your car."

Tampered. The word crashed into her like a wave. Sabotage had crossed her mind yesterday, but only as a remote possibility. Now he'd made it real. "You think someone messed with my brakes. Why didn't you tell me this sooner?"

"I tried to, last night at dinner, but you didn't want to talk about your car."

Her shoulders bunched with tension. She had antidotes for anxiety — think positive, analyze the situation, and bake something. This morning, she'd need all three.

"Old cars have problems. The wire or fuse, or whatever the warning light uses, could have jiggled loose when I went off the road."

258

So much for positive thinking. Now for analysis. "Did the mechanic say if the damage to the brakes was deliberate?"

"He won't even look under the car until Monday. You can call the police. They might light a fire under him or even look at it themselves."

"I'll call the chief after breakfast." She nibbled on her muffin. It tasted like sawdust. She crossed to the refrigerator and took out two eggs.

"You're cooking eggs?"

"I'm letting them warm up before I use them to make macaroons. But if you want eggs, I can —"

"Nope. This will do me." He pointed to the croissant and a cheese pastry on his plate.

She returned to the table. A headline in the newspaper caught her eye — MURDER FOLLOWS HATE CRIME. She snatched up the paper and read the lead.

The murder this week of Bayport real estate agent Nadia Westrin came a day after an incident that would have been called racist if Ms. Westrin hadn't been white. On Sunday night a wood tennis racket was set on fire on her lawn in a grotesque parody of a Klan threat.

A friend of the victim speculated that the racket burner escalated from vandalism to murder. A police spokesman would not comment on the possibility that the fire and the murder were related. .

Val flipped to the page where the article continued and scanned the rest of it. No mention of Monique's name. Whew. The phone rang in the hall. A computer-generated voice came through the phone's speaker and announced the caller's ID: Mon-i-qwey Mott.

No one had taught the voice to pronounce a French name.

Val tossed the newspaper on the table. "Sorry, I have to answer this." She zoomed to the hall phone.

"Did you see the *Gazette*?" Monique's voice, pitched higher than usual, sounded on the verge of breaking.

"Don't worry about it. You're not named in the article."

"But everyone will read it and talk about it. I don't think I can handle that. I'd rather not go to the memorial service."

Wrong approach. "If you want to keep the rumors down, you have to go to the service. With Maverick standing next to you."

Her cousin said nothing for a moment. "If

you'll stand with me too."

"Of course. I need a ride there anyway. My car broke down."

"We'll pick you up. I wonder who leaked that story to the newspaper. Maybe it was that horrible sheriff's deputy."

Val doubted it. If Holtzman had leaked the information, the chief would have his hide. "Forget about the article. Just put on a good face. I'll see you later."

After Monique hung up, Val dialed the police station and asked to speak to Chief Yardley.

"The chief's not in this morning. Would you like to talk to one of the officers on duty?"

Which officer? The one who'd given her driving tips, the one who'd threatened to ticket her for her car alarm, or Holtzman? She pictured his sneer. If she filed a report without proof that someone had tampered with her car, he'd probably blame her for not maintaining her vehicle. At best, her complaint would go on a back burner. With a murder on their hands, the police wouldn't rush to investigate an incident involving no injuries.

"Just ask the chief to call me when he can." She hung up and was surprised to see Gunnar studying the DVDs on the shelves flanking the sitting room fireplace. From there, he could have overheard her on the phone.

He gave her his winning smile. "I couldn't help noticing your film collection when we walked by the shelves. A lot of my favorites from the 1930s through the '90s."

Did he leave the kitchen to study the movie collection or to listen in on her phone calls or both? "Actually, those are my grand-father's. He used to have a video rental store. I've watched a lot of them in the last few months, and enjoyed them."

She went back to the kitchen and cracked the eggs into a bowl. They hadn't warmed up long enough, but sometimes a baker had to compromise. She turned on the oven to preheat.

Gunnar sat at the table. "Aren't you going to finish your muffin?"

"Later. Right now I need to beat some-thing."

Little by little she added sugar to the beaten eggs. Meanwhile, Gunnar read the newspaper and finished his cheese Danish.

He looked up from the paper. "I read the article that upset you. Did Monique burn the racket?"

Val bit her lip. Should she lie? She folded the coconut into the egg-and-sugar mixture.

"Don't ever take up poker, Val."

Forget lying. She couldn't even manage bluffing. "Monique didn't kill Nadia. The police are wrong."

Gunnar got up, refilled his coffee mug, and positioned himself across the island counter from her. "They don't arrest people without evidence . . . usually. But let's say they make a mistake. If she didn't do it, a halfway decent lawyer will get her off."

Val stopped mixing. "You know what people will think? That she beat a murder rap by paying some hotshot lawyer. How's she going to live here then? The old-timers would remember how her father broke the law by evading the draft. Monique might as well follow in his footsteps and go into exile."

Gunnar leaned on the counter until his eyes were level with hers. "You have more reason to worry about yourself than her. You've had two close calls this week. Can you think of any reason someone would want to harm you?"

Trying to find a murder suspect other than Monique made a good reason, but Val didn't want to tell Gunnar that. "Like what? What would make me a target?"

"Hanging out with the wrong sorts."

She suppressed a laugh and smacked her

forehead with her palm. "The guys with chains and handcuffs at the biker bar. They're after me."

"I love your sense of humor, but this is serious. Any fishy people at the club? Staff, tennis players, bodybuilders?"

Luke had talked about lowlifes at the club as a joke. Gunnar wasn't joking. Did he believe the club attracted dicey types? How would a tourist and soon-to-retire government accountant arrive at that idea?

She looked straight into his blue eyes. "Okay. I'll be serious. I met a man at the club recently who's pretty shifty. My grandfather warned me not to have anything to do with this guy, but I didn't listen. Maybe I should have."

"Are you talking about me?" He pointed his index finger at his chest near the spot of sauce on his shirt, the badge he'd earned by cracking crabs.

"I want to know the real reason you're here." She covered a cookie sheet with parchment paper. "You said you were going to hang up your shingle as an accountant, but you don't act like it. People launching their own businesses are obsessed. They talk about nothing but their plans. You mentioned your venture once or twice in passing."

He turned his hands palms up. "I didn't want to bore you with my plans."

"You need a fire in the belly to start a business. You don't have it." She dropped rounded spoonfuls of the macaroon mixture onto the cookie sheet and waited for his response.

He took a deep breath. "You got me. I never had a fire in the belly for accounting, as I told you last night. I do it because it pays the bills. When I heard about Aunt Gretchen's legacy, I decided it was time for a change. Her money will give me the chance to do what I've always wanted to do."

"Which is . . . ?"

"Acting. I'll take classes, get some unpaid experience in community theater. Someday I may be able to eke out a living at it. Meantime, a small accounting practice that doesn't demand too much of my time, along with Gretchen's money, should be enough to live on."

Val filled up the cookie sheet. Accounting. Acting. As if he picked careers from an alphabetical list. Next up, acupuncture?

She should react to his revelation. Make it light, but not too flippant. "You're taking up acting now? What are you gonna do for a midlife crisis?"

He grinned. "This is it. A little early."

He went to the table and stuffed a chunk of croissant into his mouth. A French pastry gag to keep him from revealing any more about himself?

She felt as if she'd nibbled around the crust of his real story, not getting to the center of it. She joined him at the table. "You put on a good performance as a low-life Saturday night at the docks. You even fooled my grandfather. So you must have some acting talent. Go for it."

His eyes locked on hers. "The last time I ran this idea by a woman, she said I was a flake and broke off our engagement."

The matter-of-fact words didn't match his constricted voice. Maybe he still loved that woman, which would explain his reluctance to open up to Val and his token attempts at romance. She too reined in her emotions after her experience with Tony. Last night she and Gunnar had both lost control, but only briefly.

She reached across the table and gave his hand a quick squeeze. "Sorry, broken engagements are hard. Tell me about the big swarthy guy who was with you at the docks. Is he an actor?"

"Not exactly."

She waited for more details about his

companion, but none came. "Just as well he's not an actor. He'd be out of work except for the occasional pirate movie."

Gunnar laughed. "He'd do okay in *On the Waterfront.*"

"*On the Waterfront.* You know, I had a professor in college who turned down a role in it. He had a chance to jump ship and didn't do it. Instead, he stayed in grad school and spent his life teaching English."

They looked at each other, smiles growing, each knowing what the other was about to say.

Gunnar raised his finger like a baton. "Ready? One, two, three."

"He coulda been a contender." They spoke in unison, imitating Brando's dock-worker accent.

She laughed with him. Gunnar the actor appealed to her even more than Gunnar the accountant. He might not snag many leading man roles, but he could pull off the handsome rogue's best friend, the fifth wheel, or a gangster. He had a melodious voice too as Granddad had remarked on hearing it for the first time.

She stood up. "One more cookie sheet to fill." And lots more background for Gunnar to fill in.

Instead of doing that, he leafed through

the *Treadwell Gazette.* She scraped up the last of the dough and put the cookie sheets in the oven.

Gunnar rustled the newspaper and laughed. "Now I get it."

"Get what?"

"The recipes on the dining room table. Your grandfather." Gunnar spread out the newspaper on the island countertop.

A photo of Granddad popped out at her. He was grinning and wearing the Codger Cook apron she'd bought him. What the heck?

She read the headline above the photo: "CONTEST WINNER AND NEW RECIPE COL-UMNIST — THE CODGER COOK."

CHAPTER 18

Val stifled a yelp, thrust her fists into her pockets, and hoped Gunnar wouldn't notice her agitation. At least he couldn't see her face while reading the newspaper over her shoulder. She skimmed the article introducing and interviewing the new recipe columnist.

It described her grandfather as a lifelong Bayport resident, who'd served in the Korean War. As a widower for the last six years, he'd had an incentive to learn cooking. The article quoted Granddad: "Cooking's not rocket science. If an old codger like me can do it, anyone can."

A big IF, given that he couldn't cook, but a true statement.

"Five ingredients is all you need," he told the reporter, "plus a few sprinkles." The codger promised to give readers "simple, healthy recipes . . . well, mostly healthy." Asked for a rule of thumb about cooking, he said, "When in doubt, set the oven to 325."

Val coughed to cover up the combination laugh and groan that welled up in her throat. Only a few days ago, he'd set the oven to 525 and filled the house with smoke. How did he expect to get away with claiming to be a cook?

The article ended with three of the recipes he'd submitted to win the contest. Val scanned them — No Mistakes Crab Cakes, Just Small Potatoes, and Easier-Than-Pie Apple Crisp — new names for her recipes. He'd listed her ingredients, added color commentary to her directions, and claimed them as his own. Bad enough he bartered her services to contractors. At least, she got credit for that. In this case, she might share the blame for his fraud when it came to light.

"You got your cooking genes from him, huh?" Gunnar said.

Val didn't trust herself to give a straight answer. She fingered her cutoffs. "These cooking jeans? They're so old I don't remember where I got them."

"I'm back, Val." Her grandfather called out from the hall. "Somethin' smells good. Make sure you're not burning it."

Gunnar laughed. "Lessons from the master."

Val's jaw clenched. She checked the cookie sheets in the oven. "Not even close to burning." She slammed the oven door. "Thanks for bringing breakfast, Gunnar. I'm not trying to rush you, but I need to talk to my grandfather, and then get dressed for the memorial service."

"Val, have you seen the newspap—" Her grandfather stopped at the entrance to the kitchen and scowled at Gunnar. "Oh, you're here. I thought I recognized your red car parked at the corner."

"Good morning, sir. Did you enjoy the game last night?"

"Yup." Granddad looked from Gunnar to Val and back again. "I expect you enjoyed what you did too. No time to shave this morning? Or no razor?"

"Granddad." Val glared at him as he came into the kitchen.

"I can take a hint," Gunnar whispered to her. He walked past her grandfather. "Nice seeing you again, sir. Save me one of those macaroons, Val."

Val walked him to the door. "Sorry about that."

"I'm just sorry that what he thinks happened last night didn't happen." He put his

271

hand on her arm. "I meant what I said about getting away from here. If you won't go to the Bahamas, how about New York? You must have friends there."

"A few, but my friends here need me. This is my home now and —" She broke off, startled by her own words. Had her heart decided where home was though her brain still hemmed and hawed about it? Her brain took over now, feeding her practical reasons for not leaving. "I have a business to run. I can't just take off when I please."

"How about a bodyguard? I do a pretty good imitation of one."

If she needed a bodyguard, she wanted a real one, not a would-be actor playing a role. "Thanks. I'm not going off on my own. As long as I'm with other people, I feel safe."

A nerve pulsed in Gunnar's temple. "Feeling safe isn't the same as being safe. I'll call you later today."

He'd explained away some of the doubts she'd had about him, but also triggered new ones. The actors she'd met in New York had one trait in common with celebrity chefs. They performed all the time, not just in front of a camera. So how could you know what they were really like?

As she closed the door behind Gunnar, the hall phone rang. The caller ID announced *"Treadwell Gazette"* — probably a reporter following up on either the racket-burning story or the recipe contest. Val pressed Talk to answer the call and then Off to end it — a telephonic way of saying "No comment." She pressed Talk again, heard a dial tone, and left the line open. No phone calls would get through until she and Granddad had a chat.

Could she guilt him into giving up the recipe column? Probably not, but she'd try. The kitchen smelled of sugar, coconut, and vanilla. The sweet aroma calmed her. She opened the oven. Better take out the macaroons before taking on her grandfather.

He stood at the counter, lapping up the article about himself like the cat that got the cream. He pointed to the newspaper. "Surprised you, didn't I?"

She donned a quilted mitt and pulled the cookie sheets from the oven. "Doesn't it bother you to claim my recipes as your own?"

He looked the picture of wide-eyed innocence. "I view them as family recipes."

"What about the people you beat out for the columnist gig? They can actually cook. They have recipes of their own to share." Like Irene Pritchard, who'd wanted assurances that Val wasn't competing against her in the contest. She must be steamed about Granddad winning.

"They might cook better than me, but the editor decided I write better. He likes my folksy style."

Granddad wouldn't climb aboard the guilt train no matter what Val said. She transferred the cookies to a wire rack to cool. "Why did you enter the contest? It's not like you've ever shown an interest in writing a food column."

Granddad ran a finger under the collar of his polo shirt. "It's all because of Lillian, the widow Ned mentioned the other night. I met her at the senior center."

Val stared at him, amazed. "I don't understand what Lillian has to do with this. Is she into cooking?"

"Not at all. Her husband cooked. He made gourmet dinners for her every night. Now she eats at the retirement village, and she hates the food. All the fellas who live there vie to sit at her table in the dining room. I got to be top dog by inviting her to that fancy new restaurant."

"The Tuscan Eaterie." The femme fatale of the senior set just wanted to eat well. Val could relate to that. "How did Lillian like the food there?"

"She enjoyed it. Me, I thought it was

kinda skimpy and expensive. If I have to take her to places like that, my bank account will go bust. I figured if I won the recipe writer contest, I could impress her without shelling out a lot of dough."

Val waved her hand like a student with a question. "Hello. You'll have to cook for her."

"Once in a while. That's the reason for the five ingredients. I can manage simple stuff if you teach me. You have plenty of recipes with eight or more ingredients. You can put those in your own cookbook." He reached for a macaroon. "Monday's the deadline for my next column. I'm counting on you for recipes."

What choice did she have? Instead of her convincing him to give up the recipe column, he'd enlisted her as his accomplice. "I'll help you pick out recipes on one condition — you have to prepare them. That way, if someone buttonholes you on the street and asks questions about them, you can answer."

"Sounds like overkill to me, but okay." He munched his macaroon. "This is a mighty fine cookie. How many ingredients?"

"Five, but it's not my recipe, so you can't use it. I got it from a woman who lives on Maple Street, Mrs. Zachana—"

"Mrs. Z. I knew her husband. I'll drop by her place and ask if I can use her recipe. She'll probably be tickled to have her name in the paper."

At least he was asking her permission and giving her credit. After a visit to Mrs. Z's cute brick house, Granddad might do what Val had hoped a few days ago on Tuesday — fall in love with the place, buy it, and get rid of the Victorian behemoth. A compact home would be perfect for him if he lived alone. But if Val stayed for a while, it wouldn't suffice for both of them. Of course, she could always get a place of her own, but she'd miss this kitchen, not just its ample counter space, but the memories it brought back. Grandma had taught her to cook here. Val baked cookies and cakes in other kitchens, but only here did she feel her grandmother standing beside her when the oven gave off sweet aromas. Somehow she'd find the money to maintain the behemoth, even if it meant taking in boarders, which Granddad would resist.

He plucked another macaroon from the rack. "I gotta call Ned. He'll spread the word about my column. I'll be a celebrity at the senior village."

Val laughed. Winning the contest certainly energized him and made him less grumpy.

276

"I think Lillian is just an excuse. You're writing the column in a quest for fame."

"I gotta get something out of it. It doesn't pay worth a hoot. I'm hoping they ask me to write restaurant reviews next, and I can get some free meals." He hustled out of the kitchen. A few seconds later, he shouted, "You left the phone off the hook, Val."

"Sorry."

She bit into a macaroon, crunchy on the outside, soft and sweet in the center. She arranged the remaining macaroons on a platter to take to the potluck lunch, and sliced grape tomatoes for the salad she would also take.

The phone rang several times while she was assembling the salad. Each time she expected her grandfather to report that the chief wanted to speak to her, but Granddad fielded all the calls himself.

He returned to the kitchen as she mixed the salad. "A lot of folks saw that article in the paper. They're phoning to congratulate me. I might have to take that phone off the hook myself just to have some peace."

"You'll never do that. Admit it, you love the attention."

He eyed the salad. "What's that greenish glop with the little tomatoes in it?"

She spooned some onto a small plate.

"Have a taste. Tell me what you think."

He rolled the salad around in his mouth as if tasting wine, but at least he didn't spit it out. "Not bad, but danged if I know what I'm eating."

"Hearts of palm —"

"Never heard of 'em. No palm trees around here."

"You're also eating avocados, a little mayo, and lemon juice. Onions are optional."

"Hmm. Five ingredients without onions." He tapped his temple. "Hey, if I put a salad recipe in my column, I won't have to cook, just chop, and I'm good with a knife." He held out his plate. "Give me some more so I can decide if I like it."

"Sorry. It's going to the buffet lunch we're having after Nadia's memorial service today. The macaroons are also going." Val covered the salad with plastic wrap and stowed it in the fridge. "I'll add the onions to the salad later if I have time. Right now, I'd better shower and get ready for the service."

Half an hour later, Val came downstairs, dressed for the memorial service in a black skirt and a cream top.

Granddad was sitting at the dining room table, poring over recipes. "Got a call from the police while you were showering. The chief said to tell you he knows about your busted brakes, and he's looking into it."

"How did he find out?" Either the garage mechanic or Gunnar must have contacted the police.

"He didn't say. How come you didn't tell me about the brakes? Or being run off the road Tuesday night? And you didn't wake me when you heard noises in the middle of the night."

"I didn't want to worry you." She headed for the kitchen. "I need to chop onions."

He followed her. "I looked at your recipe. You left it on the counter. It calls for red onions. I think you should use green onions instead."

She wheeled around. "Now you're trying to teach me to cook. Winning that contest is going to your head."

"I'm making a suggestion. Green onions won't overpower the salad. Red ones will."

She opened her mouth to object, closed it, and stared at him. "You're right. I should have thought of substituting green onions."

"Here's another thing you should have thought of." Granddad sat at the breakfast table. "Going after a murderer can get you in trouble. The police want you to stop, and I do too."

"They would rather arrest Monique and

close the case." She took a bunch of green onions from the fridge. "And don't try to convince me she's guilty."

"I bet she asked you to help her, though, and that's putting you in danger." He pointed his index finger at Val. "If she wants to prove she's innocent, let her do it herself."

By doing it herself, Monique would increase speculation that she'd murdered Nadia.

"I'm sure her lawyer advised her against doing that. Don't worry, Granddad, I'm not walking around accusing people of murder. I'm just asking questions about Nadia." Val sliced through each green onion lengthwise. "I've learned a lot about her in the last few days. I should have taken the time to get to know her better, instead of just writing her off. I wish I'd returned her call the day she was murdered."

"You want to make it up to her by solving her murder? That's guilt gone haywire."

"Guilt's hard to control." No one knew that better than Val. She'd come to Bayport with a plateful of guilt and a side order of regret for the life she'd left behind in New York. Four months had passed, and she still couldn't get rid of the leftovers. "You can't assume my car problems have anything to do with Nadia's murder."

"I'm just glad your car's in the shop, and you can't drive for the next few days." He stood up. "You need a ride to the memorial service?"

"Monique and Maverick are coming by for me." Val cut the onions crosswise into semicircles. "By the way, Mom and Dad phoned this morning and missed talking to you. When they call you later, don't mention the murder or Monique. It might ruin their vacation."

"Okay." He waggled his finger at her. "Don't you go playing detective at that lunch."

At the memorial service, Val sat on one side of Monique, Maverick on the other side. The chapel filled quickly. Nadia's nearest neighbors, Irene and Roger Pritchard, flanked their son, Jeremy. The real estate folks occupied two rows. Downtown merchants showed up, including Luke and Darwin. Nearly every row had Bayport tennis players or club staffers sitting in it. Also present, two men resembling vultures more than mourners: a reporter, who tried to buttonhole people as they arrived, and Deputy Holtzman, who fixed his eyes on Monique.

During the opening hymn, Bigby charged

in. He walked up and down the center aisle, looking for an empty seat with the same intensity he doubtless showed when looking for empty land to build on. As the singing stopped, he lowered himself into one of the folding chairs lining the walls.

The minister addressed the congregation with words about eternal life meant to be comforting, words he could have spoken at anyone's memorial service. Val wondered if he'd ever met Nadia.

Irene Pritchard spoke of Nadia's willingness to volunteer her time for children's charities, the money she'd raised for the March of Dimes, and the parties she'd given to bring her neighbors together. Then Althea talked about her friendship with a woman whose background and interests couldn't have been more different from her own, except that they shared a love of tennis. At one point, when Althea's voice broke, Val fought to hold back tears.

Monique nudged Val. "Look at Bigby."

The big man sweated profusely, his face strangely contorted. He squeezed his eyes closed. As Althea finished speaking, he buried his face in his hands, his shoulders heaving, though no sound escaped him. Remorse, Val decided. He was feeling remorse for harassing Nadia, maybe for killing her.

Monique whispered, "He's all broken up. He must have really cared for her."

"You think?" Val had taken it for granted that Bigby, after being rejected by Nadia, had stalked her in revenge and written an anonymous letter to expose and embarrass her. But Monique saw him differently. Val tried to shift her own perspective on Bigby. Perhaps love, not revenge, had motivated his actions. An excess of love could be as dangerous as hate.

Val sighed. People were like those inkblots psychologists used — walking, talking inkblots. They really should be easier to understand than black splotches and less susceptible to projection by the interpreter. But just when you thought you had them pinned down, they would morph, as Bigby was doing now before her eyes.

At the end of the service, the minister introduced Joe Westrin. Nadia's ex stood up and thanked them for coming in the name of Nadia's only living relatives, an aunt and uncle too frail to travel. He also announced that everyone was invited to Althea's house for a buffet lunch in Nadia's honor.

Bigby rushed out the side door, the first to leave. By the time Val made it outside, he was gone. Groups of mourners clustered on the sidewalk and along the path between it and the chapel. Val stood on the steps of the church with Monique, while Maverick joined Luke and Darwin on the sidewalk.

Monique offered to lend Val a car. "We still have our old hatchback parked at Maverick's shop. I could drive that, and you could drive my van."

"Thanks, I can use a car. How about you keep the van and I drive the hatchback?"

"The door locks don't work, and the air conditioner is dicey."

"Doesn't matter. I'll only use it for short hops."

"We might as well pick it up on the way to Althea's house. We'll leave whenever Maverick stops hanging out with the boys over there." Monique pointed with her chin toward her husband. "On second thought, maybe you shouldn't take the hatchback. It could be bad luck."

"Bad luck?" Val echoed. She wasn't superstitious. Broken mirrors and black cats didn't worry her, but after the last few days, not to mention her automotive history, she wasn't anxious to drive an unlucky car. "What do you mean?"

Monique brushed lint from her black dress. "The last person who drove the hatchback was Nadia. She borrowed it a few weeks ago."

The car borrowing no longer surprised Val. She might be the only person whose car Nadia hadn't driven. "Why did she want your car?"

"Probably to haul something that would have messed up her leather upholstery." Monique beckoned to Maverick. He either didn't see or ignored her. "I found out what Maverick was doing Monday night. He left Philadelphia sooner than I expected."

"Where'd he go?"

"Casino-hopping in Atlantic City." Monique rolled her eyes. "How dumb is that? No one wins at a casino except the house."

And the man who needs an alibi. Maverick had lucked out, his face on casino surveillance cameras the night his mistress was murdered. "So Maverick's really into gambling. I remember him talking about the NCAA championships at the café. It sounded like he had a lot of money riding on the game."

"For the Super Bowl, he didn't just bet on the game, he bet on the toss. He can't even go to a funeral without consulting his bookie. And until a month ago, he played poker two nights a week, usually losing big."

"Hello, ladies." The reporter Val had seen

inside the church swooped down on them. "I'm Terry Barnes from the *Treadwell Gazette.* Val Deniston and Monique Mott, if I'm not mistaken. Mind if I ask you a few questions?"

Val recognized his name from the byline on this morning's article. "Mind if I ask you about your sources?"

He ignored her. "I understand you've been helping the police with their inquiries into the murder, Mrs. Mott."

Monique turned rigid and pale.

Val stepped between her and the reporter. "I'm sure everyone in Bayport is helping the police any way they can."

"But some people might be able to help more than others." He maneuvered around her and addressed Monique. "Were you and, uh, your husband close to the deceased?"

Monique stared down the reporter. "Not really."

Val took her by the elbow. "Let's grab Maverick and leave."

In the van Monique twisted toward the backseat where Val sat. "We'll drive you to the boatyard to pick up the hatchback, but then Maverick and I are going home. I can't face the luncheon at Althea's. There's nothing you can say to change my mind. Don't even try."

Ten minutes later Val climbed into a canary yellow hatchback parked in Maverick's boatyard. Ugly car, but it ran. She tested the brakes on the road back to town. No problem there.

The problem was in the rearview mirror. A midnight blue sedan kept pace with Val's car, braked when she did, and made the same turns she made.

CHAPTER 19

Val slowed down, hoping for a better look at the car tailing her. The sedan kept its distance, too far away for her to read the license plate or see the driver through its tinted glass. How long had the car followed her? She hadn't noticed it on the way to Maverick's boatyard, but why would she? She'd spent the time talking with Monique, not looking out the back window.

A pickup truck pulled out of a side road behind her car. She could no longer see the sedan in her mirror. She steered into the housing development where Althea lived, the pickup still behind her. When she turned into Althea's cul-de-sac, the pickup and the dark sedan went straight. Val released a deep breath. Maybe the sedan hadn't followed her after all. Gunnar had made her jittery with his warnings. She parked the hatchback, grabbed the cooler containing the luncheon food, and hurried up the steps to

Althea's house.

Althea answered the door. "Come on in. Drinks are in the kitchen."

Val held up the cooler. "I have my contributions to the buffet and Monique's. Where do you want the food?"

"Dining room table. I know whatever you made will be great. What did Monique prepare for us?"

"Deviled eggs with a twist. She added puréed beets to the egg yolks, which turned them pink. Then she topped them with Gorgonzola cheese and pickled carrots. That's her version of comfort food."

Althea groaned. "Luckily we also have real comfort food. Chatty baked bread, and Bethany made a potato salad. Luke is bringing sandwich ingredients. All I had to supply were the drinks and the veggie platter."

Val put her arm around Althea's shoulder. "Nadia would have appreciated all this. And you gave a wonderful tribute to her during the memorial service."

Althea looked down. "It's the least I could do for her."

"This may seem like a strange question, but did she ever borrow your car?"

Althea's head whipped up. "How did you know? She wanted my station wagon last month. She said she had to pick up something that wouldn't fit in her trunk." Althea turned away to greet the next person at the door. "Talk to you later."

Maybe Nadia borrowed cars to haul things around or maybe that was just an excuse. Either way, it was odd behavior in the weeks, or possibly months, before her murder. The police should look into it.

Val put her salad and Monique's eggs on the dining room table. She set the macaroons on a sideboard with other desserts.

Chatty motioned to her from the kitchen and tugged her out the back door. "I don't want anyone listening. Did you see the article in this morning's *Gazette* about the arson and murder? Wasn't it great? That reporter was putty in my hands. He wrote exactly what I wanted him to." Chatty grinned broadly enough to give herself the laugh lines she seldom permitted her face to display.

Val stared at her. "You told him all that stuff?"

Chatty's eyes, outlined in black to match her lacy sheath, opened wide. "I planted disinformation to take the heat off Monique. The *Gazette* reporter who cornered me at the club Thursday night asked me to confirm that Nadia had an affair with the husband of a tennis teammate. Instead, I confused the issue. I said it wasn't a husband, but a brother of a teammate, and it wasn't an affair, but a fizzled romance. Then I needed to divert his attention with something even more sensational. That's why I told him about the racket burning."

Thereby drawing the reporter's attention to the incident incriminating Monique, but Chatty didn't know she'd done that. "And the part about the arson and murder being connected. Did you tell him that too?"

"The icing on the cake. You agreed that Bigby must have set the racket on fire."

"I did not." Val's words came out louder than she intended. Two women looking at Althea's flowers near the back fence turned toward her.

"Well, you didn't disagree with it. You said he made a good suspect in the murder. I decided to smoke him out."

"You're the one who's smoking something, if you think that Bigby —"

"Did you see him at church? He's breaking down already. He's afraid the police are on to him." Chatty gestured toward the house. "Notice he's not showing his face here. He's probably at the station confessing right now."

"I doubt it." Val couldn't convince Chatty of the harm she'd done without telling her that Monique had burned the racket. "Let's go back inside."

Chatty followed her. "You're too pessimistic, Val. Wait and see how this plays out before you criticize. By the way, I saw the announcement about your grandfather. Who knew he was an expert cook?"

Not a soul. Val returned to the dining room as Luke arrived with a huge platter.

"Here comes more food." Chatty made space on the table for Luke's platter.

He set it down with a flourish and removed the plastic wrap. "There you go, ladies. Sandwich meat and cheese straight from the diner. The bread's coming up." He left the room, clutching a wad of clear plastic.

Chatty wrinkled her nose. "Hmm. I thought everything at the diner came from the fat vat or the greasy grill. Not that this stuff's any more healthy." Chatty's citrus cologne fought a losing battle with the scent of garlicky smoked meat.

Val took a pickle from the edge of the meat platter. "Nadia ate there sometimes. She must have ordered a salad, nothing from the vat or the grill."

"I wonder if vintage French fries still decorate the floor."

"It was clean yesterday when I ate there.

Sweeping is Jeremy Pritchard's job, and he takes it seriously."

Chatty popped an olive in her mouth. "Nadia was trying to coax that kid into getting a GED. That's asking a lot of him. He's great with mechanical things, but not reading and math."

"People overcome learning difficulties. What's the source of his problem?"

"Lack of oxygen during birth. That's what I heard. He —" Chatty's eyes widened as she glanced toward the living room on the other side of the hall. "Irene's beaming daggers this way. She couldn't have heard us talking about Jeremy. I wonder what's eating her."

"Those daggers have my name on them." Val wanted to apologize to Irene for Granddad's ruse, but as his accomplice and enabler, she couldn't do it without feeling hypocritical. She'd better just stay out of Irene's way. "I hope the memorial service didn't upset Jeremy. He was there with Irene and Roger, but I don't see him here."

Luke bustled back into the dining room with plastic baskets of bread and rolls. "Jeremy's at the restaurant helping with lunch. Should I tell him you were looking for him, Val?"

"Doesn't matter. I'll catch him some other time."

"We're shorthanded right now. I've got to get back there myself."

As he left by the front door, Chatty headed to the living room. "I'll let everyone know lunch is served and start herding them in here."

Bethany joined Val and surveyed the table. "Isn't this gorgeous?"

Val handed her a plate. "Dig in. Someone has to be first."

"You take a plate too. I don't want to be the only one eating." Bethany piled her plate with ham rolls, salami slices, and pickles. "You know, I feel I'm finally at peace with Nadia. She did me a favor."

"What do you mean?"

"Now that I have a different partner, I see what I missed. Yumiko and I are equals on the court. When I played with Nadia, she was always in charge. We were in a rut from playing together too long." Bethany studied the vegetable platter. Skipping over the celery canoes, she culled a radish rose. She pointed at the cheese cubes and carrot sticks on Val's plate. "That's all you're going to eat?"

"I'll have some nibbles now and make a sandwich later. Is Bigby here?"

"He has to work this afternoon. Construction's running late."

A more plausible explanation for his absence than Chatty had given. "He looked really upset at the service."

"Bigby's got a gruff exterior, but he's a softie inside. He gets very emotional at family reunions. Let's see, what have I missed here?" Bethany mounded potato salad and Val's avocado salad on her plate. She circled the dining table again. "I have to bulk up because I'm starting the cabbage soup diet tomorrow. It lasts seven days. People shed pounds like crazy on it."

"I believe it. Eating cabbage in water for a week would kill my appetite." Val took her plate into the living room.

The young real estate agent she'd met in Nadia's office broke away from her colleagues. "Hey, Val. I was hoping I'd see you here."

"Hey, Kimberly."

"I wanted to thank you for the referral to Mrs. Z. She listed her house with me. In case you're interested, her name ends in 'a.' You added an extra letter to it."

Val might have mixed up some of the interior vowels, but not the consonant at the end. Maybe Nadia had made a mistake in her notes. "The last thing Mrs. Z needs is another letter in her name."

Kimberly giggled. "I also tracked down the Wilsons, the couple Nadia saw in her office on Monday. They wanted to buy a big old house in town. I met with them this morning."

"You have another new client then. Congratulations."

"Nadia gave them some addresses, so they could like drive by and take a look. And guess what? One of those addresses was 175 Grace Street. Isn't that where you live?"

"Yes." Val drew out the syllable. "But I don't know why Nadia would have given them my address. The house isn't for sale."

Kimberly looked stricken. "That's too bad. The Wilsons told me Nadia tried to call you while they were in her office, to find out when you might sell, but you weren't home. They decided to drive by anyway, and they loved your place."

"Ah. That's why Nadia called me Monday." Nothing to do with the murder. Just real estate business as usual. Val felt as if one of the clouds hanging over her had floated away.

"If you change your mind about selling —"

"The house belongs to my grandfather. I'll let you know if he decides to sell."

Kimberly went into the dining room with her colleagues. Val set her plate on an end table.

Irene approached her, gripping a sweating glass of water or maybe gin on the rocks. She looked as if she might use it to give Val an ice-cold facial. "You lied to me about that contest."

Val tensed, ready to duck liquid and verbal missiles. "I wasn't lying. I didn't know my grandfather entered it until the paper announced the result."

"I don't believe you. He knows nothing about cooking. He's fronting for you."

Val was glad to see most of the guests clustered in the dining room. The three women talking at the far end of the living room couldn't overhear this conversation as long as she and Irene didn't raise their voices. "Why would I do that?"

"What else are you lying about?" Irene spoke through teeth tight as a vise grip. "You were up to something at Nadia's house the morning she was found dead. The police chief's protecting you because he's your grandfather's buddy."

Val stopped breathing, taken aback by the wild accusation. Two heartbeats later, she gulped air. Was Irene accusing her of destroying evidence or even of murder? "What are you suggest — ?" She broke off as Irene marched away and joined the group of three women.

Val resisted the urge to follow Irene and demand an explanation, counting her blessings instead: no ice water on her face or clothes. She needed a moment to calm down. She went out the kitchen door and walked toward the back fence.

Irene had a lot of nerve to make accusations based on nothing. At least Val looked for a motive before viewing people as suspects. Only yesterday she'd toyed with the idea of Irene as the murderer, but without accusing her to her face. Maybe Irene believed in a good offense as the best defense.

Val smelled tobacco smoke. Irene's husband, Roger, stood under a tree, puffing on a cigarette. He looked as surprised to see her as she was to see him. If she didn't talk to him now, she might not get another chance. She'd have to take the risk that he would lash out at her as Irene had.

"Hi, Roger. Sad day, isn't it?"

The wiry man with thinning gray hair gave a single nod that she took as both a greeting and a response to her question.

Undaunted by carrying on a one-sided conversation, she forged ahead. "I talked to

298

Jeremy yesterday. He's really taking Nadia's death hard."

Roger exhaled smoke. "He would do most anything to please Nadia. It's weighing on him that he couldn't make her happy lately." He took another puff on his cigarette.

Val hoped he'd say more once he exhaled, but he didn't. "Nadia could be hard to please sometimes."

"That's the truth. She kept at Jeremy to get a better job. Why should he change jobs when he likes what he's doing?" He looked at Val as if she could explain Nadia's behavior.

"I don't know." It didn't make sense that Nadia had pushed Jeremy into the diner job and then urged him to leave it. "Maybe she heard about a job with more prospects."

"Change ain't always good." Roger dropped the butt of his cigarette and stepped on it. "I hope it's good for your granddaddy. I wish him luck. Irene says he can't cook. She thinks only women can, but I make a darn good barbecue myself."

"Most famous chefs are men. I'll tell my grandfather what you said."

Roger ambled back to the house. Val followed a minute later, still unsure whether to trust his explanation of the disagreement between Nadia and Jeremy.

Once inside, she cornered Joe Westrin, Nadia's ex.

He pumped her hand vigorously. "It's good to see you, Val. Sorry I didn't return your call, but things have been hectic. You wanted some information about Nadia for the club newsletter?"

"I don't want to take up your time now. Any chance we can get together later?"

"I'll be at our — I mean Nadia's house to gather papers this afternoon. I'm her executor. You want to come by the house around three-thirty?"

"Um . . . okay." Though she didn't care to return to the place where she'd found Nadia dead, she'd rather not wait any longer to talk to Joe.

Granddad wouldn't approve of her meeting alone with anyone, especially one of his five suspects. The police, though, had eliminated Joe as a suspect. That was good enough for Val. She hit the buffet and indulged in foods she didn't stock at home for fear of tempting her grandfather: soft cheese, salami, chocolate truffles.

CHAPTER 20

Val climbed the steps to Nadia's front porch and tried not to think about the last time she rang the bell here.

Joe opened the door. "Come on in. I just made coffee. Would you like a cup?"

"Not for me, thanks." The rich food she'd eaten at Althea's house had left her slightly queasy. The acid in coffee would make her feel worse.

"I'll grab a cup. Have a seat in the living room. I'll be right with you."

At least Val didn't have to make a return visit to the kitchen. She went through the archway into the living room, sat on the overstuffed sofa, and looked in her handbag for a pen and paper. If she concentrated on recording Joe's words, she might forget where she was. The only paper she found was the small spiral book with Nadia's tennis team notes that Kimberly had given her. She turned it to the first blank page as Joe settled into an easy chair.

She jotted notes while he talked about his first encounter with Nadia on the Virginia Beach boardwalk, her enthusiasm for living on Maryland's Eastern Shore, and their shared enjoyment of tennis.

Joe clutched his coffee mug and shook his head. "Hard to believe she's gone. I called her at the office Monday. I never thought that would be the last time I'd talk to her."

"Did she tell you what happened the night before?"

"About the burning racket? Yeah. She should have contacted the police. She never liked dealing with them on account of what happened when she was a kid."

Val couldn't imagine Nadia in trouble with the law. "She had problems with the police?"

"Her father called them about a noisy party next door. The cops overreacted and arrested some people for disorderly conduct. The neighbors blamed Nadia's folks and harassed them."

"Harassed them, how?"

"Phoning in the middle of the night. Letting their Dobermans loose when Nadia was playing outside. Her family had to move to get away from it."

That explained Nadia's reluctance to tell

the police about the racket burning and a possible stalker. Had she confided in her ex about the stalking? "I think something was bothering Nadia, even before the racket fire."

"She didn't mention anything to me, but I found a strange e-mail message on the printer. I'll show it to you. Maybe you'll know what it's about." He took a paper from an antique secretary desk in the corner, handed it to Val, and went back to his easy chair.

She read the message: Hi Nadia, We love our vacation house on the bay. Thanks for helping us get it at a price we could afford. I ran the two samples you gave me through my gas chromatograph. Except for the red dye in the pink sample, the components in both are the same. They match what's in a product we supply to drugstores and small resellers. Let me know if you need more information. — KC

According to the message header, kcarlson at obp-labs had e-mailed it early Monday morning. Val wrote down the sender's e-mail address and "gas chromatograph." She handed the paper back to Joe. "It doesn't mean anything to me. Did you try contacting the sender?"

"Nah. I hate to bother somebody just to satisfy my curiosity."

Val had no such qualms. She'd follow any lead, however remote, to help her cousin. She put the spiral notebook away, hoping to encourage Joe to talk off the record. "It's wonderful that you and Nadia stayed friendly after your divorce. You didn't hold it against her."

His neck and head moved forward like a turtle's. "You mean that she didn't hold it against me."

"The divorce was your idea?"

"Yeah, I pushed for it. Things had gone stale after fifteen years. It might have been different if we'd had kids. We had a baby who died. Neither of us could get past the loss."

"I'm sorry."

"Thank you. We tried everything, including the test-tube approach. Didn't work." He interlaced his hairy fingers. "We just found out my fiancée's pregnant. That's one reason I called Nadia Monday, to let her know the good news."

Val's mouth dropped. "How did she take the news?"

He rubbed his eyes. "I couldn't bring myself to tell her on the phone. I figured I'd wait until the next time I saw her."

Okay, that made him less than a hundred percent dense and self-centered, just ninety-nine percent. Yet Nadia stayed friendly with Joe after he abandoned her for someone fertile. Maybe the divorce was a relief for both of them. If what he'd just said was true, Joe didn't have a motive for killing his ex-wife. He was a man on the verge of marriage, looking forward to having a child.

Val stood up. "I won't keep you any longer. I know you've had a bad week. Thanks for taking the time to talk to me."

"I was going to ask you to stop by anyway. Nadia's will says that her friends should each choose a knickknack to remember her by." He gestured at the shelves holding Nadia's collection of miniature houses. "Take your pick."

"I really wasn't such a good friend. I don't feel I should —"

"The people she played tennis with were some of her closest friends. Please. Take something."

Val approached the shelves. The brownstone tempted her as a reminder of her first home in New York. She started to reach for it but switched course. Her hand closed over the Victorian house that resembled Granddad's. "Thank you, Joe. I'd like this one."

He walked her to the door. "Take care, Val."

She took his advice literally. On her way

home she checked the rearview mirror several times. No blue sedan trailing her now. Good. The ground had shifted under her enough for one day — Gunnar telling her to leave town and Granddad recruiting her as a recipe ghostwriter, tough Bigby shedding tears and nice Joe dumping his wife, Chatty striving for disinformation and arriving at the truth. On top of that, this morning's *Gazette* article increased the pressure on Monique. The day had brought tremors rather than seismic shifts, but tremors often presaged an earthquake. A big shakeup opening new ground might be just what the situation needed. Otherwise, the police would arrest Monique, and the media would try her in short order.

Val pulled into the driveway and joined her grandfather on the front porch.

He sat in a wicker armchair, his feet propped up on a matching ottoman. "I was snoozing out here, opened my eyes, and saw you drive up in a mutant banana. I figured I was dreaming."

She laughed. "It's Monique and Maverick's old car. I'm borrowing it until mine's fixed." She sat on the porch railing. "You're going to have to cross some suspects off your list. Maverick has an alibi. He's on surveillance tapes in Atlantic City casinos at the time of the murder."

"Hmph. Does he have a twin brother?"

"He's an only child. Nadia's ex, Joe, is also in the clear. He hasn't been nursing a grudge. Contrary to what everyone thought, he divorced Nadia, not vice versa."

"She's not around to contradict him. Unless there's proof of that, I'm keeping him on the list — him and Monique, Bethany, and Gunnar." He ticked off his suspects on four fingers and pointed his thumb up. "I could use one more. Five's a nice round number. How many suspects do you have?"

"A single definite one. I'm still rooting for Bigby." Today she was less certain of his guilt than yesterday. She at least had Irene as a backup if he came up with an alibi. And now, thanks to the e-mail Joe had shown her, Val had a new angle to pursue. She opened the screen door. "I'll be working on the computer for a while. Then we can tackle dinner."

"Plug in the phone if you want to answer it. I unplugged it to stop it from ringing. Too many people want to talk to me now that I'm a newspaper columnist."

She waggled her finger at him. "Be careful what you wish for."

She plugged the phone in, turned on her laptop in the study, and found a website for

OBP Labs, where Nadia had sent samples of something. OBP stood for Organic Beauty Products. The company manufactured cosmetics and personal care products for resale under private labels. Resellers could buy OBP products in gallon or even five-gallon jugs and decant them into smaller containers.

Val and Nadia both knew someone who sold organic beauty products — Chatty. Could Nadia have sent one of Chatty's products for analysis?

Val studied images of the empty bottles and jars OBP marketed to resellers. The small ones looked exactly like Chatty's containers for facial products. The larger bottles resembled those on display at the big drugstore in the Midway Shopping Plaza. No wonder Chatty had snatched back her bottle of "pink silky stuff" when Val pointed out its similarity to what she'd bought at the store. Chatty offered services that stores didn't — a free facial and lots of gossip. That entitled her to charge more, but perhaps Nadia thought Chatty was ripping her off.

Val calculated the return on a gallon of moisturizer divided into four-ounce bottles and sold for the price Chatty charged — eight hundred dollars on an investment of a hundred dollars. A similar product, possibly the same one Chatty sold minus the dye, cost a third as much at the drugstore. Nadia might have made the same calculation. Most people would merely stop buying an overpriced item. They wouldn't go to the trouble of proving they were being over-charged as the meddling Nadia had done.

She routinely checked e-mail at every op-portunity. She'd probably read the OBP Labs message Monday morning before hitching a ride to work with Chatty. Had Nadia demanded a refund from her or threatened to expose her high mark-up? Chatty would lose customers if Nadia broadcast that a nearby store carried the same products at a much lower price. How far would Chatty go to save her reputation and her business? Val's queasiness returned at the thought of Chatty as a possible killer. All along she'd assumed someone she didn't like or barely knew would turn out to be the culprit, not a woman on her tennis team.

The hall phone rang. Its computer-generated voice announced the caller's ID — Luke Forsa. Maybe he was calling, like everyone else in town, to congratulate Granddad. She answered the phone.

"Hey, Val. It's Luke. You going to the concert at the park tonight?"

She hadn't planned on it. But if she stayed home, she'd just brood about Chatty. Listening to music would give her a chance to relax and take her mind off the murder.

"Why not?" she said into the phone. "What kind of music?"

"A jazz group. Can we meet there? They start playing at eight, but I might be stuck at the diner 'til eight-thirty."

"Okay, I'll see you there." She'd have no trouble finding him. This time of year, it stayed light until nine. "I'll sit somewhere near the fountain."

She clicked the phone off. She ought to check for messages that came in while Granddad had the phone disconnected.

Most of the messages were for him. She saved those. Gunnar had called her and suggested they go to the concert in the park that evening.

Rats. She'd have preferred his company to Luke's. On second thought, a dose of Luke could be an antidote to Gunnar. Luke wasn't stagestruck. He didn't dramatize. He wouldn't spend the evening talking about sabotage and urging her to leave town.

She called Gunnar back, left a message that she'd already made plans for the evening, and suggested they get together tomorrow.

Granddad came in from the porch. "Who phoned?"

"Luke. He asked me to meet him at the park tonight for the concert."

"Hmph. In my day, we picked up our dates. We didn't invite them to meet us places." Granddad stroked his chin. "Luke. He's my fifth suspect. I should have thought of him sooner."

Val laughed. "I see a pattern here. Gunnar and Luke show an interest in me. I go out with them. Therefore they must be murderers. Or do you have some other reason for thinking Luke killed Nadia?"

"You gotta watch out for men who don't treat their mothers right. He makes Rosie do too much. Restaurant work is for young people. She should retire."

"Maybe she doesn't want to retire. She's like you. She wants to keep her hand in. Speaking of which, we'd better start cooking dinner. Did you pick out a recipe?"

Of course not. He left it up to her. She chose an Orange Pork Tenderloin recipe and modified it for chicken tenders. She made him do most of the work. After dinner, he patted himself on the back and offered to drive her to the park for the concert and pick her up.

"I don't want you going anywhere alone

after all the trouble you had the last few days."

She should have taken Gunnar's offer to serve as a bodyguard, given that her alternative was a man in his seventies.

As they were about to leave the house, she spotted the family that lived down the street. They carried lawn chairs and a blanket, probably going to the outdoor concert. "I'll go with them, Granddad, and come back with either them or Luke. I promise I won't go anywhere alone."

She hurried out of the house before he could object and fell into step with nine-year-old Tiffany, a tomboy who reminded Val of herself at that age. As she chatted with the girl, Val glanced behind a few times to check if anyone had followed her in a car or on foot. She saw no one.

The family stopped at the ice cream parlor. Val licked her double chocolate ice cream cone with chocolate sprinkles and felt some of the tension leave her body.

Tiffany's family joined some friends at the park. Val sprawled on her grandfather's army blanket. The sound of water splashing in the fountain relaxed her. She watched the crowd gathering for the concert.

Bigby O'Shay picked his way around strollers and folding chairs, stopping now and then to glad-hand someone, like a politician bent on reelection. Val went on alert when she saw him coming toward her.

The evening wouldn't be as relaxing as she'd hoped.

CHAPTER 21

Val scrambled to her feet as the man who'd been her number one murder suspect for the last few days approached her. She didn't want him standing over her or, worse yet, sitting next to her on the army blanket. "Hello, Bigby."

He fingered the gold chain around his neck. "I have to talk to you. I — uh — want to explain."

"Explain what?"

"Why I was rude to you the other day. I thought you were out to smear Nadia, but Bethany tells me you're helping the police find her murderer."

Val groaned. No wonder she'd become a target with Bethany spreading that rumor. "Bethany's wrong about that."

He hooked his thumbs on his belt loops. "She said you'd deny it."

Darn. Any direct questions to Bigby, such as where he was the night of the murder, would only confirm what Bethany had said. Indirect probing might work though. "This morning's service for Nadia was very moving, everyone talking about her charity work and how much they'd miss her. You looked like you were missing her too. I'm sorry for your loss."

Bigby inhaled loudly and focused on the fountain. "I didn't realize how much she meant to me until she was gone."

Val forced herself to look sympathetic. "People often don't realize things until it's too late. Whoever sent Monique an anonymous note about Maverick's affair with Nadia would be shocked by what happened as a result."

His bloodshot eyes bugged out. "What do you mean?"

"Monique was upset about the note and told everyone what Nadia had done. After that, people shunned Nadia. Someone burned a racket at her place. Then she was murdered. One person made an accusation, and everybody jumped on the bandwagon. Like the Salem witch hunt." Okay, she'd left logic in the dust, but Bigby didn't seem to notice.

"I . . . I wrote that note."

"You did?" Val's surprise was genuine. She hadn't expected him to admit it. "Why?"

He gulped as if swallowing a big bitter pill. "To break them up. I didn't have a chance with Nadia as long as Maverick was around. But once his wife reined him in, I figured Nadia would be lonely."

And Bigby would be there to catch her on the rebound. But faced with rejection, he might have decided that if he couldn't have her, no one could. Val finally had a theory that made sense of Bigby's behavior. Obsession, not resentment, explained why he sent the anonymous note and possibly killed her.

"Hey, Bigby! I'm over here." A woman waved her arm in a wide arc at Bigby. She wore a spangled hot pink halter top and short shorts with a roll of belly flesh overhanging them.

Bigby's date for the evening? Easy to see why he'd find the physically fit Nadia more attractive. She also had better taste in clothes than the woman in pink.

"Coming." He gave his date a halfhearted wave and then turned back to Val. "Nadia wasn't an empty-headed chick. She had a lot character. I hope her murderer rots in hell."

He shuffled away, no longer working the crowd, his head and shoulders bowed. Val almost felt sorry for him. If he was the murderer, remorse was eating at him. If he wasn't, she'd just given him the mother of all guilt trips by blaming him for a chain reaction that ended in Nadia's death. Even if he hadn't killed her, his anonymous note had kicked off a vendetta that made Monique a suspect. He deserved to feel miserable.

Val scanned the audience as the musicians tuned up. She recognized some neighbors and a few club members she'd served at the café, but other wise everyone was a stranger — locals she hadn't yet met and tourists visiting for the weekend. A few loners stood out in the crowd of couples and families. A man with glasses and a gray mustache hovering at the edge of the park caught her attention. He wore jeans and a navy turtleneck with long sleeves. Most of the crowd had bare arms and legs. Maybe he'd covered up to avoid being mosquito bait.

By the time Luke joined Val, the concert was half over, and the musicians had gone on break.

"Sorry I'm late." He parked himself next to her on the blanket. "I got bogged down at the diner."

"Business must be good."

"We're short on staff. The kids who usually help us are away at beach week." He stretched out, crooked his elbow, and rested his head on his hand. "What's with your article on Nadia? Got any leads on her murder?"

Great. Yet another person assuming she was on the trail of the murderer. "I'm focusing on Nadia's life, not her death." Tonight, though, she wanted a break from both. One surefire way to change the subject, ask a man about himself. "Your mother said you used to live in Baltimore. What did you do there?"

"I worked for a restaurant supplier. I had to move here after my father died. The diner leaked money for years. He dipped into savings to cover the expenses. Nobody knew 'til he died that their retirement fund was empty. And he let his life insurance lapse."

"Ouch." She leaned back, resting her head on her hand and faced him, a mirror image of his position. "What about selling the place? Wouldn't that give your mother enough money to retire?"

"She doesn't want to retire. She likes to cook and talk to people. The diner's her life. I'm going to make sure she enjoys it as long as she can."

She heard a fierceness in his voice that contrasted with his usual breezy tone. So much for Granddad's notion that Luke was treating his mother badly and forcing her to work. "You're a good son."

"I wish my father could hear you say that. He had me down as a good-for-nothing. My sister was the perfect child. But what has she done for Mom? Squat. She came to my father's funeral and went right back to Seattle."

"Mom" and "my father" — Luke's word choices showed where his affections lay. Val sat up and wrapped her arms around her bent knees. "It's a long way to the West Coast. My brother lives in California. We don't see much of him or his family."

"Did you ever get hold of Jeremy?"

"Not yet. You must treat him well. According to his father, Nadia tried to talk Jeremy into giving up his job for a better one, but she couldn't convince him to leave the diner."

Luke's mouth turned down with skepticism. "First I've heard of it. I don't want to hold anybody back, but a better job just isn't in the cards for that kid."

Nadia had either seen more potential in Jeremy or concealed her real reason for urging him to change jobs. "Maybe she thought you were going to fire him, and she wanted to spare him the humiliation."

Luke gave her a you-must-be-kidding look. "No way I would fire him. People who sweep the floor with that much enthusiasm are hard to find."

Val had trouble reading Luke. She couldn't tell whether he appreciated Jeremy's hard work or was mocking him for enjoying a menial task.

As the music started, she spotted Chatty conversing with two older women whose jewelry and makeup would have suited a concert at Carnegie Hall better than one at the town park. Clearly they could afford Chatty's high-end beauty products. Why had Nadia gone to the trouble of sending one of those products for testing unless she intended to act on the test results? She might have confronted Chatty about it Monday morning, when she'd also shown Chatty the burned racket.

On Monday night Nadia had welcomed someone arriving at her door. She would have let Chatty in, though not Bigby because he'd stalked her . . . or so Chatty had claimed. Val cringed. How easily Chatty had convinced her of Bigby's guilt and thrown up smoke screens after the murder. While in front of a TV camera, she'd diverted suspicion from the tennis team toward Nadia's real estate colleagues. After that, she'd told a newspaper reporter that the police would soon arrest the racket burner for murder.

Val watched Chatty hand business cards to the two well-heeled women. Did she have an alibi for the night of the murder? Probably not. As a single mother, she spent most nights at home with her fourteen-year-old son. But she could have left him alone for as long as it took to murder Nadia. Motive, means, opportunity — Chatty had them all.

Val's eyes stung with tears. The downside to sleuthing — finding a friend guilty. Though she'd run to the chief with her suspicions about Maverick and Bigby, she would hold off on telling him about Chatty. For a change, she would think through a theory before sharing it.

She wiped her eyes with the back of her hand and forced herself to forget about Nadia and Chatty for the rest of the concert.

Twice before the music ended, she caught Luke looking at her. Then, during the encore, she felt his hand on her neck. When she turned, he kissed her, holding the back of her head with one hand. She smelled his aftershave, an overlay on the cooking oil that clung to him. Twenty years ago, his kiss had surprised and excited her. She hadn't known what to do with her arms, leaving them to flail at her sides. Now, though, she knew how to use them.

She pushed him away, the heels of her

hands against his shoulders. "When you asked me to meet you, I didn't think —"

"You can't blame me for kissing you. I couldn't help myself."

She almost laughed. He'd used those exact words the last time. Amazing how puppy love imprints every detail on your memory. Tonight he'd kissed her in front of an audience at twilight. She hoped anyone who saw that also noticed her rebuff him.

When the encore ended, Tiffany scampered toward them. "Val, you gonna walk back with us? You promised."

Val hadn't promised, but Tiffany's parents might have seen her push Luke away and sent the girl to give Val an excuse to ditch her date. Val saw no reason to string Luke along when she preferred Gunnar's company.

She stood up. "Thanks for suggesting the concert, Luke. I'll head back home with my neighbors."

Luke's face turned stony. "Sure. Enjoy the rest of your night." He stood up and disappeared into the crowd.

"Race you to your house," Tiffany said as they turned the corner onto Val's street. She darted away.

Val trotted at an easy pace behind her.

The girl's parents and younger brother brought up the rear.

Tiffany bounded up Granddad's porch steps, stopped short, and suddenly ran back to the sidewalk, her face contorted in fear.

Val felt a jolt of adrenaline and dashed toward her. "What's wrong?"

Tiffany grabbed her hand. "I didn't know you had dogs. They sound mean. Do they bite? Is that why you never let them out?"

"They're in the house?" When the girl nodded, Val imagined Granddad fending off canine attacks. She ran to the porch as her grandfather opened the front door. He looked calm despite the furious barks coming from inside the house. "Are you dog-sitting, Granddad?"

He grinned. "In a way. When Ned moved to the senior village, he forced his dang-fool motion detector on me. RoboFido. It makes a racket when anyone comes near the house. I'll turn it off."

Val explained the barking to Tiffany and her family. The girl insisted on meeting RoboFido.

The device sat on the floor near the front door's sidelight. Tiffany frowned at it. "It's just a box. It doesn't even have fur."

Granddad patted the girl on the head. "This dog is less trouble than the furry kind. Never needs walking. Want to see how it works?" He pointed to a dial on top of the box. "This is the on-off switch and the volume control. The other dial lets you pick different sounds."

Tiffany took to the role of DJ and strung together a medley of doggie tunes — a woofing solo, a baritone-and-bass barking duet, and a snarling chorus by hounds of the Baskervilles. Tiffany's little brother howled along with the hounds. Her parents had to drag her away from the gizmo.

Granddad closed the door behind the family and gestured with his palm up toward RoboFido. "How do you like our pet?"

"We need a dozen in a house this size." Val unplugged the device. "One's better than none. I'll put it in a back window facing the darkest part of the yard."

She also made sure the lights near the front and side doors were on. She'd heard nothing unusual outside the house last night, either because she'd slept soundly or because the driving rain had discouraged anyone from creeping around. No rain tonight.

After getting ready for bed, she decided against sleeping in her own room. It faced the backyard. She'd surely hear the sentry barking, but she wouldn't hear any noise from the driveway or the front. She took her pillow and a light blanket to the sofa in the sitting room, read until she couldn't keep her eyes open any longer, and fell asleep.

She dreamt of driving through a fierce windstorm that denuded the trees. Her tires crunched over piles of dry leaves. She woke up and still heard the crunching sounds from her dream. They came from under the side window. She parted the curtain and could barely make out the yellow hatchback in the driveway. No light came from the fixture near the side door. A loose bulb for the third time this week? No way. She decided against turning on the lights in the house. They wouldn't help her see into the darkness outside, just make her visible to anyone out there.

The crunching noises stopped. Then a crescendo of barks reverberated through the house. Fido had detected motion in the backyard.

"Val?" Granddad said from his bedroom door. "What's happening?"

"Someone's out back. Call 911. Tell them to send the police. Then lock yourself in your room."

The barking stopped. Val grabbed a flashlight from the kitchen and peered out the dining room window. She saw a dark figure run from behind the house toward the front. A second figure pursued and tackled the first one.

Val ran to the side door and cracked it open. Her flashlight illuminated two men on the ground between the car parked in the driveway and the backyard. They thrashed and slugged each other. One wore a dark turtleneck like the man she'd noticed at the park tonight. The other guy, also in dark clothing, wore a tight-fitting cap.

The man in the turtleneck rolled on top of the other guy and punched him.

If Val didn't act, the police might find a man beaten to a pulp in her driveway.

CHAPTER 22

Val searched the closet near the side door for something to hurl at the men and break up their fight. No wrench. No hammer. Her old tennis racket would have to do.

She opened the side door, flashlight in one hand, racket in the other.

"Look out, below!" Her grandfather yelled from an upstairs window. Whatever he threw made a volley of soft thuds at the front of the driveway, nowhere near the men fighting toward the back.

She aimed her flashlight at the fighters and crept toward them. The man in the turtleneck had his hands on the other guy's throat. She couldn't stand by and watch someone being choked.

Val gripped the racket to hit her target with the frame instead of the strings. She leaned over the men on the ground. Pretend it's a first serve. Wham.

Despite a blow to the head, the big guy in

the turtleneck still pinned the other man down.

Val swung again, a forehand to the husky man's neck. Whack. The blow stunned him enough that the guy underneath pushed him off, scrambled up, and kicked the husky man in the groin. Turtleneck grunted and curled up.

Val trained her flashlight on the kicker. His face was smeared with something black. She couldn't make out his features. He shoved her.

She fell backward. The racket and flashlight flew from her hands, and her head hit the soft earth of her flower bed. The man who'd pushed her disappeared into the night.

A startled cry came from the front of the house, guttural noises, and then a string of curses. The voice sounded like Gunnar's though she'd never heard language like that from him.

"Gunnar?" she shouted.

"Val? What's going on?"

She found her flashlight on the ground, stood up, and trained it on him as he sidled past the yellow car toward her.

"Hey, you're blinding me." He shielded his eyes with his hands.

A clean face, not blackened. She lowered

the flashlight. He wasn't the man who'd shoved her. "Two guys were duking it out in my yard. One of them's groaning on the ground. The other one pushed me and ran off. Did you see him?"

"He fell in your driveway near the street. I tried to grab him. I fell too, and he got away. Did you throw tennis balls all over the front?"

"I did." Granddad's voice came from behind Val. "To trip you guys up."

Gunnar stopped dead in his tracks. "Sir, is that thing loaded?"

Val turned to find Granddad wearing pajamas and carrying a shotgun. "Oh, shi— I mean, shoot." She saw him raise the gun. "I mean, *don't shoot!*"

He braced the gun against his shoulder and aimed it at Gunnar. "That other fellah got away before I loaded it. It's ready to fire now, so don't try to run. Call the police, Val."

"I told *you* to call them." Val could reach high C when she was angry. Never before had she hit high banshee.

"I had to go upstairs to find my gun and ammo. They were in the closet behind your bucket of old tennis balls."

"I'm callin' the cops now." The bass voice came from the house across the driveway.

"How am I supposed to sleep around here?"

Val could have asked her neighbor the same question when he ran a chain saw at dawn. "Thanks, Harv—" She broke off as he slammed the window down.

Val beamed her flashlight at the hulk on the ground. With the light on his face, she saw his dark mustache and bushy eyebrows.

"It's the pirate." Granddad swung his gun toward the man. "Avast!"

Gunnar leaned over the man. "You okay, Vince?"

The reply included a string of unprintable words. Val caught the gist. Vince was mad as hell, but not severely injured. Now that Val knew he didn't need medical attention, she wanted answers from Gunnar. "What's Vince doing in my yard?"

"I asked him to keep an eye on you today."

"I saw him at the concert keeping an eye on me." Though he'd disguised himself with glasses and powdered his mustache to look older. Had he followed her all day? "Does he drive a dark blue car with tinted glass?"

"Uh-huh." Gunnar squatted next to the man. "Can you get up, buddy?"

"Stay on the ground," Granddad said. "I have a gun on you."

"What the hell's going on?" Vince rubbed the back of his head. "I was on top of him,

Gus. And then something hit me from behind."

Val moved closer to Gunnar. "Why did he call you Gus?" Either her serve to the head had concussed Vince into a memory loss, or Gunnar had lied about his own name, along with probably a thousand other things.

Vince sat up. "First I got hit in the head. Next something hit me in the neck. Then the guy kicked me in the balls."

"Why were you fighting him?" Gunnar asked.

"He was piling up paper along the foundation."

Val aimed her flashlight toward the house. Sure enough, crumpled newspaper. "That was the crunching sound I heard. But why — ?"

"He headed for the backyard and set something down." Vince pointed over his shoulder. "Then the dogs started barking, and he took off. Check out the backyard. I bet you find a gasoline can."

A gasoline can. "Arson?"

Val could hardly believe it. RoboFido had scared away an arsonist, and she had clobbered the wrong person. Or had she? Maybe Vince was the arsonist, trying to blame someone else for what he himself had done.

Granddad lowered his gun. "You can get

up now. A pirate who saves my house from an arsonist can't be all bad."

"A pirate?" Vince scratched his head and stood up. "I was getting ready to tackle him when the dogs went crazy. He ran, and I jumped him. Man, that guy was strong. Built like steel. With all that barking, I expected a dog to bite me on the ass. Instead, somebody hit me." He turned to Val. "You?"

Val chewed her lower lip. "I'm sorry. I just wanted to stop the fight."

"Why didn't you hit the other guy?" Vince rubbed his neck.

She heard a siren in the distance. Lot of good it did to call the police. The fight was over, the arsonist gone. She turned to Gunnar. "All day I was afraid someone was stalking me. You should have told me about Vince."

"I didn't know how you'd react. I wanted you to leave town, and you wouldn't go. I talked him into keeping an eye on you. You couldn't object if you didn't know about it."

"If you thought I needed protection, why didn't you do it yourself?"

"You blew me off this morning when I offered. And I tried to spend the evening with you, but you had other plans. I came here to relieve Vince."

The siren cut off as the squad car pulled up in front of the house. By then Granddad had disappeared into the house with his gun. Wise man.

"Police! Don't move!" The command came from behind a torch that turned night into day. "What's the problem here?"

Val recognized the voice of the officer who'd responded to her car alarm two nights ago. "Officer, it's Val Deniston. Watch your step in the driveway. Someone was sneaking around the house tonight, and my grandfather emptied a bucket of tennis balls to trip him. These two men tried to catch him, but he got away."

"Which way?"

Gunnar pointed. "Across the street and between two houses. Five minutes ago."

The officer approached. "What'd he look like?"

Val hadn't noticed much about the man she'd seen only by flashlight. "Dark clothes, a tight cap. His face was smeared with charcoal or something."

Vince piped up. "Height about six-two, weight around two hundred. Muscular build."

"And who are you?"

Vince whipped a badge out of his pocket.

"Vince Palminteri, Drug Enforcement Agency. Your chief knows we're operating here."

The policeman checked Vince's ID and then eyed Gunnar. "Are you DEA too?"

"No. Here's my driver's license and government ID." He surrendered two cards.

Lights blazed in two houses across the street. For the first time Val realized how little she was wearing. Her elongated T-shirt left lots of leg exposed. "Officer, I'd like to go inside and put on some clothes. The two guys know more about what happened here than I do."

She left the men in the driveway, unplugged RoboFido, and patted him. Such a good watchdog. Her grandfather emerged from his bedroom in overalls and his pajama top. She told him his pirate worked for the Drug Enforcement Agency. He went back outside.

By the time she changed and returned to the driveway, another squad car had arrived with a policeman she didn't recognize. The officer tagged a can of gasoline as evidence. Gunnar was still there, but Vince had gone.

"What weapon did you use on Vince?" Gunnar asked.

She spotted her racket near the flower bed

and brandished it. "The only thing I could find."

"He's lucky you didn't find a crowbar. I can't wait to tell him what hit him. He left when the neighbors started coming out. He has to keep a low profile."

Because he worked undercover. So how did Gunnar come to know him? Before she could ask, the cop with the weather-beaten face approached her. "You have a smashed lightbulb in your side fixture. That's the one I tightened the other night."

"Our visitor got tired of unscrewing it night after night. Any chance a police car can stay until daylight in case he comes back?"

"We'll patrol the area, but if other calls come in, we have to respond. We've had a couple of arsons in the last month or so, but never more than one a night."

She sighed. If the arsonist wanted to finish the job, he could call in a bogus emergency to get the police out of the neighborhood.

Gunnar touched her arm. "Go get some rest. I slept earlier. I'll be on your front porch in case you need me. If the guy comes back, I want to be where I can see and hear him."

She went inside, found a light coverlet,

335

and brought it out to him. "Take this in case it gets cool toward morning." She sat next to him on the porch steps. "Is your real name Gus?"

"A nickname. My initials are G.U.S."

"You're on nickname basis with a DEA agent?"

"I've worked with Vince on some cases. I'm with IRS Criminal Investigation. My job is tracing laundered money."

Now that had the ring of truth to it. Unlike his other stories — opening an accounting practice, Great-Aunt Gretchen's will, his acting ambitions. "Are you working with him now?"

"Not right this minute."

An evasive answer, but she was too tired to care. "I'm going to sleep." She stood up.

He held the screen door open for her. "See you in the morning." He gave her a gentle kiss that left her disappointed.

Had she been too cool toward him? Not that she wanted the passionate kisses of last night. Tonight she longed to be cradled and hugged.

She turned on the motion detector at the back of the house. "Whatever your limitations as a pet, Fido, you will not be the dog that didn't bark in the night."

The next morning when she looked through the front window, she saw Gunnar stretched out in a makeshift bed — a cushioned chair, an ottoman, another chair. He'd kept his word and stayed all night. Reliable? Yes. Truthful? Not so much.

She made coffee and tried to make sense of last night's attempted arson. Her house could have been the random target of the arsonist who'd started other fires near Bayport.

She didn't buy it. Too many coincidences: the arson coming on the heels of the road bullying, the noises outside her house on Thursday night, and the brake tampering. If the same person had been responsible for all those incidents, he'd targeted her specifically.

The coffeemaker sputtered and gurgled. According to Vince, the would-be arsonist had been over six feet tall, around two hundred pounds, and "built like steel." Three men she knew fit the description — Bigby the house builder, Darwin the bodybuilder, and Luke with his barbell and beer physique.

She reviewed her recent encounters with

each man in the light of last night's attempted arson. The coffee aroma cleared the cobwebs from her brain. She saw now what she'd missed previously. The man targeting her feared she could connect him to major crimes.

Before she went to the police with her conclusions, though, she'd try them out on Gunnar. He'd better not have woken up and sped away in his Miata while she was making coffee. Last night he'd given her only part of his story. He still had plenty to explain.

CHAPTER 23

Val took coffee and a plate of biscotti to the porch.

Gunnar was moving the wicker furniture back in place. His jeans and navy T-shirt didn't look bad after a night spent on chairs, but his bloodshot eyes suggested he hadn't slept much.

He smiled anyway. "Good morning."

"It's a great morning. There's a cool breeze, and I think I know who last night's arsonist was." She handed Gunnar a mug and leaned against the porch railing. "The pro at the club, Darwin, owns the sporting goods store in town. When I was there Tuesday, he overheard me talking to a friend and got jumpy when I used the word *arson*. That would make sense if he set the fires the officer mentioned last night, the recent arsons around town. Also, he matches Vince's description of the guy trying to set a fire here last night."

Gunnar rubbed his stubbled chin and raised an eyebrow. "Overhearing one word — not much of a reason to target you."

"Guilty people often overreact. The time line fits. Right before I was run off the road, my car was parked in front of Darwin's shop. Easy for him to follow me. He's supposed to be a car expert, so he could have tampered with my brakes. When that didn't sideline me, he resorted to arson. He couldn't do it Friday night because of the rain, but last night was perfect."

"Too bad you didn't see his face last night. Not that I'm disputing your post-game analysis. I'd still like to know what else you —" Gunnar stopped talking as a black Crown Victoria pulled into the driveway behind the yellow hatchback. "You have company."

Chief Yardley climbed from the car. "Heard you had a spot of trouble here last night."

Val set her mug on the railing. "I did, and you're just the person I want to see about it."

The chief mounted the porch steps and thrust his hand out to Gunnar. "Earl Yardley, Bayport police chief."

"Gunnar Swensen. I've heard about you, sir."

340

"Likewise. I just talked to your DEA buddy. He said I might find you here." The chief sat on a wicker chair. "Where's your granddaddy, Val?"

Uh-oh. Val hoped the DEA man hadn't told the police about the crazy geezer waving a gun and calling him a pirate.

She opened the front door and peered down the hall to her grandfather's room. "Sleeping in after last night's excitement, I guess. His bedroom door's closed."

"How about some coffee?" the chief said. "I'll have it black. And take your time in the kitchen. Give us five or ten minutes here."

He was using the coffee as an excuse to get rid of her. Good to know that he had a reason other than Granddad's shotgun for showing up here. She went inside.

Granddad emerged from his room off the hall. "Why didn't you wake me up? I got stuff to do today."

"Chief Yardley's on the porch. He's looking into what happened here last night."

"Good. He'll get the fella who tried to burn my house down. The two of us, we need to start cookin'. I got recipes due tomorrow."

Never mind that Val had someone trying to maim or kill her. She followed her grandfather to the kitchen, took out the ingredients for banana muffins, and gave him some tips on mixing the batter. By the time she returned to the porch, only one man sat there.

She gave the chief a mug of coffee. "Where's Gunnar?"

"I sent him to his B&B. He needed a shower and a shave. He'll be back soon."

"Did you vet him?"

"I know he works for the feds. You want to know about his personal life, hire an investigator." The chief sipped his coffee. "He told me you suspect Darwin of arson and tampering with your brakes."

She sat on the porch railing. "I suspect him of more than that. I asked Darwin if anyone had ordered a wood racket recently. He has some on display in his shop. I didn't say anything about the weapon, but if he killed Nadia, my question might have panicked him."

"First you tried to convince me Maverick Mott did it. Then Bigby O'Shay. I can't keep up. Why would Darwin murder her?"

If the chief couldn't keep up now, Val better not hit him with her suspicions about Chatty and Irene. She'd stick with Darwin for now. "Maybe Nadia found out he was the arsonist, and he silenced her."

"You're saying he committed murder to

cover up a property crime?"

"Okay, it's a feeble motive." That wasn't the only weakness in the case for Darwin as the murderer. He'd have needed access to the burned racket to make a murder weapon that resembled it.

The chief's cell phone rang. He unhooked the phone on his belt. "Yardley . . . Oh, yeah? . . . I'll meet you at the station. We'll go there together." He put the phone away and stood up. "Darwin owns a silver SUV. That doesn't mean he was the one who ran you off the road. We're going to talk to him and find out where he was that night and last night."

"And the night of the murder?" She took the chief's grunt as agreement. "Can you keep me in the loop? I'm scared of the guy."

"I'll put a patrol in the neighborhood." He pulled a card out of his wallet. "Here's my cell phone number. Call me in an hour or two, and don't go anywhere alone. Not even to church."

She spent the next ten minutes on the sidewalk fielding questions from neighbors about the night's events. As they dispersed, she glanced at her watch. She'd better check on Granddad's cooking project.

She zoomed into the house. Judging by the aromas inside, the muffins had baked long enough. She pulled the pan from the oven.

Granddad came into the kitchen from the back porch. "Hey, what are you doing? The timer didn't go off yet. They're not done."

"The muffins were on the top rack of the oven, where it's hotter, so they cooked faster than usual."

He picked up her recipe card from the counter and waved it. "This didn't say which rack to put them on."

"True, but it's a good idea to check baked goods five minutes before they're supposed to be done because the baking time varies with the stove and the altitude."

"How am I supposed to know that?"

After yesterday, when his joy over the recipe column made him gripe less than usual, he had plenty of pent-up grumpiness like a pressure cooker giving off steam.

"Here's another tip. To test a muffin or a cake, press gently on top." She demonstrated. "If it springs back like that, it's finished baking. If it stays dented, put it back in the oven."

"Those things should be written down." He threw up his hands. "Where are the ten commandments of cooking? And can you boil them down to five?"

Val laughed. "You just taught me some-

344

thing. My recipes take too much for granted. When I write my cookbook, I hope you'll tell me what's missing."

"I'm glad my ignorance is worth something to you."

He sounded more like Eeyore than ever.

The doorbell rang. "That's probably Gunnar." She couldn't let him see the kitchen. Eggshells, banana peels, and sugar sprinkles decorated the counter, along with batter drippings that a Jackson Pollack wannabe might envy.

Granddad waved her away. "Go sit outside with him. I'll bring you some iced tea and muffins."

"Thanks." Her grandfather might still balk at welcoming Gunnar into the house, but at least he was willing to feed him on the porch like a stray cat. She left the kitchen.

Gunnar broke into a radiant smile when she joined him outside.

Her pulse sped up. She stepped down from the porch to the front yard. "I want to see what's left of my flowers after last night's fight. I'm almost afraid to look. Banana muffins are on their way."

He followed her across the yard to the driveway. "I snagged a late breakfast at my B&B, but I'm always up for muffins."

The yellow hatchback blocked her view of

the garden. She walked past the car, surveyed the flowers planted in a bed beneath the dining room window, and yelped. "It's like a battlefield the morning after the massacre. Not a daisy left standing. The daylilies are totally crushed too."

"It could have been worse." Gunnar didn't show much sympathy. "The house might have burned up with you and your grandfather in it."

"I know. I really appreciate what you and Vince did last night." She resisted the urge to hug him and walked to the far end of the driveway to inspect the vegetable garden. "Oh, good. The tomato plants escaped destruction. Now I won't have to kill Darwin with my bare hands. I can wait for justice to take its course." She headed back to the porch.

Gunnar pointed to a plate of muffins, a pitcher of iced tea, and two glasses on the porch table. "Where did that come from? The elves?"

"Granddad elf. He's busy in the kitchen this morning." Val sat on the glider, hoping Gunnar would sit next to her.

He took a wicker chair facing her. "Before the police chief stopped by this morning, you were talking about what happened in Darwin's shop. Tell me more about it, who

346

was there, what was said."

This sounded like a business meeting. No wonder he was wearing pressed khakis and a button-down shirt. Val felt underdressed in her jeans skirt and knit top, the same outfit she'd worn for her last interrogation. Better to have Gunnar than the sheriff's deputy questioning her.

She gave him a detailed account of her visit to Darwin's shop and her conversation there with Chatty. He didn't react until she got to the part where the football star and Darwin came out of the backroom.

Gunnar sat forward in his seat. "Did the kid have a racket?"

Val closed her eyes and pictured the scene in the shop. "He was carrying something inside a zippered racket cover. I assumed it was a racket, but I only saw the cover. Right after that, Chatty and I talked about arson. Darwin looked startled."

"Then what happened?"

"The other customers left the shop. Darwin tried to sell me a new racket. I said I might want to order an older model and asked about the kind of rackets people special-ordered from him."

"The kind of rackets? Oh, you were trying to find out if anyone ordered a wood racket."

"What?" Either he was psychic, or someone had blabbed.

"I called Vince when I left your house this
morning. He and the police chief exchanged
information on their cases. Vince told me
about the murder weapon. He said no one
knew about it except you and the police."

At least Val wouldn't have to dance around
the subject of the weapon any longer. She
reached for a muffin. "If Darwin murdered
Nadia, my questions about wood rackets
would have worried him. That might explain
why he came after me."

Gunnar frowned and shook his head. "Or
he didn't like your curiosity about his
special orders, especially after the other
things you said in the shop."

"What other things?" Val munched on the
muffin.

"Vince's investigation involves an arson
and a hit-and-run."

"And when I said 'hit-and-run' at the
sports shop, Darwin moved in closer. He
looked as if he was waiting to hear more,
but I stopped talking when I noticed him."

"You also talked about backroom transactions. I'm beginning to think he's the man
Vince is after."

DEA agents went after only one type of
criminal. "You mean Darwin's in the drug

trade. Where does the hit-and-run fit in? The sheriff's deputy kept bringing it up."

Gunnar left the wicker chair to sit next to her on the glider. "A guy named Ramirez was hit and killed by a car a few weeks ago. He had no ID on him. The police ran his prints and found out he was wanted in Delaware for drug dealing, mostly steroids and party drugs. He lived in a house on a cove near here. It burned down the same night as the car hit him. Arson."

Val felt as if she had random ingredients she couldn't possibly combine into a single dish. A hit-and-run, arson, drug dealing, Nadia's murder. How did all these things fit together? "Did Ramirez torch his own place to get rid of drug evidence before he was run down?"

"The arson came after the hit-and-run. The same person could have done both, possibly to destroy evidence about the suppliers and customers Ramirez had. The fire was started with wadded newspapers soaked in gasoline, same as what the arsonist tried here last night."

"Assuming Darwin's the arsonist, how do you connect him to the hit-and-run?"

Gunnar poured iced tea until it overflowed a glass, his mind apparently on something other than a cold drink.

He blotted the spill and chugged enough iced tea to give himself brain freeze. "Ramirez died on the way to the hospital. Before that, he was talking gibberish, half-Spanish, half-English. The EMT heard something that sounded like the number ten followed by the letter S."

Why had Gunnar hesitated before mentioning this detail? "Ten-S. A license plate?"

"The police thought that at first, but it turned into a dead end."

"Tennis. That's the connection to Darwin." But not just to Darwin. Val frowned. "Wait a minute. Is that why you turned up at the club?" And why he nearly drove off the road when she told him a woman from her tennis team was murdered?

"Vince was already working undercover as part of a joint task force investigating drug traffic on the Eastern Shore. He needed help to follow up on the tennis angle and the money trail. He knew me. We'd worked together once before. He requested I be detailed here."

The phone calls that made him drop whatever he was doing had probably come from Vince, summoning him back to his duties. "So when you roamed the docks with Vince, you were both working undercover to find drug dealers."

"Yup. He was checking on the boating traffic. The water route's the obvious way for drugs to come into this area. The Chesapeake and its tributaries have thousands of miles of shoreline. Vince focused on this area because Ramirez was killed around here."

The wind blew Val's hair in all directions. She tucked it behind her ear and wished her churning thoughts were as easy to anchor. "I'm trying to make sense of all this. Assuming Ramirez was trying to say 'tennis,' Darwin's a suspect because he's a tennis pro and sells rackets. From that, you want to connect him to drug-dealing and the hit-and-run?" She shook her head. "That's a *ten*uous chain of reasoning."

"You may give us the missing link. What do you remember about the guy who picked up the racket in Darwin's shop?"

"Football player from the high school, just taking up tennis. It struck me as odd that someone new to the game would place a special order for a racket. One racket's as good as another for a beginner." But what if he'd picked up something besides a racket? "Special orders. They could be drug transactions taking place in the backroom."

Gunnar reached for a muffin. "That's what I think."

351

"It's a fancy system for passing drugs. Why do it that way?"

"Darwin hides his profits. He's probably got an inventory of old rackets he's paid next to nothing for. He sells them at high prices to certain regular customers. The drugs go out with the racket. As far as his books go, he's bought low and sold high, a legit business practice."

"Why would Darwin kill Ramirez?"

"Drug dealers find lots of reasons to blow each other away. Ramirez could have complained about the quality, refused to pay, or even blackmailed Darwin."

Val watched a woman ambling along the sidewalk with a sailor-suited boy. A collie, his fur ruffling in the breeze, kept pace with them. "Moms, kids, dogs — they belong in Bayport. Murderers and drug dealers don't. Let's get rid of them."

"I'm working on it. I'll put the DEA on to Darwin. They'll want to talk to the football player who ordered a tennis racket. You know his name?"

"Kyle. The team captain. I don't know his last name, but most people in town probably do. High school football's big around here."

The woman, the boy, and the collie passed by the house. A gust blew the boy's hat off.

Gunnar jumped up off the porch and scrambled after the cap rolling down the street. He picked it up and presented it to the little sailor. The boy donned the cap and then shook Gunnar's hand by way of thanks. The dog extended a paw, which Gunnar also shook.

Careful, Val told herself. Tony had been good with kids and dogs too. Hardly a sign of a steadfast character.

Gunnar returned to the porch. His phone chirped as he sat down on the glider. While he took the call, Val chewed a muffin without tasting it.

He closed the phone and slipped it into his shirt pocket. "That was Chief Yardley. Darwin wasn't home. His girlfriend said he left before midnight and never came back. Assuming he came here to set the fire, he might be afraid you recognized him. He's on the run."

A lump of muffin stuck in Val's throat. She washed it down with iced tea. "I'll be glad when they catch him."

"It may take time. Sheriff's deputies and the state police are on the lookout, but he could be three states away by now."

"What comes next? You tell me to take a plane for the Bahamas?"

"You're more likely to run into Darwin in

the Bahamas than here." Gunnar squeezed her hand. "The police are watching his house and this neighborhood. If he comes back, they'll catch him."

"I hope you're right." She stood, walked to the porch railing, and scanned the sky. Only shades of gray, her least favorite color. "It started out a beautiful morning, but it sure has changed."

Gunnar joined her at the railing. "I can trust you to keep our talk private, right? Drug investigations are sensitive. You never know who's involved."

"You can trust me." But could she trust him? Together, they'd worked out the answer to one question: Why had Darwin stalked her? The question obsessing her for the last five days remained unanswered: Who murdered Nadia? "Could Nadia have somehow gotten on to Darwin? Maybe he murdered her too."

"Oh. That's the other thing the chief said to tell you. Darwin has an alibi for the night of the murder. His girlfriend said he was at a bar with her. The bartender confirmed it."

Val covered her ears. "Stop. I'm tired of hearing about people with alibis. I'm even beginning to think it's a sign of guilt. Darwin could have hired a hit man to kill Nadia while he was in a bar."

"His legitimate business and his illegal operations are tied to tennis rackets. He'd be stupid to commit a murder with a racket or hire someone to do that."

"Darwin's not known for his brains, and he's practically a one-man crime wave. Drug dealing, car tampering, arson, and hit-and-run. He's guilty of everything except murdering Nadia? That's hard to believe."

"His crimes fall into a pattern. He uses cars and fire as weapons, first against Ramirez and then against you. He was afraid you knew about his other crimes, which all go back to the drug dealing." Gunnar glanced at his watch. "I've got some work to do on this case. With what you told me, I think we can crack it. You've been a great help."

His lips grazed hers, a touch of skin, light and swift. No heart.

She grabbed his wrist and kept him from going down the porch steps. "Don't leave yet. You owe me some answers."

CHAPTER 24

Gunnar held up the wrist Val's hand encircled. "No need to shackle me. I won't run away from your third degree unless it goes on too long. What do you want to know?"

She could ask him to list every lie he'd told her, but that might take longer than either of them wanted to spend in each other's company. She released his wrist. "You said Vince was keeping tabs on me all day Saturday. When did you decide I was in danger?"

"Friday, when you told me about your brakes failing."

He'd made sure she was never alone from then on. He'd shown up at her door Saturday morning, unshaven, his clothes rumpled, spots on his shirt from Friday night's crab dinner. It shouldn't have taken her this long to figure out why. "You didn't go back to your B&B Friday night."

"I spent the night in my car, watching your house. I thought you might be in danger and shouldn't be alone."

"Which is why you tried to spend the night even closer to me. In the house. In my bed. Of course, I didn't know I shouldn't be alone. I thought something different was happening between us. Does the handbook for an IRS agent have a chapter on seduction?"

"Am I supposed to apologize? I hoped you'd want to . . . but you didn't." He ran his hand through his hair. "Listen, it's been hard for me to balance things for the past week. I liked you a lot, but I had a job to do. Now it's all out in the open, and we can —"

"The past week?" Another layer of fog in her brain lifted. "I get it. I finally get it." The words of a dying man explained Gunnar's interest in her and why he'd hesitated to tell her those words.

"What?"

"A Spanish speaker's T is like our D. What Ramirez said probably sounded more like 'dennis' than 'tennis.' Vince concentrated on the docks, and you focused on tennis and a woman whose last name starts with a similar sound — Val Deniston." She backed away from him. Until today, she'd have

357

described his eyes as blue, but now they reflected the color of the overcast sky. Chameleon eyes.

"Put yourself in our shoes. A few months ago, right after you moved here, the drug situation got worse in this area. Your last name sounds like what a drug dealer started to say before he died. I believed you were innocent after I got to know you. I just had to convince the DEA."

Excuses, excuses. "Exactly when did you get to know me? Yesterday you asked me who I hung out with, as if you expected me to name my lowlife friends."

"I feel like I'm playing tennis and can't get a serve in. I open my mouth, it's a double fault."

She could wield a tennis metaphor too. "At least you knew all along who was on the court, but I just found out. You, undercover investigator. Me, target of investigation. But now you have your culprit. The game's over."

She marched into the house, slammed the wood door behind her, and flopped on the sitting room sofa. How stupid of her to fall for Gunnar. Friday night, he'd kissed her passionately, not out of passion, but because he wanted to come in out of the rain.

Her grandfather came into the room from

the kitchen. "I'm going to the supermarket to pick up a few things. Do you want to know which recipes I'm trying today?"

She shook her head. "I trust your judgment. I should do that more often. You were right about Gunnar."

Granddad's bushy white brows rose halfway up his forehead. "You mean he murdered Nadia?"

"Of course not. He was working undercover here, tracing laundered money. That's why he came to the Eastern Shore, and why he'll leave once he finishes his assignment."

"Can't say I'll mind seeing the back of him. Stay inside while I'm gone, Val, and don't open the door to strangers."

Val turned her hands palms up. "What am I, six years old? The chief already warned me to stay put. I know I'm under house arrest."

She dead bolted the front door behind him and went into the study. Nadia's spiral notebook sat on the desk, open to the page where Val had jotted information about the company that analyzed cosmetic samples. No point in speculating on whether Nadia's research had given Chatty a motive for murder. The chief wouldn't listen to more speculations. When she talked with him at the police station Wednesday, he'd stressed one simple fact about the crime — only someone who'd seen the burned racket could have made a duplicate of it to use as the murder weapon. She'd argued against this theory at the time because it made her cousin look guilty. But since then, she'd come across others who'd seen the prototype of the murder weapon.

She turned to a blank page in the spiral book and wrote Luke, Irene, and Chatty. Val added Monique to the list, drew a line, and jotted Bigby with a question mark after it. She'd already worked out how he could have seen the prototype, by raiding Nadia's trash.

Of the five people on the list, Monique definitely had no alibi. What about the others? Val pulled the card with the chief's cell phone number from her pocket and called him.

"Hey, Chief, it's Val. Anything new?"

"Darwin's SUV turned up. Abandoned on a country road about twenty minutes from here. We're still looking for him. He might have arranged for someone to pick him up."

She sighed. Darwin was probably out of the reach of the local police by now, but if the DEA wanted him, they might catch him. They could cast a wide net. "By the way, Chief, did you have a chance to check on

Bigby O'Shay's alibi?"

"Did you forget I'm running a police department here, not a PI service at your disposal?"

"But he was stalking Nadia." Maybe. Val reminded herself she had only Chatty's word for that.

"I'm trying to find the man who was stalking you. Right now, you're keeping me from doing that."

"Sorry. I won't take up any more of your time."

She hung up and looked at the page where she'd written the five names. She couldn't cross off any of them yet. She tossed the notebook onto the desk. Strange how the pages at the back, like those at the front, were crinkled at the edges. The middle pages looked flat, unused.

She opened the notebook from the back. Nadia had written on fifteen pages. Val flipped through them. Each one had a date at the top and a list of six to ten addresses. No two pages had the same set of addresses, though some addresses appeared on more than one page. The recurring addresses were all highlighted with a yellow marker.

What did these notes mean? An organized person like Nadia might divide a notebook into sections for different topics. Dated pages with comments about tennis matches in the front of the book, dated pages with addresses at the back. The dates at the front corresponded with the tennis team's matches from April through June. Those in the back covered random days from the same period, the most recent one last Monday, when Nadia had borrowed Kimberly's car and left the spiral notebook in it. On the previous Wednesday, she'd borrowed Chatty's car. Val turned the page. Sure enough. That date appeared in the book. These notes might relate to Nadia's car switches.

Val flipped through the pages again. A few of them had no highlighted addresses on them. On some pages, three or four highlighted addresses appeared under one date, but not necessarily the same three or four always together. Other pages had only one address highlighted. Did the highlighted addresses have any significance other than all of them occurring more than once?

The doorbell rang. Val jumped up. Her grandfather's caution against answering the door to strangers echoed in her mind. She peered out the study window. Her cousin stood on the porch in her church clothes, a calf-length beige skirt and a white top. Val opened the door for her.

Monique handed her a grocery bag. "I went by Althea's to pick up my serving dish. She gave me leftovers from yesterday's buffet to share with you."

"Come in." In the months since Val moved here, her cousin had been in the house only once. Val had invited her and her children for homemade ice cream while Granddad went to an Orioles game. Granddad and Monique mixed together like vinegar and oil, only when forced and not for long.

Monique followed Val to the back of the house, apparently taking no notice of the recipes strewn on the dining room table or the chaos left by Granddad in the kitchen. "What happened last night? I heard rumors at church about police cars on this street."

Val carried the mixing bowl with the muffin batter residue to the sink. "We scared off an arsonist last night, before he had a chance to start a fire." No shocked response from her cousin. Not even curiosity about who was included in Val's "we." Monique must have already known about the arson attempt. From church gossip or another source?

Monique gripped her by the shoulders. "A few days ago, I asked you to help me. Now I'm asking you — I'm begging you — to stop. Give up trying to clear me and go

363

back to cooking. I couldn't live with myself if you got hurt because of me."

Val shook off Monique's grip, rinsed a sponge, and wiped the counter. "The police don't think the arson had anything to do with Nadia's murder."

"It's not just the arson. Someone ran you off the road and messed up your car." Monique grabbed the sponge from Val. "Stop cleaning and listen. I have a lawyer. He'll hire a private investigator. I don't want you in the middle of this."

Val folded her arms. Her cousin could have warned her off yesterday, when they'd spent time together in the car and at Nadia's memorial service. What brought this on today? Val had a suspicion. "Granddad called you this morning, didn't he?"

Monique threw the sponge in the sink. "He never asked me for anything before now. I was the invisible relative, invited to funerals but otherwise ignored. I couldn't turn him down, especially since he's right."

"Don't worry. From now on, I'll leave the questioning to the police."

"I'm back, Val." Granddad called out from the front of the house. He stopped in the kitchen doorway. "Oh, we have company." He raised an eyebrow at Monique.

She gave him a barely perceptible nod.

Val interpreted their silent messages, Granddad asking if Monique had completed her mission and receiving confirmation. "Monique brought us leftovers from yesterday's potluck, more than enough for lunch."

"Good. I need a break from my own cooking."

Val stifled a laugh. She could use a break from his cooking too, given the mess left behind the two times he'd tried to cook.

"Congratulations on your newspaper column," Monique said. "I'm looking forward to reading it."

"Thank you kindly." Granddad set his grocery bag on the counter. "Why don't you join us for lunch, Monique?"

Monique looked as startled as Val felt. "Um . . . sure."

Even if Val's snooping didn't lead to Nadia's murderer, at least it was leading to a truce between two family members.

Nadia's name never came up during lunch. Instead, the conversation revolved around Monique's children and Granddad's column. Val's thoughts, though, wandered from the table talk to the notebook's list of addresses.

After lunch she detoured into the study as she walked Monique to the door. "I want you to look at something." She showed her cousin the back pages of the spiral note-book.

Monique glanced at them. "Nadia's writing. Where did you get this?"

"Someone in her realty office found it. Do the addresses listed on those pages mean anything to you? Look at the highlighted ones." Val handed her the notebook.

Monique leafed through the pages. "They're spread out. Four in or near Bayport, two in Treadwell, and two even farther away, in Easton. I don't know where this last one is, Marsh Drive."

"I'll look it up online." Val sat in front of her computer, entered the address on Marsh Drive, and studied the satellite map that came up. "It's a small road that dead-ends at the bay. The place looks like a waterfront property, big house, expensive. I'll try the addresses in Treadwell and Easton." She pinpointed the properties and zoomed in on the images.

Monique peered over her shoulder. "They're all big homes too. They might be going on the market. Maybe Nadia gave sales pitches for them. I'll drive by the Bayport addresses and let you know if I see any For Sale signs outside them." Monique jotted the addresses on a slip of paper.

"Look at the dates on the pages. Could

any of them be the day Nadia borrowed your hatchback?"

Monique leafed through the pages in the spiral and glanced at the wall calendar hanging over the desk. "Could have been this one." She pointed to a page with an early June date and two highlighted addresses on it.

The highlighted addresses were clustered in the first half of April, early to mid May, and early June. Had anything special happened on those dates?

After Monique left, Val checked back issues of local and regional newspapers online, focusing on the dates corresponding to Nadia's highlighted addresses. The newspapers covered county and town government meetings, Chesapeake Bay environmental issues, local crime, and human interest stories. She also skimmed the front pages of nearby city papers. The *Baltimore Sun* and the *Washington Post* featured the Middle East crisis, Congressional disputes, and violence at home and abroad. In half an hour of browsing the newspapers online, Val found no common threads among the dates with highlighted addresses.

Her cell phone rang.

Monique briefed her on the addresses she'd copied from Nadia's notebook. "One's an older two-story house, nicely kept. No signs in front. It's the type of place Nadia might have sold, unlike the next one I drove by — a bungalow with sagging gutters and moss on the roof. She wouldn't have made much commission on that."

Any commission is more than no commission. "What about the other addresses?"

"Commercial real estate, not residential. One belongs to a mortgage settlement company. The other's a garden apartment complex. Nadia didn't sell commercial property."

"Thanks, Monique. Talk to you later." Val hung up and stared at the spiral notebook.

Maybe the notes would make more sense if she isolated the information. She copied the eight dates with highlighted addresses on a blank recipe card.

Granddad poked his head in the room. "What are you doing?"

"Trying to figure out what certain dates have in common." She handed him the card. "See if anything strikes you about them."

He sat on the sofa in the study and adjusted his reading glasses. "They start when the blue crab season starts, and the baseball season."

"People watch baseball and go crabbing

368

on a lot more days than those listed there. Anything peculiar to just those dates?"

He rubbed his chin. "Nothing that fits all of them. The ones in early April and early June are around basketball finals — the NCAA and the NBA. The May dates are right before the Kentucky Derby and the Preakness in midmonth. The Belmont, the third Triple Crown race, is in early June."

"Same time as the French Open tennis tournament." Nadia would have followed tennis, but Val had never heard her mention other sports. "Can you think of anything besides sports?"

"Two big World War II anniversaries — VE-Day on May 8 and D-Day on June 6. Nothing big like that in April." He looked up from the paper and shrugged. "These dates look random to me."

The hall phone rang, and the caller ID announced the Bayport Police. Val rushed to answer it.

"I have news for you." Chief Yardley's voice sounded flat with no hint of whether he had good or bad news. "We're not announcing this yet. We've just notified the next-of-kin."

Her stomach clenched. Bad news. Another murder?

Chapter 25

Val clutched the phone so tightly she hit buttons and heard tones of protest. "Chief, you still there? Who's dead?"

"Darwin. Facedown in the river. Lucky his body snagged on some roots. If he floated into the bay, we wouldn't have found him that fast."

The knot in Val's gut loosened a little, but didn't totally unwind. "Was he murdered?"

"Hard to tell with a drowning. Could be accident, suicide, or murder. We have to wait for the autopsy. Even then we might not know for sure."

Ramirez, Nadia, and now Darwin. Three suspicious deaths. "Did you find anything connecting Darwin to the arson attempt here or the hit-and-run?"

"Nothing definite. His SUV had recent body work, consistent with damages from running someone down."

"Maybe Nadia found out that Darwin —"

"No new theories on Nadia's death. Not 'til we figure out what happened to Darwin. By the way, we found Darwin's fingerprints on your car — evidence that he tampered with your brakes. You don't have to worry about him coming after you again. You're safe."

"Safe from Darwin." Safe from arson and sabotage, though Monique wasn't yet safe from a murder charge. "Thanks for letting me know, Chief."

Val put the phone down and sprawled on the sofa in the sitting room.

Granddad sat in his recliner, his feet propped up. "What's the latest?"

She filled him in on her conversations with Gunnar and Chief Yardley that morning and told him how the manhunt for Darwin had ended. While she talked, the room darkened. She looked through the window at the sky. Thick clouds had descended, blocking the sun.

Granddad nodded off. She was too keyed up to nap. Her relief that Darwin could no longer harm her gave way to worry about what his death meant. An hour ago she would have bet on him as Nadia's murderer. Now the odds had changed. She ticked off the possibilities. One: Darwin killed Nadia, and then died by accident or suicide. Convenient, but improbable. Two: Nadia's death and Darwin's had no connection to each other. A coincidence, but possible. The hit-and-run victim, a known drug dealer, might have had friends who retaliated against Darwin. Three: Nadia's murderer also killed Darwin, remained at large, and might strike again. The likeliest scenario.

Bits of conversations from the last two days echoed in Val's mind.

Nadia kept at Jeremy to quit his job. You added an extra letter to Mrs. Z's name. Maverick can't even go to a funeral without consulting his bookie. Darwin would be stupid to commit a murder with a racket.

Sherlock Holmes could solve a mystery with fragments like that, whereas she would mix them together like cake ingredients, pop them in the oven, and pull out a half-baked theory about the murder. Maybe she lacked a key ingredient. Sherlock tuned into silence as well as words. In "Silver Blaze," the dog that didn't bark in the night spoke volumes to him. Had she missed a telling silence, words not spoken?

She tiptoed to her desk in the study and opened the spiral notebook to her list of suspects. She reviewed her conversations with each of them since the murder. All but one of them had asked how Nadia had died.

372

Besides already knowing the answer, what would keep someone from posing the obvious question? Shock, distraction, the assumption that Val didn't know the answer. Too many possibilities for the chief to accept the "question not asked" as a sign of guilt. By itself, it proved nothing. Did any other clue point in the same direction?

Gunnar's words about the weapon drifted through her mind. *Darwin would be stupid to commit a murder with a racket.*

But someone who had nothing to do with tennis would be smart to commit a murder with a racket. For the last five days, Val had asked herself why the killer used a racket. She finally grasped the logic behind it. The weapon made sense if the murderer wanted the police to focus their investigation on tennis players instead of where they might otherwise look.

Val glanced at the names she'd written in the spiral notebook. Removing the tennis players left her with only two suspects, Irene and Luke. Yet she couldn't eliminate Chatty or Bigby. Either could have made a duplicate of the burned racket to frame the person who'd set it on fire. That left Monique as the only one who wouldn't want to frame the racket burner. Didn't that make her the least likely suspect? The chief would reject this reasoning, though, because it presumed a logical murderer, not one crazed by jealousy, anger, or another strong emotion.

No point in contacting Chief No-New-Theories Yardley yet. Val still couldn't come up with a full explanation of who had murdered Nadia and why.

She needed to clear her mind, stop obsessing about the suspect list, and do something else. She hadn't yet written the article about Nadia for the newsletter, but at least she had a theme for it — how Nadia mentored young people. She'd done that with Bethany on the tennis court, even though Bethany didn't give her credit for it. Nadia had also helped Kimberly, the young real estate agent, and Jeremy.

Jeremy. Val smacked her forehead. She was supposed to talk to him about Nadia this afternoon. She swiveled the desk chair toward the front window. No rain yet, but dark as dusk. If she hurried, she might beat the storm. She took Nadia's spiral notebook on the off chance that Jeremy would recognize the addresses or know why Nadia had borrowed cars. Val scrawled a note to her grandfather telling him where she was going.

Ten minutes later, she turned into the

Cove Acres development just outside the town limits. Some mailboxes had addresses on them, others only names. She cruised by several neo-colonials before spotting L. Forsa and J. Pritchard on the mailbox. Luke's house had a detached garage with windows on the second story, an air conditioner protruding from one of them. Jeremy's apartment. Nice that he had a place of his own and some privacy, even if he lived above a garage.

Val checked both sides of the street. If she'd seen any cars parked nearby, she'd have gone back home without talking to Jeremy. She wouldn't want to knock on his door while one of her suspects, his mother, was visiting.

Val parked the yellow hatchback in the driveway, blocking the door to the double garage. She peered in the garage window. Enough room for two cars, but only Jeremy's delivery van was parked inside, not Luke's BMW. No need to worry about another of her suspects interrupting her talk with Jeremy.

The breezeway between the garage and the house gave her a view of the cove beyond the backyard. The gunmetal gray water reflected the ominous sky. She wouldn't beat the storm after all. She climbed the outdoor staircase to the garage apartment and rapped on the wood door. While she waited for an answer to her knock, fat raindrops splashed on her and splattered on the wood stairs.

Jeremy inched the door open. He bit his lip. "Um, hi." He looked as if he didn't know what to do with someone standing on his threshold.

She smiled. "Hi, Jeremy. Can I come in?"

He pushed his dark-rimmed glasses up his nose and opened the door wider.

She stepped inside the efficiency apartment. Any male between fifteen and twenty-five would feel at home here. Posters of sports cars and rock stars covered the available wall space. A wood bench made an altar for audio and video equipment.

"Wow. This is a neat place."

"Thanks." Jeremy stole a look at the baseball game on the TV and then muted the sound. He perched on the edge of a brown vinyl lounge chair.

She sat on a sagging plaid sofa, reminded him she was writing about Nadia's life for the club newsletter, and asked about his happiest memories of Nadia.

"She used to read to me and act out the story. She made me laugh. And she stayed with me when Mom and Dad went away on vacation. One time, she climbed a ladder to rescue my cat from a tree limb." He took off his thick glasses. "I loved Nadia. She was good to me."

"The other day you told me she asked you to do something. What was it?"

Staccato raindrops beat down on the roof. Jeremy stared at the ceiling. "She wanted me to stop working at the diner and get a better job. She said clearing tables and making deliveries was boring, but I don't mind. I like working there."

So Jeremy's father had told the truth about Nadia's campaign. Val leaned forward. "What did your mom and dad think about Nadia's idea?"

"They said I didn't have to listen to her. She could be a busybody. I told her that, and now she's dead." He buried his face in his hands.

He looked so forlorn that Val wanted to hug him. But how would he react to a hug? No way to know. Best to leave him alone and give him a minute to compose himself. She walked to the window.

Rainwater streamed on the driveway.

Jeremy came up behind her. "Have you been following me?"

His loud voice, inches from her ear, startled Val. The kid sounded paranoid. She sidestepped away from him. "What do you mean?"

"In that car." He pointed to Monique's yellow hatchback.

Val chose her words carefully. "It's not mine. I borrowed it from someone. You've seen it before?"

"When I was making deliveries. It was right behind me, everywhere I went." He squinted at her. "But you weren't driving it. The lady behind the wheel had long, black hair."

That sounded like the wig Nadia had worn while driving a borrowed car last Monday. Maybe she'd disguised herself and driven various cars because Jeremy would have recognized her and her Lexus in his rearview mirror.

Val returned to the sofa. "Come sit next to me, Jeremy. I want to show you something." She reached into her tote bag for Nadia's spiral notebook, opened it to the page dated the day of the murder, and passed it to Jeremy. "Take a look at these addresses. Do they mean anything to you?"

Jeremy frowned briefly and then his eyes lit up. "I made deliveries to these places one day last week. That's the route I took."

Val flipped the notebook to a page with four highlighted addresses on it. Jeremy recognized those addresses, saying he made frequent deliveries to them. Nadia had followed his delivery van occasionally, tracked the addresses of the diner's regular customers, and highlighted them. The busybody who'd sent Chatty's lotion for chemical analysis wouldn't hesitate to pry into Jeremy's work. Something must have aroused Nadia's curiosity about the deliveries.

Val took a stab. "You were very close to Nadia, Jeremy. I bet you told her things you never told anyone else. Did you talk to her about your deliveries?"

Jeremy's fingers writhed like worms. "About the money. I never open the envelopes, but some coffee spilled. I took the money out to dry. It was a bunch of hundred-dollar bills. I asked her if I should take the money back to the house where I made the delivery."

"What did she say?"

"To put it in the envelope and give it to Luke." Jeremy crossed his arms and hunched, hugging himself as if he wanted to shrink away. "She said not to tell him I opened the envelope."

A few more details and Val would have what she needed for the chief. "Do you use envelopes for all your deliveries?"

Jeremy nodded. "Luke staples a bill and

an envelope to each delivery sack. People put their money in the envelope. One time, before we used envelopes, someone didn't pay enough, but I didn't know who. Now I don't have to keep track of how much I get at each stop."

Transporting envelopes filled with big bucks made Jeremy a possible robbery target. *Nadia kept at him to quit his job.* When she couldn't convince him to give up his job, she must have decided to tackle the problem from the other end. Armed with a list of the diner's regular customers, she could threaten Luke with exposure unless he stopped using Jeremy as a courier.

A courier for what? Drugs? Nadia wouldn't have let a drug dealer into her house, especially one she was going to threaten. She must have suspected a less serious crime.

Maverick can't go to a funeral without consulting his bookie. Monique had said that while watching her husband talk to Luke and Darwin.

Gambling. Granddad had hit on the common thread among the highlighted dates in Nadia's notebook. Jeremy's deliveries to frequent customers had peaked in the days surrounding major sporting events. Nadia could have figured that out too, or Maverick might have told her Luke was his bookie. Yet illegal gambling was such a minor crime that Luke wouldn't have committed a murder to cover it up. As a teenager, he'd run a poker game. Maybe he ran a high-stakes one now, the game Maverick had given up a month ago. Something else had happened a month ago — the hit-and-run. Hmm.

Jeremy squirmed in his chair. "Do you want something to drink?"

Val stood up. "No, I'm going to leave. I don't want to block the driveway any longer, in case Luke wants to park in the garage."

"He's already home."

"His BMW wasn't in the garage when I came." She looked out the window. "And it's not parked on the street."

"He has a garage behind the house where he keeps the BMW. This garage is for the diner van and for his cabin cruiser in the winter. In the spring he hauls it to a river-front lot he owns. He has a dock there."

"Is that his only boat?"

"He has a canoe he uses on the cove."

That canoe could have come in handy the night of the murder. The cove was part of the creek that ran behind Nadia's house.

Val opened the door of Jeremy's apartment and watched the rain come down in sheets. At least she wouldn't have to fumble with the keys. Monique had been right about the car locks not working.

Jeremy handed her a shabby umbrella. "Take this. It's bad out there."

Val dashed to the car. She managed to close the umbrella and stow it in the backseat without getting more than a few drops on her. She buckled up.

The door opened on the passenger side. First she saw the gun and then the face of Nadia's murderer.

CHAPTER 26

Val stared at the gun, her hands rigid on the wheel. Her heart pounded like a tom-tom.

"Drive." Luke slid across the bench seat and shoved the barrel of the gun against her ribs. "Don't go out the main entrance. Take the gravel road at the end of the street."

Val's mouth dried up. She gasped for breath.

"Drive, bitch!" He poked her harder with the gun.

She started the car, turned on the wipers and the lights, and shifted into reverse. Could she escape from the car? Her seat belt was buckled. Even if she slowed down or stopped, she wouldn't be able to make a quick leap. Better to keep driving and wait for a chance to attract someone's attention. Eventually, this road would intersect a main artery with more traffic on it. Luke wouldn't risk shooting her with witnesses around.

"Take a right up ahead." He pointed to a

narrow lane.

Damn. No main road after all. She shivered in a cold sweat. Would the gun go off by accident if she hit a bump on the unpaved road? Luke held it steady, his finger on the trigger.

"Would you put that gun away? It makes me nervous." Maybe she could trade on his attraction for her. She slowed down. Their eyes met. "Luke, please. You can trust me."

"Where'd you find that list of addresses?"

She froze. "Addresses?"

"Give up the bluff. I hear everything that goes on in Jeremy's apartment."

"What, you bugged his apartment?"

"He belongs to me. If someone tries to turn him against me, I'll find out. That's why I moved him next door."

Val remembered Luke saying the move was Nadia's idea. He'd hoped to conceal his interest in monitoring Jeremy. "And everyone thought you were being kindhearted, fixing up an apartment for him."

"That's me. Kindhearted. Taking care of the village idiot." He shifted the gun so it no longer gouged into her. "It's such a neat set-up. A dimwit carries piles of money, never notices, and wouldn't take it even if he did. Then some coffee spills, and I got a pair of nosy bitches poking around."

A jolt of fear hit Val. She couldn't expect better treatment than the other nosy woman. Luke didn't have a soft spot for her. He'd wanted her information not her company, asking her for an update on the murder investigation every time he saw her.

He rummaged in her tote bag with his free hand. He pulled out the spiral notebook and flipped the pages. "Ah, here it is. Nadia said she had my customers' addresses. I couldn't find it in her house. Where'd you get it?"

She'd better not mention Kimberly, or he might go after her too. "Nadia left it behind at the club."

"She was wrong about one of these addresses. The mortgage place ordered subs once a week. No special pick-ups or deliveries there." He put the notebook in his jeans pocket. "I could understand it if she wanted a piece of the action, but her 'free Jeremy' crusade made no sense."

"Why didn't you let him go? He can't be that important to you."

"Once he was out of it, there was nothing to keep her quiet. She could go to the cops anytime. I couldn't let that happen. Mom depends on me."

The good son. "I see. You're just taking care of your mother." That's how he salved whatever little conscience he had.

"Make a right turn up ahead. Nadia didn't feel a thing, you know. I opened a bottle of expensive wine, like the one she gave me when I bought my house from her, and slipped a sedative in her drink."

Luke, the good murderer. Could Val say anything to convince him not to murder her? "Nadia had a personal interest in Jeremy. I don't. I'm not a meddler like her."

Luke poked her with the gun. "Don't take me for a fool. You want to nail Nadia's murderer. I knew you were trouble when you baited Darwin about the hit-and-run and arson."

"Until he tried to set my house on fire, I didn't think he was guilty of anything except stupidity."

"Stupidity is right. I paid him to make sure there was no trouble at my poker game. One night he brings a Hispanic with him. The guy waves a gun and holds me up for the night's take."

Ramirez. "You sent Darwin after him."

"I told him to get my money back and make sure the guy never comes to the game again. So what does he do? Runs the guy over."

The last pieces of the puzzle clicked into place. If Nadia ever told the police about the money Luke collected via the diner's deliveries, they'd look into his income sources. Not only his sports betting operation might come to light, but also his high-stakes poker game and Darwin's role as muscleman. Under police questioning, Darwin could claim that Luke ordered him to eliminate Ramirez.

"Darwin went to you for help, didn't he? Last night after he tried to set fire to my house."

"He was afraid you recognized him. He figured the cops were watching the roads. Wanted me to take him by boat to Annapolis, where he had friends who'd hide him."

As soon as Darwin attracted police scrutiny, Luke had to get rid of him, pushing him overboard far short of Annapolis. And Luke planned the same end for her. She had a vision of the medical examiner slicing into her bloated body. Her throat burned. Her mouth filled with something bitter. She had to make her move before they reached Luke's boat.

She glanced sideways. He sat in the middle of the bench seat, and he wasn't belted in. Chef Henri, also without a seat belt, had gone to the hospital with a bunch of broken bones. Like Henri's vintage car, this old hatchback had no airbags. Could she do on purpose what she'd done by accident a few months ago? Could she duplicate a crash? Not as precisely as Luke had duplicated a racket to use as a weapon. In this crash she might suffer more than minor injuries, but anything beat what he planned for her.

She scanned the road ahead and saw the faint glow of headlights. Perfect. She'd want someone to call for help when she crashed the hatchback.

Her palms sweated on the steering wheel. If she kept talking, Luke might not notice her growing anxiety. "Where did you get the wood racket?"

"From Mom's attic. It was my father's."

Of course. "Your mom told me he played tennis." And Luke had said she never threw anything away.

The headlights of the approaching car glimmered. A few hundred yards ahead, a tree with a hefty trunk stood in a field, just off the road to the right.

She pressed on the accelerator. *Come on, hatchback.* Once she went off the road, the car would have to go fast not to bog down in the mud.

"Slow down!" Luke yelled.

She eased off the road toward the tree still fifty yards away.

Luke grabbed the wheel, forcing the

hatchback to swerve to the left. Val saw
nothing but the headlights of the oncoming
car.

CHAPTER 27

Val flashed back to the icy road last winter. Seconds before the accident, Chef Henri fought her for the steering wheel as Luke was doing now. This time she wouldn't let the man sitting next to her take charge.

Adrenaline surged through her. She wrenched the wheel back to the right and slammed on the brakes.

The tires squealed. The car skidded off the road, throwing Luke sideways. Val aimed the right side of the car toward the tree trunk. No way to avoid it now. She took her hands off the wheel, covered her face, and braced herself.

The car whammed into the tree trunk. Her body pitched forward and snapped back.

She opened her eyes. Luke was slumped on the seat, his head tilted sideways. Blood gushed from his forehead. He must have hit the windshield. Val unbuckled her seat belt with a shaking hand.

Where was the gun?

Val spotted it on the floor between Luke's left leg and her tote bag. Luke groaned. She thrust the gun in her bag and opened the car door.

A middle-aged man and a pudgy woman hurried toward her from across the road. The woman carried a huge umbrella in one hand and a cell phone in the other.

The man helped Val get out of the car. "Are you all right?"

"I'm okay, but he needs an ambulance." She pointed to Luke. "And I need the police."

The woman held the phone up. "I've got 911 on the line."

After the café closed Monday afternoon, Val reached up to put a bowl on a top shelf. Pain stabbed her neck and shoulder like a long-bladed knife. She moaned.

"Let me do that." Monique came around the counter. "I'll clean up here. You sit down, drink your iced coffee, and finish telling me what happened last night."

Val could talk about it with barely a shiver now. The first few times she'd described the crash, to the police and Granddad last night, and to Bethany and Chatty this morning, she couldn't stop trembling. She'd decided to tell Chatty nothing about Nadia's research into cosmetics. Legally Chatty could set whatever price she wanted for her products. Val would never buy the products, but any woman undaunted by those prices had money to burn.

Val climbed onto the stool that Monique had just vacated. "Where did I leave off?" The painkillers made her groggy without killing the pain. At least they dulled it a bit.

Monique slid the iced coffee toward Val. "You told me about the crash. How badly was Luke hurt?"

"Nothing major wrong with him, just a gash in the head and a concussion. The hospital released him this morning, and the police have him in custody. They'll charge him with Nadia's murder." Val hoped he hurt as much as she did or, better yet, more than she did. "Sorry your hatchback won't recover."

Monique waved away the apology. "It died for a good cause. Nadia must have been crazy to let Luke into her house. Why didn't she go to the police instead?"

"She just wanted to get Jeremy away from him and didn't expect Luke to kill her for that. She took him for a small-time crook. That's all he was until Darwin killed Ramirez, making Luke an accessory to a major crime."

"This morning Maverick told me why he wouldn't go back to the poker game. He saw the gun Ramirez brought to the game." Monique wiped down the food prep counters. "Some people call gambling a victimless crime, but if Luke hadn't run a poker game, three people would be alive."

"And he wouldn't be in custody." Val sipped the last of her iced coffee. "Last week he said that Nadia did a good deed by helping Jeremy get a job. I remember thinking she wasn't killed for her good deeds. But in a way, she was. She tried to protect Jeremy."

Monique came around the counter and sat next to Val. "Nadia was a strange mixture of good and bad."

"Like most people."

"I've forgiven her, you know, for what she did with Maverick. But I don't know if I can forgive myself for what I did to her. If I hadn't set fire to the racket, maybe —"

"No. Luke would have killed her anyway. He'd have used a different method."

"But I wouldn't have been the chief suspect. I'm grateful for what you did, Val. You risked your life to help me."

Val swiveled the stool to face her cousin. "We're family."

"Yes, and you belong here in Bayport. Don't even think about leaving." Monique stood up. "Need a lift home?"

Val thanked Monique for the ride and climbed out of the van. No sign of Granddad's Buick. Maybe he'd gone fishing, taking advantage of the first pleasant weather in a week. She breathed in the clear air, stood under the oak tree in the front yard, and peered at the blue sky through the leaves. The tree had roots so large they surfaced in the lawn. She propped her foot on a sturdy root. *I belong here.*

A truck from the Treadwell Nursery rumbled along the street. It stopped in front of the house, reversed, and backed into the driveway.

Val crossed the lawn and shouted over the engine noise. "What are you doing?"

The driver poked his dreadlocked head out of the truck window. "We got plants here for 175 Grace Street."

Her grandfather wouldn't buy plants. "Are you sure you have the right address?"

"Deliver and plant. That's what it says here. It's all paid for." The driver waved his clipboard at her and jumped from the truck. "The name on the order is . . . Gus. Anybody here by that name?"

A peace offering from Gunnar. She couldn't refuse it. "You're at the right place."

The driver and his assistant unloaded plants from the back of the truck. Val checked out the daylilies. Healthy and fuller than the ones that had fallen in combat Saturday night. Instant garden. Better than no garden. Yes, she'd let other people lay down roots for her, as long as she decided where they should go.

She pointed to the flower bed. "Plant the daisies in front and the daylilies behind them."

She was still directing the planting when Gunnar appeared in the driveway. Her heart skipped a beat. She hadn't expected to see him ever again and wasn't sure she wanted to.

His brow furrowed. "I heard about the crash, Val. Are you okay?"

"I'm so stiff I move like the Tin Man. The doctor says it'll ease up." She rubbed the back of her neck. "The chief told me you left for Washington yesterday."

"I rushed back here as soon as I could. I wouldn't have left if I thought you were in danger."

"I wouldn't have let you stay." She gestured with her thumb to the flower bed.

"What's with the plants? Damage control by the DEA or the IRS?"

Gunnar shook his head. "Thank Great-Aunt Gretchen."

"Can we just stick to the truth?"

"It *is* the truth. Look." He pulled a folded envelope from his shirt pocket. "They finally probated the will. I think Gretchen would like it if some of her money went toward a garden."

Val scanned the letter from a law firm. According to the terms of Gretchen Swensen's last will and testament, Gunnar could expect a legacy. Val wasn't completely convinced. You could make letterhead on a laser printer.

He searched her face. "Don't tell me you didn't believe in Great-Aunt Gretchen."

"Let's leave that aside for the moment. You didn't need to spend her money, or yours, on my garden."

He shrugged. "Call it a way of making up for mistakes."

The way she'd tried to make amends for prejudging Nadia? "I finally realized you can't make up for mistakes. You have to forgive yourself and move on."

"I could do that better if you forgave me."

"Oh, you're forgiven, but not because of the plants. Having a gun poked in my ribs put everything in perspective. Let's go sit on the porch." His radiant smile made her feel better than the painkillers she'd swallowed.

"Chief Yardley briefed Vince and me on what happened. That was a lucky accident you had with Luke holding a gun on you."

"I'm lucky he went to the emergency room, not me." She hadn't told anyone she'd aimed the car at the tree, not even the police. The less said about the crash, the better. "Were you right about Darwin selling drugs from his backroom?"

"He had steroids and party drugs hidden in his storage area among the shoeboxes. Unfortunately, since he's dead, he can't lead the DEA to his suppliers."

Val climbed the porch steps. "Was Luke involved with drugs too?"

"The police have no evidence that he even knew about Darwin's drug dealing. They'll get Luke for the murder, thanks to you."

She sat in a cushioned wicker chair. No glider. Too many moving parts. Today she didn't want any of her parts moved. "Luke told everyone he kept the diner going for his mother when he was really using it as a front for gambling."

"And a way to launder money. He rang up phantom cash sales." Gunnar sat on the glider. "The juice from sports gambling gave him a steady income most of the year. Spring through fall, he ran a poker game for locals and guys who came here to fish and hunt."

"How much was that worth to him?"

"Five bucks a hand times twenty-five hands an hour. Depending on the number of tables, he could take in as much as five thousand a night in cash. Enough money he'd want protection."

"Enter Darwin, the muscleman." Enough rehashing. "What's next for you, Gunnar? Is your assignment in Bayport over?"

"Like I said, I'm leaving my job to open an accounting practice and study acting. You didn't believe me, huh?" When she said nothing, he continued. "I always told you the truth, but I couldn't tell you the whole truth."

Val still had her doubts. She'd fallen for too many stories lately. "If you were serious about acting, you'd head to New York."

"Broadway, here I come? Not yet. I can study acting at the University of Maryland. There are community theaters around here and lots of theaters in the Baltimore-Washington area." He leaned toward her, his elbow on his crossed knee and his chin cupped in his hand. "Can we start from scratch? As friends. With the whole truth."

She held out her hand to shake on it. "As friends." A good first step.

He pointed toward the sidewalk. "Your grandfather's back."

Neither of them had noticed the Buick pull up at the curb.

Granddad climbed the porch steps and gave Gunnar a half wave. "Hope you're not staying long. My granddaughter's hurtin' and needs some rest."

"I was about to go." Gunnar stood up. "Feel better, Val. I'll call you."

Her grandfather took off his fishing vest and tossed it on the glider. "I thought he left town already."

"He may stick around, Granddad. He's talking about opening an accounting practice here and studying acting."

Granddad looked like a silent movie actor miming surprise, his mouth agape and his hands in the air. "Him an actor? With that face, he better stick to voice-overs." He folded himself into the wicker chair that matched hers.

"I have something to tell you," she said. No one else would appreciate it. "While I was driving with Luke, I remembered every detail of the accident last winter. The car was spinning on ice. I turned into the skid and got traction. Chef Henri panicked, grabbed the wheel, and sent the car spinning again. His fault, not mine."

Granddad gave her a thumbs-up. "Now you can finally let it go."

She nodded. No more guilt. No more fretting about whether she'd tried to maim Henri. She felt like a new person. Unlike Granddad, she didn't have a new name to mark her rebirth. "So, Codger Cook, did you try all the recipes for your column and meet the deadline?"

"I got them in on time. I tried them when you cooked them. Didn't need to fiddle with them myself, except to add my secret sauce before I turned them in."

"You mean you added a dollop of attitude to my recipes." Like Chatty added a smidgen of dye to make her cosmetics unique.

He folded his arms and sat back. "I call it style."

"Style matters. I'd have known Luke was the murderer sooner if I'd paid attention to Nadia's style of writing names. The night she was murdered, she was on the phone with a client, taking notes on a house, when Luke called. She wrote F-O-R-S-A-L on her notepad under the house details."

"For Sal?"

"I thought it was the start of a 'For Sale'

400

ad. When I went to her office, I saw how she wrote her clients' names on the master schedule, always the person's last name and first initial. All caps with no spaces or punctuation."

Granddad tapped his forehead. "Forsa L— Luke Forsa. I can see why you missed that."

"I even had a second example. Nadia jotted the name of her other caller, Mrs. Z, the same way. I gave Mrs. Z's name to a real estate agent, who told me I added an extra letter to it. If only I'd checked, I'd have found out the extra letter Nadia wrote was Mrs. Z's first initial, K."

"That wouldn't convince a jury Luke was guilty."

Val shifted in her chair, felt her muscles protest, and stifled a groan. "By itself, it proves nothing, but it reinforces the other clues — the weapon, Nadia's car switching, the notes in her spiral book, and what Luke didn't say. He never asked how Nadia was murdered."

Granddad held up his hand with fingers splayed. "Five clues. It took you a while to figure them out."

"I guess solving murders, like cooking, takes practice."

While Granddad could practice cooking

any time he wanted, Val couldn't expect more shots at sleuthing. What were the chances of another murder in a peaceful small town?

RECIPES FROM THE CODGER
COOK NEWSPAPER COLUMN

MYSTERY SALAD

When I first saw this salad, I recognized the little tomatoes. The other ingredients were all a mystery to me. Turns out the mushy green stuff was avocados and the white disks were hearts of palm. Now I've heard tell of avocados, but I never knew palms had hearts. The whole mess tasted pretty good, though.

Hearts of palm from a 14-ounce jar, drained and cut crosswise into 1/4-inch slices
2 cups diced ripe avocados (2 Haas avocados)
1 cup small grape tomatoes, halved
1 tablespoon lemon juice
1 tablespoon mayonnaise
[Salt and pepper, optional]

Throw it all in a bowl and taste it. Add salt, pepper, and more lemon juice if you like.

Serves 6.

JUST SMALL POTATOES

Use plain ole spuds for this dish, not ones with fancy names like russets, creamers, or fingerlings. Parmesan cheese straight from the canister works great. If you have a hunk of Parmesan and want to grate it, knock yourself out, but I can't guarantee the potatoes will taste as good.

Preheat the oven to 375 degrees.

6 medium to large potatoes
1/4 cup flour
1/4 cup grated Parmesan cheese
1/4 teaspoon salt
5 tablespoons melted butter

Pour the melted butter into a glass baking pan (13 × 9 × 2 inches). Combine the flour, cheese, and salt in a plastic bag. Peel the spuds and cut each into eight pieces. Dip 'em in cold water, throw 'em into the plastic bag a few at a time, and shake. When the pieces are coated, plunk those babies in the pan, flat side down, nestled in a single layer. Bake for an hour, turning them after half an hour to brown another side.

Serve them in the baking pan. If you want the pan to look pretty, you can add parsley sprigs.

Serves 6.

No Mistakes Crab Cakes

"Less is more" when it comes to crab cakes. The best ones contain crabmeat and just enough other stuff to make the crab stick together. No bread crumbs, mayo, veggies, and sauces needed.

1 pound fresh lump crabmeat, picked over to remove any shells
1 beaten egg
1 teaspoon Old Bay seasoning, or to taste
2 tablespoons flour plus enough for coating the patties
4 tablespoons olive or canola oil

Gently mix the first four ingredients. Shape the mix into four patties. Put the patties on a plastic-lined plate, covered loosely with more plastic wrap, and chill them, 30 minutes in the fridge or 15 minutes in the freezer. If you skip this step, the patties may break up in the pan, which mars their beauty. They still taste fine, though.

Pour the oil in a large skillet and heat it at medium. Dredge each crab cake in flour right before putting it in the hot oil. Turn up the heat to medium-high. Flip the crab cakes carefully when you see that the underside has browned around the edges (5-7 minutes) and brown the other side. Serve with lemon wedges.

Serves 4.

GRAND BERRIED PORK

A lot of my friends have teeth that nature didn't supply. This dish suits them just fine. The meat's real tender. It's grand berried pork for grandparents. You can use the same recipe for pork chops, but only if you and your guests have good choppers.

1 1/2 pounds pork tenderloin
2 tablespoons vegetable oil
3 cups fresh cranberries
3/4 cup sugar
2/3 cup water

Wash the berries, discarding any mushy ones. Slice the pork into 1-inch thick pieces, and press the pieces between wax paper, flattening them to 3/4 inch. Dry the meat with a paper towel if you want it to brown — and you do. Heat the oil in a large skillet at medium heat. Brown one side of the meat. When the meat pieces no longer stick to the pan, they're ready to turn. Brown the flip side of the meat for a few minutes. Drain the fat and juices from the pan.

Add the cranberries, sugar, and water to the meat in the pan. Stir. When the mixture comes to a boil, reduce the heat. Cook covered, with the mixture at a slow boil, for 20 minutes, turning the pork pieces halfway through. If it looks like the cranberries are sticking to the pan, add water. Salt the dish to taste, serve with white rice, and pass the cranberry sauce as a topping.

Note: For six 3/4-inch thick bone-in pork chops, simmer an hour or until the chops are tender.

Serves 4-6.

EASIER-THAN-PIE APPLE CRISP

This recipe, with five main ingredients plus optional sprinkles of cinnamon and salt, is for people with at least one sweet tooth in their mouth.

Preheat the oven to 350 degrees.

6 cups thinly sliced, peeled apples (about 5 medium or 3 large apples)
1/2 cup flour
1/2 cup brown sugar
1 cup chopped pecans or walnuts
1/2 cup softened (not melted) butter
[Pinch of salt and sprinkling of cinnamon,

optional]

Put the sliced apples in a shallow, square baking pan (8 or 9 inches). Sprinkle with cinnamon if desired. Cover the pan with foil and bake the apples for 20 minutes.

Mix together the flour, brown sugar, and nuts. Add a dash of salt if desired. Mash the softened butter into the mixture with a fork if you're finicky, and with your fingers if you're not. Mighty good lickin'. When the apples have baked for 20 minutes, cover them with the crumb mixture.

Bake uncovered for 30 minutes or until the topping is golden brown.

Cool the apple crisp for at least 30 minutes unless you want blisters on your tongue. Serve it warm or cold. Add vanilla ice cream or whipped cream to make your sweet tooth even happier.

Serves 6-8.

DE-LISH ROCKFISH
The Chesapeake Bay rockfish goes by the name of striped bass in other regions. Call it what you like, it's Maryland's official state fish

and a favorite of bay anglers. Rockfish is delish no matter how you cook it. This recipe uses fillets topped with a simple sauce that seals in the moisture. You can use the same recipe for any firm white fish or even salmon.

Preheat the oven to 450 degrees.

4 rockfish fillets 4-5 ounces each
1/4 cup reduced fat mayonnaise
2 tablespoons grated Parmesan cheese
2 tablespoons chopped green onion
1/2 teaspoon Worcestershire sauce

Combine the mayonnaise, cheese, onion, and Worcestershire sauce.

Shoot some cooking spray into a pan large enough to hold the fillets. Put the fish in the pan, skin side down if it has skin. Spread the mayo mixture over the fillets.

Bake for 12-15 minutes or until the fish flakes.

Serves 4.

MRS. Z'S E-Z MACAROONS
Your tongue might twist if you say the name of this recipe fast three times. For sure it will

sing when you taste these cookies. Most macaroons are made with egg whites. The whole eggs in this recipe make for golden nuggets.

Preheat the oven to 350 degrees.

2 eggs
1/3 cup sugar
1 teaspoon vanilla extract
1 tablespoon of grated lemon zest
1 7-ounce bag of shredded sweetened coconut

Beat the eggs in a bowl. Add sugar slowly while stirring. Mix in the vanilla and lemon zest. Fold the coconut into the mixture. Be sure to break apart any large lumps (unless you want lumpy macaroons). The mixture should look moist and glossy.

Line two cookie sheets with parchment paper for an E-Z cleanup. Drop heaping teaspoons of the mixture onto the sheet, spacing them an inch and a half apart.

Bake 12-15 minutes or until the edges and some coconut shreds turn light brown. The center of each macaroon should still be soft.

Slide the parchment onto racks. Remove

the cookies when they're cool and start eating.

Yield: 30-36 cookies

Adapted from a recipe by Jayne Sutton in *Cookies Unlimited* by Nick Malgieri.

A LOT O' STRATA

A strata is a layered casserole. Folks compare it to quiche, but it's a lot less trouble and a good way to get rid of stale bread. Like the Codger Cook, this dish needs its rest. You have time between mixing and cooking to take a nap or even get a good night's sleep. With this recipe you can feed brunch to a crowd. For LESS O'STRATA, use half the ingredients and a smaller pan, but stick to the same sleep and bake time.

Preheat the oven to 350 degrees.

1 pound bulk sausage, turkey or pork, spicy or not, depending on your taste
6 eggs
2 cups milk
Stale bread: French, white, wheat, or whatever
1 cup grated sharp cheddar
[1/2 teaspoon salt, optional]

Brown and drain small chunks of the sausage.

Beat the eggs with the milk and salt if you use it.

Cube the stale bread and spread it in a single layer at the bottom of a 9x13 inch pan. Sprinkle the sausage and the cheese on the cubed bread and pour the egg and milk mixture over the top.

Refrigerate overnight or a minimum of an hour.

Bake for 45 minutes.

Serves 8-10 for breakfast, brunch, or lunch.

ACKNOWLEDGMENTS

Though too many cooks may spoil the broth, many experts enhanced *By Cook or by Crook*. I'd like to thank the Police Department of Chestertown, Maryland, for information on how crime scenes are handled within their jurisdiction and on the roles of various law enforcement units from the town, county, and state in the investigation. I'd also like to thank D.P. Lyle, M.D., for clarifying the medical and forensic issues in my murder scenario. Any mistakes in the book are mine and not the fault of those who shared their expertise with me.

When I needed assistance to test a scene for the book's first chapter, the initial response was a bemused question: "You want to do *what* with a tennis racket?" Once over that hurdle, my friend, John Fay, guided my use of a hatchet, and my son, Paul Corrigan, made sure my controlled burn didn't go out of control. I also owe

413

John thanks for the fish recipe the Codger Cook renamed and adapted.

My gratitude goes to the many generous veteran and newbie authors in Sisters in Crime and their Guppy subgroup. They taught me much about writing and publishing mysteries and led me to my agent, John Talbot. Thanks, John, for shepherding my proposal. I'd also like to thank my editor, John Scognamiglio, for taking on a new writer based on a proposal and making me part of Kensington.

Special thanks go to my friend and writing partner, Carolyn Mulford. She read more versions of this book than anyone else and offered insights and suggestions that improved it at every stage. Thank you to the Maryland mystery writers who critiqued an early version of the manuscript: Mary Nelson, Helen Schwartz, and Sylvia Straub. I'm grateful for the helpful suggestions of the Virginia Sisters in Crime who read the completed manuscript: E.B. Davis, Sherry Harris, Maureen Klovers, C. Ellett Logan, and Robin Templeton. My friends and family gave thoughtful comments: Susan Fay, Elliot Wicks, and the Corrigans: Nora, Paul, Toni, and Rob. Mike Corrigan read early and late versions and supported me in every way as I wrote and rewrote. He never once asked, "When are you going to finish that book?" Or if he did, I've forgotten it. I won't, however, forget what I owe to those who helped me with this book. Many thanks.

The employees of Thorndike Press hope you have enjoyed this Large Print book. All our Thorndike, Wheeler, and Kennebec Large Print titles are designed for easy reading, and all our books are made to last. Other Thorndike Press Large Print books are available at your library, through selected bookstores, or directly from us.

For information about titles, please call:
(800) 223-1244

or visit our Web site at:
http://gale.cengage.com/thorndike

To share your comments, please write:
Publisher
Thorndike Press
10 Water St., Suite 310
Waterville, ME 04901

LC